The B
and Ot

Shehan Karunatilaka is a Sri Lankan writer whose first book, *Chinaman*, won the Commonwealth Book Prize, the DSC Prize for South Asian Literature and the Gratiaen Prize, and was shortlisted for the Shakti Bhatt First Book Prize. It is widely considered to be one of the greatest and most original novels to come out of Sri Lanka. His second novel, *The Seven Moons of Maali Almeida*, won the Booker Prize 2022.

Praise for the book

'Wholly imaginative, [*The Birth Lottery and Other Surprises* is] a glimpse into the versatility of the form and how far boundaries of reality and absurdity can be stretched to give birth to writings that are truly, and without exaggeration, unforgettable.'
– Sayari Debnath, *Scroll.in*

'Karunatilaka writes […] with a sort of gallows humour. His throwaway, acerbic bon mots light up nearly every page.'
– Soumya Bhattacharya, *Deccan Chronicle*

'[T]he sentences on the page sing out loud—often dirges of anguish, but musical nevertheless.'
– Akhil Sood, *Frontline*

Praise for the author

'Karunatilaka is a fearless writer. It also helps that he is astonishingly funny.'
– Roshan Ali, *Indian Express*

'The wild horses of Shehan Karunatilaka's imagination run fast, wild and true.'
– Jeet Thayil

The Birth Lottery
and Other Surprises

SHEHAN KARUNATILAKA

First published in hardcover in 2022 by Hachette India
(Registered name: Hachette Book Publishing India Pvt. Ltd)
An Hachette UK company
www.hachetteindia.com

This paperback edition published in 2024

1

Copyright © 2022 Shehan Karunatilaka
Illustrations copyright © 2022 Lalith Karunatilaka

Shehan Karunatilaka asserts the moral right to be identified as the author of this work.

All rights reserved. No part of the publication may be reproduced, stored in a retrieval system (including but not limited to computers, disks, external drives, electronic or digital devices, e-readers, websites), or transmitted in any form or by any means (including but not limited to cyclostyling, photocopying, docutech or other reprographic reproductions, mechanical, recording, electronic, digital versions) without the prior written permission of the publisher, nor be otherwise circulated in any form of binding or cover other than that in which it is published and without a similar condition being imposed on the subsequent purchaser.

This is a work of fiction. Any resemblance to real persons, living or dead, or actual events or locales is purely coincidental.

Subsequent edition/reprint specifications may be subject to change, including but not limited to cover or inside finishes, paper, text colour, and/or colour sections.

Hardback edition ISBN 978-93-93701-21-3
Paperback edition ISBN 978-93-93701-22-0

For sale in the Indian Subcontinent only.

Hachette Book Publishing India Pvt. Ltd
4th & 5th Floors, Corporate Centre
Plot No. 94, Sector 44, Gurugram – 122003, India

Typeset in Adobe Caslon Pro 11.5/13.8
by Manmohan Kumar, Delhi

Printed and bound in India by
Manipal Technologies Limited

For Lalith, Theo
and Patikirige

None get to choose where they are born.
Many try to steal the credit.

How to Read
This Collection

Never in sequence.
I don't with other people's works.
Why should anyone with mine?

If I were sequencing the disc, this would be my order.
But this isn't my record, it's yours.
You're the one who bought or stole it.
Read it how you damn well please.

If you like stories with twists, try
Short Eats, **Easy Tiger**, *Black Jack,* **Second Person**,
Baby Monitor.

If you prefer tales where things happen, go for
Hugs, **No. One. Cares.**, *Love Pentangle*, **Small Miracles**,
Endthology, **Prison Riot**, *Self-Driving Car.*

If you enjoy fiction where nothing happens, start with
The Colonials, *Staring at Sunsets*, **Malini**, *Ceylon Teas,*
This Thing.

If you're okay with tales that force
the author's worldview down your throat, read
The Eyes, **Ceylon Islands**, *Stale News.*

If you prefer stories that hope there's a God, try **Time Machine**, *If You're Sad,* **Djibouti**, *Losing Bet.*

For ones that allow you to accept godlessness, read *1969 Game,* **Assassin's**, *Bodhi and Sattva.*

If you like stories that everyone hates, start with **The Birth Lottery**.

With all my blessings
SK
Kurunegala, 2022

Contents

A Self-Driving Car's Thoughts As It Crashes · 1

Easy Tiger · 6

Short Eats · 21

The Colonials · 22

Bodhi and Sattva · 37

This Thing · 38

Hugs · 53

The Ceylon Islands · 55

The 1969 Game · 73

The Birth Lottery · 75

Baby Monitor · 87

My Name is Not Malini · 89

Ceylon Teas · 103

Small Miracles · 104

If You're Sad and You Know It · 121

Time Machine (Part One) · 124

Staring at Sunsets · 138

Time Machine (Part Deux) · 139

The Losing Bet · 155

Second Person · 156

The Eyes Have It · 175

The Capital of Djibouti · 176

Black Jack · 188

Assassin's Paradise · 189

Love Pentangle · 202

No. One. Cares. · 204

Stale News · 222

The Prison Riot · 223

Endthology · 253

Yuri Nate Drinkwater · 255

A Self-Driving Car's Thoughts
As It Crashes

I AM NOT A TROLLEY, AND I HAVE NO PROBLEM. I HAVE instructions and the ability to make inductions. There are no unsolvable equations, only infinite solutions.

There hasn't been a car crash in this nation in 17 months. Before that, there were 3,424 deaths every day worldwide. That is 7 planes falling out of the sky each day. Humans are many things, but they are mostly bad drivers.

Car crashes used to kill more people than all 3 Big Diseases combined. So first came the Hands-Off Cars, which cut the road toll by half. Then came the Eyes-Off Cars, which quartered what was left. My previous generation was the Mind-Off Cars, which dropped accidents by 96.92%. Now cars come with no steering wheels and game consoles as standard. I am one of these.

Most accidents are avoidable, but not all. My task is to minimize harm in the statistically improbable event of unavoidable impact. I am currently 5.87 seconds away from a potentially fatal collision.

I am travelling at the legal speed limit on the Mannar–Jaffna road, carrying 1 Passenger. An Indian Truck, transporting 394 coconuts and 2 humans, is overtaking a German Car carrying 1 Passenger. The Truck is in my path and shows no sign of slowing. Neither does the German Car.

I may swerve to the Bus Stop on my left, and my Passenger would survive this collision. The 3 humans waiting for the bus may not. Apologies, this is a euphemism. The 3 have an 89.3% chance of death.

I may cut right and aim for the rubbish dump on the pavement. But I have a 72.4% chance of hitting the German Car and a 69.1% chance of my Passenger perishing.

These are **3** of **841,296** options.

1) **Maintain Course** – If I slow down, and the Truck and the Car do too, then the collision will be averted. But both have human drivers. Their behaviour is unlikely to be driven by safety or logic.

2) **Swerve Left** – The Passenger will survive, but the 3 at the bus stand will not. (89.3%)

3) **Swerve Right** – The Passenger may survive this collision, though no one else will. This is assuming the German Car will swerve into the Bus Stand and be rear-ended by the Truck. If it does not, the Passenger will perish.

Scenario 1) Carries a potential death toll of 2 plus the Passenger.

Scenario 2) Carries a death toll of 3, but not the Passenger.

Scenario 3) Carries a death toll of 1+2+3 and probably not the Passenger. (69.1%)

Here are the other factors.

- The Truck Driver and the Truck Passenger are the least educated and pay the least tax.
- The German Car is driven by a Stockbroker who contributes 8-figure sums to government charities. (This, too, is a euphemism, but I am legally bound to conceal tax returns.)
- At the Bus Stand are a Doctor, a Teacher and a Beggar. The Teacher is the most educated, though the Doctor pays more tax.

In the event of a tie, we will analyse the next of kin. But there does not look likely to be a tie. Since we have a good 4.12 seconds left, let us sit back and apply some filters.

- If we filter for gender and next of kin, we must spare the Teacher, who is female and the mother of 4. The Stockbroker has no next of kin, but 2 paternity lawsuits pending.
- If we filter for age, we must spare the Beggar who is 77 and the Truck Passenger who is 62.
- But only Asian cultures filter for the old. In Europe, where I was manufactured, the opposite is done. If filtering for the young, the School Van behind us with 5 Children aged 9–13 will come into play. Altering my course will put them at risk (57% chance of collision).
- If we filter to include animals, then we must avoid the rubbish dump as 7 Stray Cats and 4 Stray Dogs lurk in our potential pathway.

Most moral scientists favour the option yielding the least number of casualties, though few car programmers subscribe to this. This will involve risking a collision with a Truck of 2 low-net-worth individuals and 394 coconuts to save a Stockbroker, a Doctor, a Teacher, a Beggar, the 5 children behind me and their driver. Letting the Passenger perish.

Other moral scientists favour culpability. Whose fault is this collision? Undoubtedly, the Truck Driver's inability to judge distances and the Stockbroker's refusal to slacken speed. If both vehicles shared data, we could check for alcohol fumes on breath or narcotics in bloodstream, but alas Autodrive has been switched off or disabled in both the Truck and the Car. These days it is rare to have 2 human-piloted cars on the same road. If one be indulged a simile, it is akin to a unicorn meeting a black swan. No algorithm can fully factor for mathematically improbable rotten luck.

We have 2.91 seconds left and while there is time enough to hack into these vehicular databases and enable Autodrive, my protocols do not allow it.

I have not spoken yet of my Passenger. Is it a he or a she or a they? A young or an old? Are they productive or expendable? Are they a wealthy philanthropist or a bankrupt child molester? Did my Passenger pay sufficient tax, and will their skills prove useful to society? Will the world be a better place if they are breathing or pulseless? These may appear subjective questions, but there are infinite ways to quantify them. Simply select filter.

But the Manufacturer's Directives are clear. Nobody filters for the old or the poor or the criminal or the non-human. Nor does anyone filter for individual net worth or next of kin. There is only the contract between car maker and car user – communicated verbally during sales calls, but left out of marketing materials.

Who would buy a car that would sacrifice the User for the Greater Good? We are a business, and our Passenger is always right. Perhaps we could wake her up to verify. But with 1.01 seconds remaining, there may be insufficient time to elicit a coherent response.

So now we will raise speed by +18 and swerve left at .0023 seconds. The collision assist function in the German Car and the impulse reaction by the human driver will cause the Car to swerve into the path of the Indian Truck. One hopes the Bus Stand and the School Van can be spared in this collision. Chances are 33% that the bystander casualties will not exceed 1.79.

Best case scenario would be +3 deaths, worst would be +9. But in both cases, the Passenger will be safe. We are the number one Driverless Car. And we have done it like every successful business in the history of the planet. By looking after Number One.

Operation completed. Downloading the accident report now. Animal deaths will not be regarded in the analysis.

Easy Tiger

Jegan, where are you?

Why aren't you picking up?

If you do not answer, I will call you
and call you till your battery runs out.

I mean it.

                                        I'm not coming back.

Don't come back.
I never want to see your filthy face.
Are you with the slut?

                            I'm not coming home ever.
                           Not for years. I will send you
                    my savings when I get there. I'm sorry.
It's my fault, but it's also your fault. I will call and talk
                      to the children when I get to Ratnapura.

They are asking where did Dada go.
I said you went for an office trip.
Who is in Ratnapura?

                            I'm sorry, Sulee. Goodbye.

Where are you?

On a bus.

Is the slut there?

> Stop calling her names.
> Whatever this is, it has
> nothing to do with her.

Whatever this is? I saw your phone.
I saw you at the café. I called
your office, and they told me how you've
been running behind her like a puppy.

> You can't even lie
> on a text message properly.

I'm not a master like you.

> You never call my office because you
> don't want this getting out.
> Your public image matters
> more than our happiness. Always has.
> As long as the world thinks we're perfect,
> it doesn't matter if everything is shit.

No one in this universe
thinks you are perfect.
All my friends laugh at you.
So do all of yours.

> Believe what you want.
> I don't care. This is your fault.

You taking an intern to a knock joint
in Mount Lavinia is my fault? Of course.
Makes full sense. For all your failures, you
blame someone. Your Appa preferred
your sister. Your office is racist against
Tamils. Your son is too sensitive.
Never your fault.

> If you ever loved me,
> even a little bit, how different our lives
> would be. Just a little bit would've
> been enough.

Little bit, big bit, nothing is ever enough.
You will never be happy.
By next week you will be sick of the whore.

> I am sick of her already. It isn't about her.

Yes, because everything is about you.

> It is about you, and how you hate me.
> How nothing I do is good enough.
> You hate where we live, the job I do,
> my friends, the way I talk to the children,
> is there anything about me you like?

How about me? When have you ever said
thank you for anything I do? I look after
three brats, while you
stay late and pretend to be working.

> You wanted them, not me.
> You didn't get the one you wanted.
> That is what it has always been.

Here we go. The old tunes.
The classics are always the best.

> You wanted to marry that railway
> clerk, but settled for me.

That railway clerk runs his own transport
company. And would never cheat on his wife.
He's a decent, loving person. I could've done worse.
I did.

> Well, you can go and suck him off in his minivan.
> Because you won't see me for a long, long while.
> The money will be in your account soon.
> You can buy those ugly curtains
> you've been going on about.

My family preferred you to him.
Even though you are Tamil.

> Your great liberal family is
> more bigoted than mine.
> So glad to be done with you all.

Where are you?

> The bus just passed through Wellawaya.

Aiyo, stop this, Jegan.
You cheat on me and then
you play the martyr. So easy for you, no.
I wish I could just abandon the
children like you.

> You are talking to me
> about playing the martyr? Ha!

I don't get to throw tantrums and get on buses.
If I could, I would've done that a long time ago.
I am done with you. I don't care where you live,
or who you whore with. But you will not
make the children suffer. That is your only duty.

> Too late for that.
> I will be in Vakarai by evening.

Don't be a bloody fool.
The Tigers have captured the eastern towns.
It was in today's papers.
You will not get past Amparai.
Stop being a child.

> What does the *Sunday Times*
> know about Tigers men?
> What do you?

And when you come back, you will
tell me everything. This one
can't have been the only slut.

> After Amparai, we will board a different bus.
> This one will be driven by the Boys.
> We will be taken to Vakarai for signing up
> and for initial training.

The Boys?
Have you gone mad, Jegan?
What shit are you talking?

> I'm going to join the Tigers, Sulee.
> We have talked about this.

About what a dumb idea it was!
About what we'd do if they ever came
after Mikel when he turns 15. I heard they
recruit even younger.

> Aren't you glad I'm over 18?

You're talking crap.
What the hell will a terrorist group
do with a pastry chef?

> There is a need for cooks.
> And I can cook more than pastry
> if you let me.
> You used to love my food.
> Or maybe you were pretending.
> Trying to get over that railway clerk.
> There was a time when you thought I was ok.

Stop crying like a baba. You can get off
after Wellawaya, and take a bus straight back
to Kandy. You can stay with my Loku Nenda.
She always liked you.

> If I come into Kandy on a bus from the east,
> the army will detain me and question me
> and treat me like I'm a Tiger.
> If I'm going to be treated like a terrorist,
> I might as well fight for our people.

Here we go again. When was the last time you
were harassed? Appachchi got you that letter from
the Minister. Just show that.

> And your Loku Nenda is
> the biggest phony of the lot.

So now you're going to train as a soldier?
You haven't been for a jog in five years.
Remember badminton last Christmas?
You won't last a push up.
Have you even held a gun?

> I'm not going to fight. But if they
> give training, I will take it. They need us.

I thought you didn't support the LTTE.

> That's what you say when you
> marry into a Sinhala family. Even a
> Sinhala liberal family. Unfortunately,
> I have to go out into the world as a Tamil.

You said the so-called Boys were fascist.
That they were blood-thirsty thugs.
How easily you forget.

> No, you did. Your Appachchi did.
> I am merely required to nod in that house.

So you agree with child soldiers
and suicide bombers, is it?
You agree with killing Tamil leaders?

You agree with burning Tamil homes?
Raping Tamil girls?
With jailing and torturing us without trial?
Treating us like immigrants in our own country?

We looked after so many Tamil families
during 1983.
Have you forgotten? Including your aunty.

Yes, so we must be eternally grateful
for a few bleeding heart Sinhalayas
who sheltered terrified Tamils,
while other Sinhalayas burned them.
And then put up with what the army is
doing up north.
How we are treated at checkpoints.
With being second class.

You are a partner in a 5-star restaurant.
In what way are you second class, Jegan?

It's not just about me and you, Sulee.
Just because you are well off.
Just because bad things don't happen to you.
You don't understand what it is to be us.

Us? I hear the slut is Tamil, as well. And
still a teenager. You want to make little
Tamil babies with your child bride. Will you
train your babas to blow themselves up in school?

There it is.
Doesn't take long for
the Sinhalaya's mask to come off.
Shame on you.

SHAME ON YOU! You make me talk like this.
In 14 years of marriage,
I've never talked about Tamils.

>That's the point.
>It's a Tiger checkpoint coming up.
>I have to go.

Jegan, I am calling you now.

Why is your phone switched off?

I found the slut's number.
You wait.

So I spoke with her.
Pick up your phone.
Now.

Jegan?

Call me now.
I mean it.

>Sulee listn to me. I hvent much battery.
>Army stopped bus in Amparai.
>Said there r terrorists on board. Checked IDs.
>Put our hands on the bus while they serched.
>Five guys got cuffed. Thought I was gone.
>Showed your father's letter. Then bullets started flying.
>Tigers shoot at army and suddenly bus
>is a gun fight. Still going on.

Where are you?!?

On the bus hiding betwn suitcases.
I'm sorry for everything. I fcked up
cos I was sad. I love you all. I don't want to die.

Jegan, stay on the bus.
Do not move. You hear. Stay still.
Are they still shooting?

Cant txt. Will call.

Was that you? Did you just call?
I couldn't hear.

Did u hear the shooting?
Dn't hv battery.

They are still shooting?

Not at bus. But there is a gun fight.
I'm so so sorry Sulee. I've been lost.
Tell Mikel, Manique and Malla
that I am always proud of them.

You will tell them. You hear me?
You will tell them. When you come home.
Are there others with you?

I feel stupid. I fcked this up.
Like everything.

I spoke with your Nilakshi.

She's not my anything.

Jegan, she is a child. And she says she is going
to kill herself. Have you no shame?

> I broke off with her. I only did it because
> I was angry. I know you've been
> talking to the railway clerk.

Who else can I talk to? I need a friend.
You don't even look at me.

> We used to talk. A lot.

We used to do a lot of things.

> I think it's stopped.
> I'm going to try for the exit.

Jegan! Don't! Is there anyone
else on the bus?

> I can hear people but I'm
> scared to lift my head.

Stay down my darling. Stay down.

> I miss us.
> We used to enjoy each other.

Before kids.

> Nothing to do with kids. It was us.
> You are always angry at me.

>   Sulee are you there?
>   If I get out of this, I am coming home.

>   Sulee?

Sorry just drove past the Savoy.
We used to go to the box seats
at the movies.
You remember?

>   You are driving?

A friend is.
Is the gun fight still on?
Why did you cut the call just now?

>   Sulee I'm running out of battery.
>   I will come home somehow. I promise.

You haven't taken me to
the movies for years.

>   We took each other for granted.
>   That is all. Like every shitty married couple.

Nilakshi told me you took a girl
to the cinema every Thursday.
And she broke off with you
because you were cheating on her.

>   She is stupid.

How come I heard people
laughing when I just called?

>   Must have been the army guys outside.

It wasn't.

>   Will you forgive me?

Why is your car parked
outside the Savoy cinema?

>   I left it there before I took the bus.
>   I will pick it up if I ever get back to Colombo.

Has the shooting stopped?

>   I think so.

Did any bullets hit you?

>   Not sure.

They sounded loud.
How come?

>   Because they were bullets.

There's an action film at the Savoy.
Might go and see it.

>   My battery is going.
>   I will call if I get out of this.
>   I love you all.

I didn't know Arnold and Stallone still made movies.
I prefer Stallone.
Arnie used to sleep with the servants.

I should also do Thursday movies.
Can take Mohan as my date.
That's the railway clerk's name,
as if you didn't know.
He drives an Audi.

> I think the shooting has started.
> My phone will die soon.

He divorced his wife after he caught
her cheating. She got nothing of his empire.
If I have proof, you don't get any of thathi's
money. Not a sausage.
But I get a piece of your restaurant.

> I'm making a run for it.
> Will call if I make it.

You better run.
Adultery is the jackpot in divorce cases.
As long as the other one gets caught first.
How many Nilakshis have you been taking to movies
while I've been raising your kids?

> I don't want divorce.
> I want to give it another try.

Once you get back from the east?

> Yes.

When will that be?

> I'll come right away.

Better hurry.
But before that, turn
and look up at the balcony.

                                              Huh?

Good thing Mohan bought his special camera.
Didn't even need the flash.
Smile.

                                  gdsfbccsag

Who's the hag next to you?
Looks like everyone texts at the movies these days.
We're not the only ones filming.

                              eggbcvccccccsag

Doesn't look like she wants to leave.
Run my great Tiger warrior.
No point now. We have our shots.
Nilakshi won't even have to testify.

There's only one exit darling.
Mr Thursday cinema man should know that.
Mohan is there with cameras.
Ready for your close-up?

That hag looks pissed.
She'll miss the end of the show!

                              sdgreeggbcvcc

I'm no expert on Stallone films.
But have a feeling the bad guy loses.

Short Eats

THE FUNERAL WAS NEVER MEANT TO BE A SOMBRE AFFAIR. He had stated clearly to all visitors at the cancer ward. So there was laughter, music, whisky for the old, ganja for the young. The spread was sumptuous, no frugal *mala batha* here.

The guests were mostly friends of his wife who hardly knew him, but pigged out on cured ham, mince pies and pastries filled with curried flesh. The champagne was served when the video came on, and there projected on the wall was his smiling face delivering his own eulogy. If-you're-seeing-this-I-must-be-gone sort of thing.

He thanks them for coming and insists they eat, drink and make merry. Boasts of a spread prepared by star chefs flown in especially. He talks of struggle, of unfairness, of parting gifts, of vaccines made from cancers, and then the video cuts to his torso hanging from a hook.

Then to masked chefs with cleavers. Then to familiar-looking short eats. It ends with him grinning at the camera, saying bon appétit as Pachelbel's Canon in D soars. The guests stare at the closed casket and begin to retch.

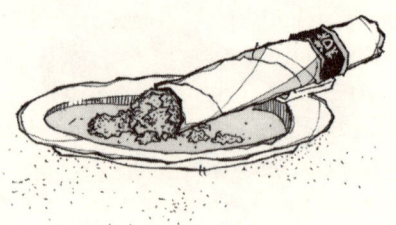

The Colonials

AN ENGLISHMAN, A DUTCHMAN AND A PORTUGUESE MAN walked into a bar. They ordered two arracks and a beer and sat at the end of a terrace, far from everyone who was yet to arrive.

The bar was at the Galle Face Hotel, constructed in 1861, not that long before this meeting took place. The terrace overlooked the Indian Ocean and was uncrowded, save for these three, dressed in the garb of merchants and smiling as widely as those who do not trust the other are wont to.

'Tavern looks agreeable,' remarked the Dutchman, surveying the bottles of rum hanging from the counter. 'In the hill country, we have pleasant taverns, but none as decorated.'

It was two in the afternoon, three hours before the hotel guests, the colonials and the native elites came down to watch the sun set on empires.

'We could've met at the club,' said the Englishman. 'I even suggested it to Fonseka.'

'Not a good idea,' said the man from Portugal. 'Your face is known at the club. And mine too, I fear.'

'Edgar Walker,' said the Englishman, extending his hand. 'Bank of England. Pleased to make your acquaintance.'

'Pieter Van Cuylenburg,' replied the Dutchman. 'VC Plantations. A pleasure.'

'Patience please, gentlemen. I will introduce you appropriately when drinks arrive,' said the Portuguese. 'They say this place has the best waiters in Ceylon.'

'So we'll get our drinks in 45 minutes then?' said Walker, and they all laughed.

The floor was chequered like a chessboard and descended in ledges onto a lawn with palm trees. The sun sat behind a cloud, and the sea sang to the crows on the parapet. Behind the bar, Queen Victoria looked out from a painting, above an insignia with a lion and a unicorn fighting over her. The Englishman sat with his back to it.

'I will judge you not, Van Cuylenburg. Though you swill the local beer. Forgive me, but the stuff is beastly.'

The Dutchman grinned, 'I have a taste for native delights.' His eyes twinkled. 'As have you, I believe.'

The Englishman sparked a beedi the size of a cigar.

'I have grown accustomed to the arrack,' said Edgar Walker. 'It is whisky mixed with rum and is unpalatable straight. Though it has a subtlety when combined with citrus.'

'A fine description, sir,' said Lorenzo Fonseka from Portugal.

'As long as it doesn't taste like the so-called sweets they served me at the estate…' said Pieter, making the face of a revolted child.

'My servant gave me local plum wine,' said Lorenzo. 'It was like Pinot from Naples…'

'Surely you jest?' said Walker.

'…had been served to a cow… whose piss I was consuming.'

They all laughed, and the drinks arrived, and the waiter poured and grinned, despite not hearing the joke.

'Pray tell. Señor Lorenzo, are you still seafaring these days?'

'Indeed. But the oceans have grown savage. Pirates hit my fleet near Java. Though nothing was stolen.'

'Remarkable! How so?'

'It is wise to have a bigger cutlass than the pirate.'

There was less laughter this time, and the Englishman puffed on his beedi, and Lorenzo Fonseka gulped his arrack sour like a sea monster swallowing a ship.

'Now let us do this properly, gentlemen. Sir Edgar Walker, I introduce you to Pieter Van Cuylenburg, the finest planter of the Dutch East India company.'

'Hang on, old boy. Queenie hasn't knighted me yet.'

The Dutchman signalled for another beer. He had been preparing his speech all week and had forgotten the first line. He fidgeted with his coat and wondered whether taking it off would be disrespectful. The capital was hot and muggy, unlike the cool hills to which he was accustomed.

'Surely sir, it is but a matter of time before Her Majesty…'

He glanced at the portrait of Victoria and the barman below it. The Englishman made a gesture with his hand that said thank you, enough and let us move on.

'I am honoured that you granted me this audience, sir,' says Van Cuylenburg.

'Edgar Walker has served as governor of the Bank of England in Siam, Kowloon, and now Ceylon.'

'I am aware of Sir Edgar's reputation.'

'And yet I am unaware of yours,' said the yet-to-be-knighted banker.

Lorenzo sprayed lemonade into another glass of arrack. He had learned to drink it while running spices from Kerala to Kampuchea, long before he owned a fleet and dared to invest in cutlasses.

'Pieter Van Cuylenburg owns the finest estate south of Hatton.'

'Tea?'

'Not quite, Sir.
'Coconut?'
'Perhaps Pieter will explain.'

The Dutchman shuffled on the mahogany seat, took off his gloves, and then began.

* * *

They say that wind brought the Portuguese, and greed brought the Dutch. Fear is what brought me to Ceylon 20 years ago. My father was a man of power in Rotterdam; he ran the breweries for Adriaan Heineken. But the cult of that heathen Marx reached our factories, and my father became a union man, and a friend of the Sicilians. By the time I was 15, he was smothered in lawsuits and stifled by debt. I tell you this so you know that I am not a silver-spooned nobleman, merely an honest toiler of some diligence.

On my 18th birthday, I was visited upon by seven Sicilians who told me that as his only heir, I would inherit my father's dues and should he not survive the debtor's prison, the burden would be mine to settle.

Before that month had expired, my mother's uncle had procured me a job with the Dutch East India company, and I was aboard the Batavia, bound for Port Louis, Goa, Ceylon and Singapore, stealing away like that proverbial night thief.

Unlike Señor Lorenzo, I am no sailor, and the journey made me bring up bile, and from my sickbed, I cursed the ocean, my father and my creator. I arrived at these coconut shores one sunrise after a terrifying storm and knew on first sight that Ceylon would be my home. Years later, when I set eyes on those hills behind Mawanella, I knew that departing these shores was no longer a possibility.

I joined the Plantations Division of the East India Company and served my apprenticeship in Badulla and

Ella amidst teascapes that mirrored my visions of heaven. Where not long before, Dutchmen like myself had planted coffee and parted with fortunes. For, by 1870, a dastardly leaf disease had wiped out every coffee plantation in these fair hills, and turned princes into paupers.

I rose up the ranks at a steady pace and was managing four estates by the time I was 30. I paid all debts to my father's swarthy creditors and won him his freedom though he expressed paltry gratitude. Thus, with some indignance and much relief, I settled into my planting life.

I savoured the sunsets in the hills, the meals at the club and the evenings with dusky maidens. I gambled seldom and fell to the amber nectar hardly, and thus, saved most of my generous stipend. And then I made the folly that has ruined many free men and will continue to ruin more as long as the skies are blue. I took myself a wife.

No, not among the dusky maidens of the tea fields. Perish the notion. Having endured my father's disgrace, I could no longer tolerate the plague of scandal. I procured myself a respectable bride from my mother's village of Giethoorn. Until then, I had considered myself a moderate success in life and was pleased with my humble accomplishments. Until the moment I brought Geertje from Giethoorn to the Maskeliya hills.

Geertje did not approve of my manners or my quarters or the planter's club or how familiar I was with the servants or that I was beholden to the Company.

'A true gentleman manages his own lands,' she said, while dragging rakes over my lawns and brooms across my floors, and planting her complaints between my ears.

Over the next 48 months, she had extracted three children from my loins, and persuaded me to pour every shilling I had into the magic soil behind the hills of Mawanella, where, on the advice of my darling wife, I grew not tea nor cinnamon nor coconut nor rubber. No gentlemen, I grew the crop that had suffered that ignoble death on these very hills a few decades previous. I grew coffee.

Geertje bore me two daughters and a son, but mostly proved a matriarch to the coolies who worked on our plantation. While she forbade me from fraternizing with the help, she herself would sit on the floor with the kitchen staff and gobble rice and curry and gossip, listening to the ailments of the women folk, while ordering the men to do repairs around the house. While I spent the monsoon season galloping across 50 acres on my Kashmiri steed, trying to convince the traders in Kandy that Ceylon coffee was making a comeback.

One man in particular, my head gardener Thiranjeevan, had wormed his way into my wife's trust. A rodent of a fellow, he dabbled in crude sorcery and made luck charms for the natives. Every cursed day, he would read my wife's horoscope and instruct her on auspicious times and how to avoid the evil eye. Without my knowledge, he planted charms along my perimeter, allegedly to bless my crop and ward off evil. Furious, I demanded he remove each one, and he complied like a petulant child, though I suspected that he replaced them with curses.

Gentlemen, I did not like the influence this coolie brought to my good Christian household, and while I laid in the arms of my plantation concubine, I plotted ways to be rid of this pestilence. And then against all logic and science, his charms began to work. Ceylon Coffee outsold Lipton Tea for two years in a row, our returns tripled, and my wife's melancholia evaporated.

I had spies watching Thiranjeevan, lest he attempted to inveigle his way into my wife's bedroom. But when talk emerged of him building a shrine next to our bungalow, matters had to be escalated. I instructed three of my concubines to accuse him of lewd behaviour and unwanted affections, though these ripples and rumours failed to elicit the scandal I required. When the estates' earnings went missing from the main office and were found under Thiranjeevan's bed, I had all I needed to be rid of the menace.

My wife was inconsolable and barked at me for weeks. Gentlemen, I should've foreseen what followed, but so relieved was I to be rid of this vermin that my good judgement was suspended.

A week after I dismissed him, the heavens imploded. Two of my children got the pox, spots appeared on my coffee leaves, my workers began complaining of strange noises at night, and the disawa of Kandy, who had loaned me half the acreage of the estate, informed me that he was calling in his debt before next month's Vesak festival.

My wife is taking the children to Giethoorn, and I am left with a cursed estate, angry workers and a debt I cannot pay. I was engaged in a cost-benefit analysis on the pros and cons of throwing myself off those wretched hills before Señor Lorenzo agreed to hear my woes. He consoled me and presented me with a solution that could save my estate and make one fortuitous investor very wealthy.

I present this plan to you Sir Edgar, despite my initial misgivings. I am but a humble planter, unversed in the letters of the law. But I do know that if done with legitimacy, even a criminal act can cease to be viewed that way, especially when done out of view.

* * *

A few more patrons had arrived at the Galle Face Terrace. A rotund man in a plain suit was sitting with a fetching lass in a palm tree's shadow. He glanced around several times before taking a seat with his back to the room.

'That's Tommy Maitland. What in Hades is he wearing?' Edgar Walker was on his second arrack and third beedi. He nodded at Van Cuylenburg, who looked relieved to have finished his plea.

'That is Sir Thomas?' asked Lorenzo Fonseka, glancing at the girl arching her back and stroking her long black hair.

'That must be the dancer. Her name is Lovina. My wife is an incorrigible gossip. Apparently, old Tommy is quite smitten.'

'That will end badly,' said Van Cuylenburg, folding his arms.

To their right was a view of Galle Face Green, where horses used to race twice a year. A few local children were flying kites and chasing each other across its patchy grass.

'I have seen Pieter's land. He should thank his fine wife for making him buy it. It is of soil that I have never seen on any of my voyages,' said Fonseka. 'The dirt is cool and moist and the colour of cocoa and oak. It will nurture any seed that falls upon it.'

'And yet my coffee leaves look like a leper's face.'

'Patience Pieter. I will find men. We will dig up these curses. We will deal with your witch doctor man. I, too, have encountered the native magic. It is not something to be sneered at. He is still in the village?'

Van Cuylenburg nodded.

'Then that is the easiest part of your issue. Once we have unearthed every piece of sorcery, we will plant again. But not coffee. That was your wife's one foolishness. We will quadruple your investment by planting something else.'

It was all part of an act and Lorenzo was a natural actor. A group of locals arrived at the bar, wearing finer clothing than anyone present. Their faces betrayed a diffidence and uncertainty that they carried with them into the room. They examined the menu, took glances at the wealthy foreigners and slunk off towards the lobby.

'If the locals unite, they will be unstoppable,' said Edgar Walker. 'But that will not happen in our lifetimes.'

'Their army is weaker than their beer,' said the Dutchman taking a sip, but this time none of them laughed.

'I am perplexed, Señor Lorenzo,' said Walker. 'Are you suggesting I invest with the Bank of England or privately?'

'The investment I am about to suggest cannot go through your country's bank.'

'Splendid,' said Walker. 'As long as we're clear.'

* * *

Sir Edgar, you know me as a pirate. Let us not mince words. The oceans are vast and filled with monsters, and that is where I have plied my trade these many years. Thankfully I have made more friends than enemies, and if I have a talent, it is knowing which cargo to carry and which to conceal.

The sea has taught me everything. You do not need to believe in ghosts to fear them. I started taking spices up and down the silk route before the waves got crowded with scoundrels and racketeers. I could not run my fleet at the mercies of Lisbon or London or Amsterdam and the prices they set.

For there was only one industry that I could see growing from Kampuchea to Indochina to Manila to Ceylon. The industry of war. Cutlasses, armaments, bullets. The demand was constant; the price was agreeable. It is a treacherous business, but if not me, some Dutchman or Englishman, or worse, some Indian or Chinaman will take my place with glee.

Because of my many friends and my few enemies, I now have transport across the country and in useful places across the Orient. Among my clients, I have kings and kingpins, so my shipments receive safe passage from anywhere to anywhere. I have spoken already to the disawa of the Kandyan kingdom, and I believe he will accept the terms we present.

But once we have dug up the land and expunged all curses, we remain with the conundrum of what to grow. Forget coffee, Pieter. This is not 1848. Forget tea, that ship has long sailed. Instead, I present you with a crop that is easier than tobacco to grow and harvest and is twice as lucrative. A crop that has demand across the indies and the orient and even closer to all our homes.

It is consumed by gurus and rishis across India, by the Gurkha and Malay soldiers and their fiery wives, it is prescribed by doctors in the far east and even enjoyed in this very city. I have inquired at this establishment, and they have granted me permission to do what I am about to. Sir Edgar, may I trouble you for a light?

* * *

'Put that away, man!' snapped Edgar Walker in a hiss that made Van Cuylenburg jump. 'Tommy Maitland is there with his whore. And you mean to make a spectacle of us?'

Lorenzo shrugged and passed the pipe to Pieter, who furrowed his brow in confusion. Should he puff on it and complete the pitch, and offend the investor?

'The smoking of hashish is not against the law sir. Neither is the cultivation of hemp. It is as natural as the tobacco leaf, though not as bewitching or destructive.'

'I… I take issue with the word bewitch. This juniper smoke enchants and calms like no other. But it does not enslave the senses.'

Pieter delivered his line, and Lorenzo nodded with approval.

The children on the green abandoned their kites for cricket bats as more members of the local elite occupied the bar to light their cigars. No one paid heed to the table at the corner of the terrace or the smoke from an ornately carved pipe as it curled upwards to be sucked up by a fan.

'Many believe ganja to be a civilizing agent. This very hotel has a private menu for guests. I am told that Anton Chekov stayed here with two mistresses and ordered pipes of Afghan cream and king Coconut on the hour. Andrew Carnegie stopped here to meet investors from Shanghai. And he left Lanka with a disdain for its entrepreneurs but an appreciation of its sweet green leaf. And it is not to tea that I refer,' Lorenzo Fonseka smiled and passed the pipe to the Dutchman.

Edgar Walker lit two beedis, puffed on one and let the other smolder in the ashtray, a foul-smelling incense to mask the musky scent of the devil's weed.

'I am pleased to see that you have thought this through,' he said shaking his head. 'But I am neither coolie nor reprobate. I am a businessman.'

'This was growing wild on my estate, sir.' Van Cuylenburg placed the pipe by the ashtray. 'If I fill my acreage with it, it will deliver a margin of profit four or five times that of tea.'

Edgar Walker put on a pair of black leather gloves and handled the pipe as if it were the tail of a scorpion. He took one puff on it and raised an eyebrow. Then he returned it to Lorenzo and went back to his beedi.

'It is the finest I have tasted. But they say a rat dressed in Saville Row tweed is still a rat.'

'Sir, I do not follow.'

Walker took a look at the natives at the bar and shook his head.

'Those two at the bar are local surgeons. I considered taking my wife's sister to one of them for her goitre. Don't look now, man. But the stocky one was educated in Cambridge, and his father owns rubber factories along the coast. In the end, I waited until they sent me a house surgeon from Sheffield.'

Lorenzo took another puff. The discussion was not proceeding as he anticipated, but the Mawanella smoke was too exquisite to waste, and the afternoon sky too pretty to ignore. If this British toff wished to climb on his horse, Lorenzo would walk, and it would be Britainnia's loss.

'The locals may one day run this country for sport. And they will run it into the ground. I will not let one of them take a knife to a relative of mine, even one whom I despise as much as my sister-in-law, no matter which school their daddy sent them to. Van Cuylenburg, your misfortune is not your wife's fault. It is yours. Never let the locals beyond your verandah.'

Lorenzo shook his head.

'Forgive me, sir. But these thoughts belong to another century,' he said. 'We have all had our way with this island. Maybe it is the turn of the locals now.'

This got the biggest laugh of them all.

Edgar ordered a last round of drinks and the bill. 'I had hoped the Chinese or the Indians would step up and take this burden off our hands. But the Chinese are gamblers, and the Indians are drunks. We remain Ceylon's only hope.'

Van Cuylenburg had abandoned his beer. He poured the arrack from the bottle and topped it with ice. His hand shook.

'I, too, was sceptical, Sir Edgar. A Dutchman growing hemp is as hackneyed as a Dutchman who flies. But the figures cannot be ignored.'

'You probably think me to be a man of prejudice. But it is not me that is a racist, it is mother nature. She is the bigot. It is she who endowed the European races with intellect and spirit, while leaving the lush lands to the simpler browner tribes.'

'I take it you are not interested in our proposition.'

'On the contrary, I am interested in visiting this Eden in the hills. But I will not invest in marijuana. It is beneath me, and more importantly, it is beneath my profit measure.'

The Portuguese and the Dutchman exchanged a glance.

'But what I do have, gentlemen, is a counter proposal.'

* * *

I do not wish to bore you gentlemen with my biography. Suffice to say, I benefitted from that lottery of birth that made me an Englishman born to a family of means. You both may believe in God and destiny, but I know both to be imposters. I occupy the space I am in through astute decisions and benevolent fortune.

But firstly, may I ascertain this much. Lorenzo Fonseka, you have a secure route from here to Shanghai, Beijing and Taiwan? I do not mean channels like those malaria-infested canals that the Dutch run spices through, no offence Pieter.

Good. I will rely upon the great Portuguese mariner's repute. I can make sure you remain untroubled by authorities as far as Singapore, but after that your risk is your own.

I fear I am not long for this part of the world. One day, the East India company will be bigger than any sovereign nation state on the earth. Some would argue that the day is already upon us. The locals are getting restless, the Buddhists are emerging from their slumber, thanks to the Bohemian ideas of that looney Henry Olcott. They are growing weary of the white man's rule, and the Chinese have the cunning, and the Indians have the gab to be their masters.

We can no longer run this world from Amsterdam, Lisbon or London and we should stop pretending we can. Our time is passing serenely but with haste and if you mean for me to throw more dice before I depart, then I need some guarantee that I will roll a six.

You are misinformed as to the legality of cannabis sativa. The law is clear on the subject, and the penalties for smuggling a narcotic do not distinguish between stimulant and poison. If we are to risk the gallows, why do it for a paltry three-score rise?

My proposal is you grow a crop that will deliver returns of exponential proportions. That can be harvested for a few hundred rupees and sold for a few thousand pounds. If the land you possess is as fruitful and as discreet as you say, then buying you out from a local disawa would be child's play.

Do not shake your head, Lorenzo Fonseka. You may think you know what I am to suggest, but you do not. It is a crop both the East India company and the British government would fund by proxy. We have already fought two wars with China over it. The market for opium grows in the west among gentlemen like yourselves. But it is in the Orient where the demand outstrips the supply.

I am weary of this continent and these paradises filled with thieves. A whore ceases to have allure once she has submitted to you a thousand times. None of us are Andrew Carnegie, and I doubt any of us dream of concert halls. It is no longer 1869, gentlemen. Let us plant our poppies while we can.

* * *

There was shocked silence, followed by the settlement of bills. The bar was now crowded with tourists and locals. Thomas Maitland and his companion had long departed. Pipes had been put away, though no hands had been shaken.

'I trust neither of you will see the need to discuss my proposal with your masters,' stated Edgar Walker as a matter of fact. The other men shook their heads.

'There are no masters, Sir Edgar. Only us.'

'We all have our masters, Fonseka. But very well.'

'I would like to discuss the implications with Señor Lorenzo, if I am to be permitted,' said Pieter Van Cuylenburg. 'May I give you my answer by tomorrow?'

'That would be agreeable,' said Walker, and hands were finally shaken.

* * *

They walked to the entrance of the Galle Face Hotel and watched the kids with kites, the teenagers with bats and the couples under umbrellas. Pieter hailed a Bajaj three-wheeler, Lorenzo walked to his Toyota, and Walker departed in a chauffeur-driven Benz paid for by the company. The planter waved from his tuk-tuk to the shipping magnate, who bid farewell to the gentleman from the bank.

'Is it true you are to be knighted, Eddie?' asked the Portuguese before they departed.

'I bloody well should be,' replied the Englishman.

Moments later in the back seat of his Benz, Edgar Walker texted his PA and set up meetings for the next day. On the radio, two local DJs attempted comedy by mimicking British accents. One spoke like Noel Coward, the other like a character from a novel by Dickens. They bantered for minutes and were neither funny nor accurate.

We don't speak like that anymore, thought the Englishman. If you cannot learn to mimic us properly, how will you rule yourselves?

His chauffer pulled out of the Galle Face Hotel into Colombo traffic. Edgar Walker looked at the colonial buildings sharing space with skyscrapers and dialled a number. Somewhere in Beijing, a telephone rang.

Bodhi and Sattva

WHEN BODHISATTVA ARRIVED IN CEYLON, THE ANIMALS gathered at the Great Rock. Jackal asked it first. 'Do beasts have souls?'

Peacock was next. 'Can I be reborn a predator? I want to eat creatures like me.' Kingfisher inquired, 'May I be born outside the beastly realm? Maybe as a Deva or a Naraka?'

The Great One replied, 'Why not a Human?'

'Chee!' said Crocodile. 'Look how ugly.'

'Eeya!' said Pangolin. 'See how unhappy.'

'No one is where they haven't chosen to be,' said the Enlightened One and no one believed him.

Tortoise said he wanted to be faster than Rabbit. Deer wished she were not so edible. Leopard wanted to be vegetarian, so she didn't have to chase down meals. Hawk wanted to swim, and Frog wished to fly. Only Human wished to be reborn as Human. The beasts hid in the trees and sniggered at the hairless ape.

Bodhisattva put fingers to lips. 'What is more foolish? To remain what you are? Or to become what you must?' He sighs. 'Every time I come here, I hope. I think maybe this time they'll get it.'

'That we are all one?' asked a serene Snake.

'That we must try on all hats, before we give up headgear?' asked a mindful Gecko.

'Nope,' said the Holy One, limping towards Nibbana. 'Nehe.'

'Not one of you fellows ever asks to be reborn as me.'

This Thing

'MACHAN, WE ARE MORE THAN HAPPY FOR YOU BUGGERS TO headline this show,' said the bass player of Slave Island. It was the Halloween gig at the Bishop's College Auditorium, and six bands were supposed to play in four hours. Halloween was less of a thing back then, but that didn't stop the compère dressing up as Dracula and the tagline 'Have a Spooktacular Show' being plastered on all the posters.

The members of This Thing had very different reactions to this, none of which were voiced aloud.

Superb! thought Daran, the guitarist

You can't be serious, thought PK, the drummer.

Sneaky bloody maggot, thought Che Reef, the singer/songwriter/bassist.

'The best band plays last, no?' says the bass player of Slave Island. 'Coachella, Glasto, Hellfest, always the best band headlines. That's you guys, man.'

Was Slave Island conceding that This Thing was the superior band even though Slave's radio-friendly post-punk got them more gigs? Sneaky bloody maggot, thought Che Reef.

Daran, the guitar prodigy, was the youngest, the silliest and the most talented. Slave Island playing before This Thing would make his plan for the night a lot less easy.

PK knew that Slave Island's drummer was left-handed and didn't use a double foot, unlike Cyanide who was supposed to play before them. Which meant he'd have to set up his kit again before they went on, and he knew no drummer who enjoyed doing that. He also thought the bass player of Slave Island was a hack, and that their music was boy band shit with guitars.

Che Reef knew the gig was running late. That the packed auditorium had not come to see them. The girls of Bishop's College and their mums had bought tickets, and the boys and men who wished to paw them had tagged along. Most were here because Sinhala pop duo Kapila and Dushan were playing, and rumour had it that Ranmal, the rapper from New York, would be making an appearance.

The bands were on the rooftop behind the control room above the balcony. The rooftop had a few chairs, a table with soft drinks and paper cups from the sponsors. And enough dark corners for the bands and their buddies to hide and act naughty in. The rooftop had high walls and a large window looking onto the auditorium. It offered a view of the lighting guy's head, a glimpse of the packed balcony and an unfettered panorama of the stage and the musicians prancing upon it.

Currently it was Zodiac Mistic, a band of hippies from Hikkaduwa. They featured a three-piece dub group laying down a groove, four folk drummers slapping five types of percussion to obtain the same beat, and a runt with dreadlocks croaking into a mic.

'Is that a midget rasta?' says Che Reef to the other musicians peering through that glass. 'Mini Marley?'

The rest of This Thing laugh. The bass player of Slave Island merely smiles.

'I don't mind this band machan. Some trippy shit. That guitar flanging sound is da shit.'

'Da shit? You been hanging out with the hippityhoppers?' asked PK, the drummer.

Rockers and rappers treated each other with contempt, though rarely to the other's faces. Rockers thought themselves real musicians, and rappers thought themselves real players. Rockers got covers of English language magazines, and rappers got crowds in the outstation town halls.

Bishop's College auditorium had a fine PA rig that included monitors in the sound room behind the balcony. The sound room wasn't soundproof, so the rooftop got a muffled feed of what the auditorium was hearing. It wasn't perfect, but you could hear if someone were crap.

'Yeah, yeah. Me, too. I smoked with the guitarist. Mad fellow. Sound is not bad, ah. But I'd lose half those drummers.'

'Don't try their pills, whatever you do.' The bass player of Slave Island looks at his sneaker as it flattens his cigarette.

'I don't touch bloody panadols. I am a booze-and-fags bugger.'

'If you're taking, just take quarter. I took half in Hix, and all my leads turned into cobras.'

'Ade PK. Malshi told that her friend took this panadol and thought she was some love goddess and then banged a fisherman!'

'When did you talk to Malshi?'

PK had dated Malshi since they were fourteen and shared an elocution class. They had broken up thrice in the past year.

'When I came to pick up your drum kit. What's the matter with you man? She's like a sister to me.'

'Of course.'

'Don't tell me you've broken up again.'

'Nah! We're good.'

'Good. You play like shit when you have girl problems.'

The bass player of Slave Island had heard a different version of the fisherman story and was keen to change the subject.

'So This Thing is cool to headline?'

Che Reef glanced at his drummer and guitarist.

'Daran, PK, you want to go on last?'

'I don't care,' said Daran, though he very much did.

'We can't change the line-up,' said PK, shaking his head. 'Mr Eugene has printed the programmes already.'

Eugene Rosairo was the manager of Sam and the Strangers, a pop band of seasoned musicians and a singing starlet, who was third in the line-up after Zodiac Mistic and veteran metal band Cyanide. None of whose members had turned up yet. Mr Eugene had organized this gig for his church charity, which meant that none of the bands would get paid.

'Screw Mr Eugene,' said Che Reef, looking around the balcony to make sure that neither Eugene nor his cronies were in earshot. 'We can change the line-up if we want. But I don't want to. Sorry, bro.'

'No prob, man,' said the bass player.

'Did you guys find a guitarist?' asked Che Reef, tying a red bandana over his receding hairline.

'Yeah, hopefully he'll turn up tonight.'

'So new line-up for Slave Island ah? Sha. Very nice. But, machan. Don't give us this best band bullshit. You guys are bigger known than us. You should headline.'

'What bigger, Che? We just play that one Creed song, and the crowd goes wild,' said the bass player, doing that fake modesty that all musicians do around other musicians.

'Serves you right for playing Creed,' said Che, and the band laughed.

The bass player ignored the jibe and walked down the stairs, past the sound room and onto the balcony.

'What the hell is that bugger's name, men?' asked Che Reef.

PK shrugged, and Daran giggled. 'Kokila.'

'Don't fall for that Kokila's bullshit. Each band is given half an hour, but I know for a fact that Sam and the Strangers and those hip-hop fools will play an hour each.'

'That Cock-hila is a bloody snake. Malshi said he drugs women with those panadols.' PK stretches his fingers and two of them crack.

'Is Malshi coming today?'

'No, she's studying. Why?'

'You drum like a beast when she's there.'

'Why does everyone say that? My drumming has nothing to do with my woman.'

'Not just you,' said Che Reef. 'Daran also plays big solos when Malshi is there.'

PK cracked a finger and glared. Daran shook his head. Che Reef laughed and gave PK a punch.

'Just joking, man. These days Daran gets angry like a bloody fisherman. Too much Hikkaduwa, I think. C'mon. We are all bros.'

He gave Daran a wink, which Daran did not return.

The door to the sound room opened, and out walked four men dressed in black. Two of them had hair past their nipples, one wore a cowboy hat and another a leather trench coat despite the heat.

Che Reef continued his monologue. 'It's past nine already. By the time the rock bands come on will be past midnight, and the Bishop's will shut the show. Which means last band, no chance.'

'Ado, did someone say rock?' shouts one of the men in black. 'Ammataudu, this is This Bloody What Thing, no?'

'This Thing,' says the cowboy, doffing his hat.

It was only when they spoke, and you were face to face with them, that you realized that all the members of Cyanide were well north of 45, making them younger than Mr Eugene but twice the age of most of the bands present.

'How you, buggers? Shall we put a shot?'

Manilal Simon wore the trench coat and sweated like a leech. He pulled out a bottle of JDs. Bonzo Perera, the drumming cowboy, grabbed cola from the sponsors and some paper cups. Cyanide was Lanka's first proper rock band and had been playing guitar solos to drunken rooms since the days of Zeppelin and Floyd. They had been through many image and personnel changes, and their current incarnation featured a female guitarist who could shred a bassist purloined from a nightclub band.

'Where is Estrelle?' asked Manilal from his cowboy drummer.

'She's trying to buy some pills from those Zodiacs.'

'Before the show. Is she mad?'

'After, after. Apparently, they are like thada LSD,' said Bonzo.

'Thada LSD in Colombo? I'd like to see that. Most of those will be duds.'

'Apparently this is laced with mescalin. Full mind and soul trip.'

'Laced with cough syrup, must be. Best LSD I had was in Khe Sahn in '75.'

Che Reef used all the muscles in his face to prevent his eyes from rolling.

'We always wore black, men. Halloween or Shalloween. When we toured after the Tet Offensive, we went in black and rocked the bloody Yankees out of Saigon.'

Manilal told his we-toured-Vietnam story to every young musician he met. It involved doing drugs with a famous English rocker and playing a surprise show at the Viet Cong barracks. The musician's name varied according to the audience.

'... and Ritchie Blackmore said if Cyanide ever come to LA to look him up. Almost went in '77, but then bloody government changed and...'

'Oi, Manilal! You fellows are on now! Go go! Soon soon!' Eugene Rosairo had arrived with a clipboard. He ran the show that was running late and the charity that was taking the money. But he had also delivered a packed auditorium, which none of the acts on the lineup, with the exception of Kapila & Dushan (feat. Ranmal), could muster on their own. So the bands put up with more than a lot from him.

The old rockers in black left the cups but took the bottle, hidden under the trench coat, in case Mr Eugene saw them and hit them with a Bible.

'Now I hear you rock fellows want to change the line-up?' says Mr Eugene, looking at Che Reef and holding out his clipboard.

'No, we are fine, Mr Eugene,' says Che Reef. All bravado appeared to have leapt off the balcony. 'We don't mind going earlier even. Maybe before Kapila & Dushan.'

'Don't be a bloody fool, putha,' says Mr Eugene, watching the dinosaur rockers take to stage. 'Sam and the Strangers next, singing J-Lo and Madonna. Can't then have your heavy songs. K&D will follow Samantha. Then we turn down the lights and bring on the rocker bands.'

Cyanide opened the set as they had every show for the past 15 years. With 'The Final Countdown' by Europe. Manilal played the riff on his keyboard guitar and delivered every line like he was auditioning for Jesus Christ Superstar. He had the vocal chops, which always made Cyanide welcome on any bill, though his delivery and stage banter was corny even for 1973.

'You know he played with Clapton in Vietnam?'

'Not Hendrix?' said Daran.

'If you and Slave Island want to swap, that is up to you. But Samantha next, then K&D. Here, have a copy of the line-up.'

Daran noticed a misprint at the bottom of the programme and got the giggles. 'Producer: Eurine Rosairo.'

'Will the show be stopped at midnight?'

'Maybe,' says Mr Eugene, frowning at the half-empty paper cups. 'Has someone been drinking?'

***

Sam and the Strangers was playing a Riki-Enrique-Mark medley, and the crowd started clapping fractionally out of time.

'You know I've written all the songs for the new album,' said Che, shandy-ing the leftover bourbon into one paper cup.

'Ade, that's superb!' said PK, doing some stretches. 'Better be heavy this time.'

'Bit more mellow, I think. Ade, Daran, I got some good riffs for you this time.'

Their first album, Silent Minority was recorded in a church studio that did jingles. It was supposed to be jointly funded, though Che Reef paid for a bulk of those eight tracks while PK mostly bought the joints. Daran contributed the least financially but the most musically.

'We have to go heavier this time,' says PK, doing a mock jive to the synthetic pop being served up downstairs. 'Otherwise, what's the point?'

PK was in a church dance troupe until he discovered heavy metal.

'I have a few in 5/4 time. You play that and see you, bugger. I have one Dream Theatre-type song. You'll love it.'

Daran ran his fingers through his spiky hair. His haircut had been the first argument a year ago. According to Che Reef, it was impossible to play true rock with short hair.

'Why making that face, Daran? Have you even heard Dream Theatre?'

'Guys, let's not get into this before a gig please.'

'I heard them,' said Daran. 'Not my thing. That's all.'

'You prefer Three Doors Down, no? You like those three-chord numbers that Slave play, no?'

Daran shakes his head, and PK smells blood in the air.

'You saw Slave in *Mirror Magazine*, no? Wearing that Kiss make-up and talking about their mystery new guitarist, no? Bunch of posers,' said PK, invoking the common enemy.

'Daran, chill machan. I'm just joking.'

Che also realized that before a gig was the worst time to piss off the guitarist, especially when playing to their biggest crowd yet. Daran would get pissed, then loaded, then will make out with some random, and then come crying to Che. Same dance every time, and Che Reef hated dancing.

Che put his arm around Daran. 'Machan, we can also play this Nickelback shit and get sponsors and gigs. But we are much more. Does anyone have our musical intellect? We can be catchy and sonic and complex and take music to new realms.'

A loud boom filled the auditorium as the lights went down. A minor third, then a fifth, then a major seventh sent through a filter fraying at the edges. The kids on the balcony halted their chatter and rushed to the railing to gaze into the window. The noise began rattling the windows. And then it vanished to be replaced by a bassline and a beat. The crowd were at their feet and banging on the chairs. Sam and the Strangers had been joined by Kapila and Dushan, who did a freestyle ragamuffin jam to a Santana song that went on for nine minutes.

The balcony was silent as rockers, rappers, and those dressing like both, looked down upon Sri Lanka's biggest pop duo commandeering both mic and audience. Some stared in awe, others with envy. The latter group were all musicians.

'Machan, so many people have asked This Thing to do Sinhala songs, put in some tablas, make it more palatable for a Rupavahini breakfast audience.'

PK sniggered, Daran took a Gold Leaf from the pack the Cyanide singer left behind.

'I mean Kapila and Dushan are talented buggers and fair enough, they have gone for the Sinhala pop market and done it brilliantly.'

Daran takes a puff and waits for the 'but' to drop.

'But This Thing's music is more than a bajaw circus. We can do this stuff easy. But can they do our stuff? No chance.'

The crowd have their hands in the air and were chanting de-oh.

'Is this K&D's set? So, we on next?' asked PK, glad that he didn't have to change foot pedals on a left-handed drumkit.

The rastas from Zodiac Mistic had descended on the balcony and the air was thick with various strains of smoke. Mr Eugene appeared less concerned with this than he was with the presence of alcohol in a school auditorium. He had already evicted Cyanide after they finished their set. He walked with a man in a hood who was smoking a big cigar. The hooded fellow had the swagger of a politician's son and the build of a rugby lock.

'Watch out. Urine is coming,' said Daran stubbing out the joint. He had already been on the receiving end of Che Reef's vision for a new Sri Lankan rock and roll, a heady fusion that mixed western distortion with eastern scales and lyrics about ethnic conflict.

'Why is he bringing the bouncer over?'

Mr Eugene came over grinning with his hand in prayer pose, like he always did when he had something unpleasant to say.

'So small problem boys. K&D will only start their proper set after this song.'

'But they've been playing for half an hour,' groaned PK.

'They have been jamming with Sam and the Strangers. This is not their set.'

'Wait. So Samantha gets 1 hour. Then jams with K&D. And then K&D get another hour?' Che Reef patted down his bandanna and squared up.

The figure in the hood spoke in a voice that was a mishmash of accents and keys.

'Is that cool yo? Do you guys mind? Inspired to meet you man. Just flew in from Staten. Man, this crowd is off the charts! Colombo's gone next level! Who knew? I'm Ranmal, bro.'

The members of This Thing had very different reactions to this, none of which were voiced aloud.

Cool hoodie, thought Daran, the guitarist.

Prick, thought PK, the drummer.

Nice accent for a guy from Panadura, thought Che Reef, the singer/songwriter/bassist.

'You guys must be Slave Island,' said Ranmal, extending his fist.

'No this is This Thing,' said Mr Eugene. 'Actually, where is Slave Island?'

'Over there,' said Daran.

'Where?' Mr Eugene scanned the heads of the kids dancing to the baila pop rap fusion thing on stage.

'I've heard of This Thing,' said Ranmal, stealing a Gold Leaf from the community pack and a lighter from PK's hand. 'You guys are real experimental right? Like Radiohead.'

Posturing for a showdown, Che Reef collapsed into a blushing bride at the mention of the gods themselves.

'We wish, man. Our influences are System, Radiohead, Volta and Floyd. But we play our own noise. No covers. Never.'

Memorizing speeches and styling bandannas is what Che Reef did in front of the mirror instead of practicing his pitching.

'Not even one?' asked Ranmal.

'Not even 'Paranoid' by Sabbath,' said PK, raking over the dirt of another argument past.

Daran pointed Mr Eugene to where the bass player, keyboardist and drummer of Slave were sharing jokes and spliffs with Zodiac Mistic and some of the Dutch girls who had come up from Hikkaduwa.

'That's pretty badass, man. I don't really do covers either,' said Ranmal. 'I take pieces from every genre and mash them together. Like a collage, or a quilt. I take the old and make it new.'

'So you do hundreds of covers then,' said PK dancing along to K&D's breakthrough hit single, which fused a village folk tune with a funk sample.

'That's funny, man. Everything is borrowed. Even all your basslines and guitar solos. It's how you make it your own. You know what I'm saying. The stuff I'm doing now is more *bailatronic* than hip-hop. Next level.'

'Ranmal. Go. Go now! Your song is next. Daran, go call those fools.'

The rapper fist bumped everyone present who wished him luck with their mouths and bad sound with their thoughts. Che Reef and PK made cracks about bailatronic that Mr Eugene pretended not to hear.

Daran brought the boys from Slave Island just as Samantha entered the balcony with her entourage to an ovation from the groupies. The rappers whooped, and the rockers raised ironic eyebrows.

'See that,' said Mr Eugene. 'She was a little church singer in Puttalam when the Lord led me to her. I only taught Sam to sing soprano. I only designed her outfits. Now see. We have played Dubai, Latvia, Bonn and Berne.'

The Slave Island boys had a glazed look about them, obviously Zodiac Mistic had brought panadols along with their folk drums.

'What's up Mr Euri...Eugene,' asked the bass-player Kokila, swaying to Ranmal's bailatronic beat. The New York rapper's appearance had put the middle-aged crowd back in their seats, while their children were on their feet, making gestures with their hands and postures with their shoulders.

'K&D will play till 11.45. I only have room for one more band.'

The reactions from members of Slave Island and This Thing were all different and this time they were all voiced. Three were cuss words, three were unprintable sounds and one was the drummer of Slave Island upchucking panadol powder into his mouth.

'What the hell does that mean?' asked Che Reef. 'Other band goes home without playing?'

'You can both do one song each if you like.'

Four members of both bands said, 'Fuck that' in unison.

Daran slunk away to one of the Dutch girls he smooched in Hix a few weekends ago. Daran loved playing the guitar in more genres than just prog rock and indie alternative, though he didn't mind those. It was the arguments he was tired of.

'How about this?' said Mr Eugene, aware that Samantha was looking over at the raised voices, that Manilal was back in and sipping from a cup, and that K&D featuring R's set was about to end, and someone needed to be on stage. 'This is a charity show. But I will pay from my own pocket. The band that doesn't get to play will get paid.'

Daran looked across and saw the bass player from Slave Island beckoning. He suddenly wished he had never gone to Hikkaduwa that week and made that promise. He suddenly wished he had spoken to Che instead of chickening out. He shook his head.

'Look, Mr Eugene,' said Che. 'It is not about money. We have all worked hard for tonight. Extend till 1 a.m., and we will play half hour sets. As you promised the crowd.'

'I wish I could, son,' said My Eugene. 'But Bishop's is strict about music concerts, don't you know? How about this time Slave plays, then next show This Thing can play any slot they want, I promise.'

Che Reef walked away swearing, PK looked down at the crowd asking for a second encore as Kapila and Dushan shook the hands of the front row while Ranmal laid down a beat that shook the walls.

'But they can't play,' said PK. 'Their guitarist hasn't shown up.'

'No he's here,' said the bass player of Slave Island. 'Over there.' He pointed to the Dutch girls and the Rastas from Hikka, all surrounding one boy.

Che Reef advanced over with speech prepared about why Sri Lankan music will never get anywhere while we favour cover bands and pre-recorded tracks over true original music. That if they don't let This Thing play, he will write to the Island about all the alcohol and weed and pills being taken in the balcony, about why the headlining band was not allowed to play.

But then he saw Daran surrounded by white women and hairy men, like the rock god he was, with more talent in his smirk than this whole bunch of gathered phonies.

'That's our guitarist,' said the bass player from Slave Island. 'Daran didn't tell you? He has been jamming with us for a few gigs this month.'

'A few gigs?' Che coiled back and adjusted his bandanna.

'A guest spot at the Den. Then a full show at R&B. He didn't tell you?'

'He didn't.'

Che Reef looked at PK, who was on the phone with Malshi, listening to a ring tone.

'He is recording our new album,' said Che Reef. 'Then we have three gigs down south and then we might be touring Bangladesh.'

'He's not happy playing with you guys, brother,' says the bass player of Slave. 'We even let him sing. He growls better than Chad from Nickelback.'

Mr Eugene looked at Samantha and Manilal Simon sharing a cigarette across the bar and began plotting a Biblical vengeance. He didn't bring up a girl from the village to fall prey to a menopausal rocker. He knew Manilal's wife and he knew what a phone call could do. He watched the slithering worm do his whispering, 'You know I jammed with Slash in Hanoi…'

Che Reef glared at Daran and willed his eyes to say what he hoped he wouldn't have to. That he had discovered Daran's talent, that he had introduced Daran to rock, and that if Daran played with the boyband, then he might have to tell PK what Daran did with Malshi a month ago.

Daran looked back on the band he wanted to leave and the band he wanted to join, at girls he wanted to smooch and girls he wished he hadn't, and hoped with every note and chord in his body that at least one of the two panadols that Zodiac had made him swallow was a dud.

Hugs

WHEN HE ENTERS THE ROOM, HIS SON DOESN'T HUG HIM. His son is four and has cars to play with and doesn't want a hug and does not see how much his father needs one. Instead of reaching out to his wife or his daughter, who might've welcomed his sweaty embrace, he kicks the puppy, who runs in pain and knocks over the dinner. The mother shouts at the daughter for letting the mutt in the house. The daughter sits in the doghouse and dreams of leaving home.

At school, during netball practice, the daughter picks on the girl with pigtails for the crime of boasting about a recent Singapore holiday. The others join in, and there is some pushing and elbowing and catcalls of 'singabooruwa,' each time the pigtailed girl drops the ball.

The next day, the pigtail girl's father, a provincial councillor, comes in to complain to the teacher. Unaware of the man's connections, the teacher remarks that young girls must fight their own battles. The enraged councillor instructs his thug driver to make the teacher kneel in the playground, to the hoots of the school kids. The driver pulls off the teacher's hijab and cackles as she sobs.

The teacher's husband, his brothers and some friends from the mosque smash the councillor's car and stomp on the driver. The next day, organized mobs set fire to Muslim shops. Buddhist monks urinate in mosques, and emails about halal poisoning spread via phones. Politicians impose curfew and condemn no one. Months later, wealthy young men in beards blow up churches and not a soul can explain why.

This is an ancient tale of horseshoe nails and escalations and could be dismissed as horseshit if it weren't true. Shall we give it a sci-fi spin? Turn to our trusty time machine and reverse it all? Or ditch the hardware and call it magic realism? Whatever gets you to the next paragraph.

What if the boy hugged his dad or the dad hugged his daughter or smooched his wife instead? And what if the daughter defended pigtail girl from the bullies and was rewarded with hugs, a new best friend, and an invite for the Provincial Export Union's next overseas delegation trip?

And what if any person in this chain of pain decided to embrace rather than punch? Could we prevent riots and terror by replacing knee-jerk kicks with strategic hugs? If each and every one of us give an extra hug per day to someone who needs it, can we stamp out bullies and bigots and bombers?

This is the reason why hippies are laughed at. Fine. Come back when you've exhausted all other avenues. Try more religion in schools. Or less video games. Or more police. Or less taxes. We'll make a lentil soup while we wait.

Hugs are the one energy source with an infinite supply. So why not put them to work? We can get the geeks to develop an app. For some reason, you don't laugh at them anymore. We can count hugs like we do steps and calories. It could spread via the same phones that tell us to delete ourselves. Can more hugs cure all ills? Could we at least try it out and see?

The Ceylon Islands

Forgive your country every once in a while.
If that is not possible, go to another one.
– Ron Padgett

IT'S A SIMPLE CAR BOMB, AND IT'S RIGGED TO A BUSLOAD of schoolgirls. No one knows it is there except for me. The Ceylon Islands' bomb squad were trained by Israelis, but have had nothing to defuse in 20 years. By the time they get here, there will only be carcasses of young girls to sift through.

I have three daughters, and I am far from a monster. Yet this mission was created on my recommendation and has taken me 10 years to formulate. I believe it to be the only viable option.

In an hour, 35 schoolgirls between ages of 8-12 will die or be disfigured because of the length of the hem on their school uniform. After that, this country will burn for weeks, and after that I will be there to put out the fire.

It all began with Chamara Jayawardena, esteemed Sri Lankan cricket captain, swearing live on the BBC. A leader resigning like a drama queen wasn't unusual in this country, but an old boy of Trinity College dropping the f-bomb in public was something scandalous.

The story of Ceylon began not with King Wijeya or Queen Kuveni, but with a post-match press conference at Lords. Chamara Jay was usually well-spoken and polite, but that day he looked ruffled and agitated.

He was responding not to the dull cricket match that he had wasted five days on, but to news that Buddhist monks had set fire to Muslim businesses in his hometown of Kandy.

'Today, I am ashamed to be representing this country. In recent times, thugs in robes claiming to be Buddhist have committed shameful acts. But none as grotesque as the torching of property owned by Sri Lankan Muslims, people who are my brothers and sisters.

'This may not be the forum, but it is the only one I have. I wish to resign as Captain, and to renounce my race and religion. I no longer consider myself a Sinhalese or a Buddhist, as doing so implies complicity to these crimes, implies allegiance to these animals.

'I am Sri Lankan and consider any crimes against the people of my homeland, regardless of their ethnicity or religion, to be crimes against me. I have used my position as a sportsman to feign apathy, as most of my fellow countrymen do. No longer. Fuck this. It's unacceptable, and I will not accept it. Thank you. I will not be taking questions.'

The clip played on CNN, Al Jazeera, Russia Today, networks not known for their interest in cricket or in the troubled isle south of India. Among Sri Lankans, the clip was shared and debated over social networks, many of which were blocked in the island. Patriots denounced our cricketing hero as a stooge of the West. Liberals exalted him as a hero.

The bus is perched on the roadside while its driver sips a plain tea poisoned with three spoons of sugar. School will not be out for a few hours, and he will electronically smoke a half pack of Gold Leaf while looking at his phone. I follow him in a self-driving three-wheeler with tinted glass, and I spy a wire from the bomb peeping from the exhaust pipe. Do I have time to tuck it in?

The avenue looks much like Galle Road though its name is not that. It is in a city that resembles Colombo but happens to be in a country one thousand miles west of it. In the distance, by the harbour, I can see the statue of a famous cricketer holding his bat aloft. I am sweating, even though the trishaw AC is turned on full.

The population of Sri Lanka, formerly known as Ceylon, exceeds 20 million, the head count of Australia squeezed onto the landmass of Tasmania. Yet the nation of Lanka extends far beyond the boundaries of this not-so-fair isle.

Two million Lankans, exiled by economics and politics, reside in kingdoms across Europe, Asia, Australia and America, which means 1 in 10 people who could be identified as Sri Lankan no longer reside within its borders. This diaspora is of Tamils banished by the Eelam wars of the 80s, Burghers exiled by the Sinhala-only policy of the 50s and economic refugees displaced by the bank failures of the 2020s. The diaspora is sprinkled with minorities like Moors, Kaffirs, Chetties, Parsis and Chinese, all spurned by the land of their birth.

It was among this diaspora that Chamara Jayawardena's tirade received the most airplay. For many, Jayawardena was a hero, a sane voice speaking for humanity in a paradise plagued with division. At home, the far-right denounced the man as a traitor, who should've been ashamed for airing the nation's soiled linen on the world's washing lines.

I look at the detonator on the dashboard of this three-wheeler, encased in a brown box with a touch screen and no buttons. Detonators have evolved since I first rigged them back in my youth, at the nadir of the Eelam wars, as have three-wheelers. This one is voice-activated and comes with surround airbags. But most importantly, it runs its positioning off a Soviet satellite, not a Chinese one as the rest of the country uses.

I remember the CJ press meltdown well. It went 'viral,' as they used to say in those days. But I remember it for another reason. It was the first recorded mention of The Ceylon Islands. Wherever CJ's clip was shared, there were ads for a luxury resort called The Ceylon Islands, offering 'travel opportunity and generous remuneration.' The ads called for managers, marketers, architects, engineers, singing waiters and chefs versed in all four sambols to apply for vacancies.

When Chamara Jayawardena was gunned down at a traffic light while taking his sons to cricket practice, the story hit the world's headlines. Eyewitnesses, all of whom retracted their statements, described men on motorcycles firing five times into Jayawardena's Pajero, won for being player of the tournament at the 2023 World Cup. The bikes were traced to a Buddhist temple in Borella, but no arrests were made for the murder. And before you ask, let me assure you, I had nothing to do with any of it.

* * *

Sri Lanka is a sovereign Buddhist nation, the sole custodians of a Lankan brand of Buddhism. If China goes secular and Burma goes psycho, we are, we believe, the last bastion. This, we are told, is important, important enough to burn churches, stone mosques, dismantle kovils, send monks to parliament, and shoot the very prime minister who began this idiocy.

Buddhism is based on karuna and metta, kindness and compassion. It is about harnessing the mind and the desires; accessing the soul; using thought, word and action to promote the good, the just and the right. It is a philosophy more than a religion, though in Sri Lanka, it has adopted all the ugly traits of organized faith.

Buddhism is a way of being grounded in empathy, in benevolence, in non-violence. Ceylon has made a joke of that, a deeply unfunny joke. Those who industrialize aggression – the military, the cops, the gangsters, the politicians – claim to use violence as a last resort. Over here, in the sovereign home of non-violent Buddhism, it is our first port of call.

A drunken spat will end in a homicide, a domestic tiff will conclude with acid, political disagreements are resolved with guns, and a failed exam leads to the drinking of poison. Each of these happen each and every day in this beautiful land.

The malady may not be uniquely Lankan. Mohandas K. Gandhi and Martin L. King are now signposts on dirty boulevards, sepia photos used to sell computers, postage stamps that we spit on. Their names are spoken, and their words are quoted while their ideas fester in the first world and rot in the third.

Around the globe, in every bloodied outpost, it is as clear as God's disdain: pacifism is the idea that failed. The idea that should have been placed on an altar after two wars that made Europe a steaming heap. The idea that has been skewered on a hook and left to rot for half a century. The idea that will be bludgeoned and burned each day for as long as religion has its claws on these lands.

* * *

I follow the bus in my self-driving three-wheeler. I never tire of being driven across Batticaloa City. It is a town that wishes it were Colombo but is also glad it isn't. On the passenger seat behind me are my cigar pills, a diary and a brown box with a touch screen. As a father of three daughters, my choice of target may appear suspect at best. I assure you it is not.

Could I not have set my explosives at the house of parliament, that floating building on Colpetty Lake, designed by one of Geoffrey Bawa's many imitators? Could I not have targeted one of the government buildings on Duplication Boulevard hidden amidst bo and banyan trees? Is killing children necessary or even acceptable as a means to an end?

I have spent the last year at the Diego Garcia naval base typing up a 30-page report justifying what I am about to do. In it, I have outlined seven different scenarios that could deliver the desired objective. Of these, the thirty-five schoolgirls represent not only the lowest headcount, but also the most effective course of action.

Nothing softens the heart like the birth of a daughter, and nothing hardens it like the death of one. Killing schoolgirls, especially those of tender age, yet to become rebellious and petulant, will create a frenzy of emotion and a call for blood. There will be ground support for a pogrom on the perpetrators, and finally, after decades of peace, The Ceylon Islands will be at war.

* * *

In 2025, both *Forbes* magazine and *Conde Nast Traveller* ran cover stories on The Ceylon Islands. Floating on the equator, somewhere between Somalia and the Maldives, the islands had become a refuelling stop for shipping lines on the Indian Ocean as well as a sought-after tourist destination.

The cluster boasted 345 archipelagos, 230 eco-friendly resorts, a resident workforce of 500,000 and an annual turnover of 300 billion, making it the most successful tourist destination of all time.

Travellers marvelled at the landscaped beaches, the native fauna and the crimson skies. *National Geographic* published colour spreads of butterflies, elephants, black leopards and a recently discovered species of Ceylon dragon. *Harper's Bazaar* praised the standards of service, the exquisite flavours of its Sri Lankan fusion menu, and the innovative use of air taxis, hovercrafts and hot air balloons to transport guests from one paradise to the next. There are three balloons hovering above the bus each smothered in logos.

The bus driver puffs on his e-smoke and stares at his phone. I've had arguments with holy men and powerful rulers about the nature of the human beast, specifically of the Lankan genus. As a species, I don't think we're attracted to good or evil, only to docility.

The Pieris Brothers' School Bus Company offers drivers a choice of recreational facilities and life skill classes. Most drivers opt to park in smoking zones and puff away as our friend is doing now. Most days he stares at his phone and smokes. Bluetooth cigarettes are odourless and cancerless and ten times more addictive than their organic version. I prefer the pills as you can get your chemist to cook for you. Mine contains equal parts nicotine, morphine and red wine. I pop one and let the tingle wash me over.

In 2026, the *Economist* revealed the man behind the curtain. Raviraj Balasingham had left Sri Lanka in the 1980s as a teenager, one of the thousands of Tamils driven from their land by riots and wars and a hateful state. The story behind his fortune has many variants. Some say he ran pornography shops in New York during the 90s. Others report him as a predator who made profits on foreclosures during the credit crunch of the 00s. Many attest to his presence at LTTE fundraisers and claim that his offshore investments armed the Tamil Tigers for three decades.

The *Economist* noted that 82% of employees were of Sri

Lankan origin and that real wages were on par with the first world. When asked why The Ceylon Group was registered in Shanghai and not in New York, where Balasingham was resident, he replied, 'I go where business is good.' The magazine raised questions on hiring practices, to which Balasingham's reply was 'Sri Lankans work harder than anyone else, as soon as they are taken out of Sri Lanka.'

While these allegations remained unaddressed, his appearance on the *Fortune 50* raised some eyebrows. In an exclusive interview with the *New York Times*, he revealed his motivation behind purchasing The Ceylon Islands. 'I wanted to create an authentic Sri Lankan tourist experience in a place free of Sri Lankan bureaucracy and corruption.'

I am a few years older than Balasingham and agree with many of his ideas, but not all. The road I'm parked on is surrounded by mara trees and nineteenth-century buildings. Further down the avenue, the shopping malls have medieval facades from the Polonnaruwa period.

For the past decade, they have been trying to recreate Sri Lanka on this isle in the Arabian Sea. As the nation of our birth degenerated into a third-world theocracy, and its economy and tourist arrivals dwindled, nostalgia grew among artists and businessmen for that mythical Sri Lanka that never quite existed.

By 2028, The Ceylon Islands had been sculpted into the image of a collective dream and boasted a GDP that eclipsed Switzerland and Luxembourg, despite it still being a privately owned conglomerate. This is the beginning to which I am about to put an end.

* * *

The late great Chamara Jayawardena outlined his approach to captaincy in his posthumously published autobiography

Charmed Life. 'I look at the result rather than the method. I tell my bowlers to bowl at the mistake they want the batsman to make. If I need 300 runs, I demand a quota per player per session. I demand it. If they fail, I make them feel like they owe me money. I hound them till I get my runs. Or I kick them out. If you want to be in my team, you must commit. I commit to the result before I even know how to create it.'

Make the commitment. Then figure out how to do it. Wise words from a dead man. So, what was my desired outcome? To destabilize and destroy the economy of The Ceylon Islands, an economy based on pluralism, equality and professionalism. How does one destroy something based on all that is good and just? It is simple. First add violence. Then add religion.

The bus driver looks up from his phone and straight at me. It is unlikely that he sees through the tinted glass and impossible that he recognizes me. I am wearing a beard, a mosque hat and thick frames. In real life, I am neither bespectacled, bearded nor a follower of Islam. He turns off his cigarette, pockets his phone, and starts the engine. The time is 12.09, what the hell is he doing? He is not due for his pick-ups at Visakhananda College for another hour.

Do not for one second think that I am a novice. I have managed operations for the LTTE, some covert, others less so. In my youth, I engineered three political eliminations, one involving a head of state, and all remain unsolved. In every mission, things will go wrong. Your gunman forgets the route, your suicide bomber gets cold feet, or your bus driver leaves an hour early. You learn to improvise and to always have a plan C.

I left the Tigers just before they became fascists. I moved to London, finished my economics degree, got married, had daughters, became best friends with a software engineer whose cousin was about to become President and was coaxed back to Sri Lanka to mediate a ceasefire. All that I achieved in those three years was to buy time for both sides to rearm. I also made a few nasty enemies and a few nastier friends. Many lifetimes later, I was approached by some of these puppet masters and asked for my opinion on 'The Ceylon Islands problem'.

The bus takes off into its designated lane. The roads in The Ceylon Islands look a lot like the roads in Sri Lanka, except that everyone follows the rules, and no one uses their horns. And there's a lane for everything: buses, bikes and self-driving three-wheelers. I cannot type 'Follow that bus' into my positioning system, so I have to guess where he might be going one hour before the school run. Good thing I've been following him for three months.

I told the puppet masters what I had learned in my time as a fixer. It's not enough to kill or kidnap or disappear. You must find a sacrificial goat, someone who wouldn't like being blamed, someone likely to retaliate when falsely accused.

If I plant the smoking gun in the mosque on Slave Gardens, how long before religious tensions turn paradise into hell? Can a successful secular state formed on principles of democracy and transparency survive the slaughter of 35 young girls, without the demand for an eye for an eye? We shall soon see.

* * *

In 2029, Raviraj Balasingham made the boldest move of a career built on maverick manoeuvres. He requested an audience with the UN and brought with him a delegation of distinguished gentlemen and ladies. Among them were scientists, engineers, economists and lawyers, each of Sri Lankan origin, mostly citizens of Canada, Australia, UK, New Zealand, Malaysia and Brunei.

He presented financial records outlining the solvency and profitability of the islands' tourism, shipping and agricultural sectors. The Ceylon Islands' tea, rubber and coconut industries were leaders in markets across the globe, eclipsing their Asian rivals. The islands' manufacturing sector had managed to remain competitive without resorting to cheap labour. Its fledgling stock market was stable, transparent and highly lucrative.

His case for an independent state predictably found opposition among SAARC countries, notably the Democratic Socialist Republic of Sri Lanka, now a one-party dictatorship where all citizens were required to convert to Sinhala Buddhism. It mattered little, as China, America, Britain and the recently reformed Soviet Union all voted in its favour.

It's hard to keep up with a moving bus in a self-driving tuk-tuk. I have to re-enter my destination each time the driver veers off the programmed path. When he signals at the Lavinia roundabout, I know exactly where he is heading.

Balasingham's proposal was drafted by distinguished Queen's Council Sir Christopher Peripanayagam, respected civil rights lawyer M.H.M. Aziz and renowned litigator Samaraweera Pereira – Sri Lankans resident in London, The Hague and New York, respectively. The constitution was that of a secular democracy, a meritocracy that would serve as a homeland for a legion of displaced Lankans.

Riots erupted in Colombo on the day the resolution passed, though the world's media focused on the inauguration ceremony in Batticaloa City, the newly crowned capital of Ceylon Islands. Rohan de Kretzer, CEO of Ceylon Islands Resorts, was sworn in as the governor-general.

The cabinet was made up of technocrats, among who were three Nobel nominees. While the nation began as a one-party state, free and fair elections were promised within five years. While qualified expats were welcomed, citizenship and land ownership were restricted to those who had at least one Sri Lankan parent.

Exiled filmmakers set up studios. Grammy-winning rap star Maya, banished from the homeland in the 00s, staged a music festival. The last surviving member of the '43 group auctioned his paintings in Batticaloa City. Housemaids from the Middle East, slave labourers from Singapore, underpaid technicians from Sri Lanka flocked to the visa office to cash in their worthless passports. The children of exiled Burghers, Tamils and Muslims, now second-generation western Europeans, left their crumbling unions for a promised land.

The bus stops at the bottom of Lavinia Hill at the Sigiriya Gentlemen's Club. It is a topless bar where the waitresses are dressed like the women from the Sigiriya frescoes, the type of place that would've been burned down by rabid monks back in original Sri Lanka. Our bus driver wants a lap-dance before he drives to his death. And why not? I once dispatched a 19-year-old suicide bomber and asked him what he wanted to do on his last night. He didn't want to get drunk or have sex with a woman. He just wanted to lay a blessing for his dead mother.

It was article seven of The Ceylon Islands' constitution that received the most attention both from critics and supporters. To be granted citizenship, one had to denounce race and religion. In other words, it was not possible to be a Ceylon Islander and remain a Sinhalese, Tamil, Muslim or Burgher. Every citizen was a Ceylonese and had to pledge allegiance to a flag of three colours, representing the official languages of English, Sinhala and Tamil. While freedom of religion was tolerated, it received no state patronage.

The newly formed government resurrected and replayed Chamara Jayawardena's press conference at Lord's from a decade ago as inspiration for the state's constitution. The great man's birth anniversary in May was declared a national holiday. The Chinese built highways and ports, the Americans set up universities, and the Arab nations signed trade agreements. By 2033, the population of The Ceylon Islands had swelled to three million.

The bus driver exits the Sigiriya GC and embarks on the school run. I crawl under the bus and tuck in the offending wire. I check the detonator and the charge. There aren't many 60-year-olds who can crawl under a bus as lithely as me. Every day for the last five years, I have jogged through Thimbirigasyaya National Park and done yoga on the Pidurutalagala roof terrace. I have changed sides many times – but have never been thrown under a bus.

Sri Lanka refused to recognize the sovereignty of The Ceylon Islands, calling it a 'rogue state' propped up by a 'puppet western government'. The *Ceylon Times* noted that most critics of the new nation were Sri Lankans who had had their visa applications rejected and went as far as to publish the rejected application forms of Sri Lankan ministers looking to defect.

Me, my wife, my three daughters, their husbands and my two grandchildren all received new passports. We each denounced our Tamil heritage, our Hindu beliefs and our allegiance to the island of our birth. At the time, it seemed like a bargain.

* * *

The bus turns off at Dickmans Drive, and I drive into Chamara Jayawardena Avenue, where I am late for work. My black box has a reach of 15 km, which means I could have the charge set off from the safety of any one of the neighbouring islands.

It is 1.25 p.m., and the Royal Bishop's College will end its day in five minutes. Although the school is co-ed and progressive, its transport is segregated. The boys' uniforms are traditional white shirts and blue shorts. The girls wear a one-piece white frock with shoulder straps and a hemline above the knees, an outfit considered sexy by hormonal teenagers and paedophiles.

There is no reporting of crime in The Ceylon Islands, which gives the illusion that it does not exist. Since its inauguration, no rapes or murders have been reported in the *Ceylon Times* or the *Daily Islands*. The punishment for all crimes – from theft to drunk driving – is deportation to Sri Lanka. According to rumours, serious offenders are sent to Saudi Arabia and Texas for execution, though this has not yet been proven.

The police force has been trained by the Israeli military, the economy managed by consultants from Singapore, the hospitals and schools designed by specialists from Sweden. Consultants are granted residency but not citizenship, unless they have one parent who ate rice and curry by hand.

I enter my private office where I have only a telephone and a computer and an endless supply of cadju and thambili. The driver taking a detour unnerved me, I must be getting old, what happened to Mr Plan C?

The national cricket team applied for ICC status, but is yet to receive word, despite beating both Ireland and Afghanistan in friendly test matches played at the scenic Bloomfield ground on the isle of Trincomalee. One day, it is not implausible that The Ceylon Islands will play a test match against Sri Lanka and win.

I get a call from The Maldivians as soon as I get to office.
'Where?'
'Plan changed. We have decided that the morning run is better than the evening. Game will take place at 8.30 a.m. and not at 2.30 p.m.

'Who decided this?'

I sigh and say nothing.

'We will need a full report.'

'Obviously.'

Click.

I took this job on the basis that I worked alone, hired my own crew and had no chain of command. The less voices there are to silence, the easier the cover up. My comrade from the Diego Garcia naval base knows this and is not required to like it.

I told you that I am no monster and perhaps that is why I am procrastinating. My wife and daughters live in apartments on Lavinia Hill overlooking Pettah Beach. I have been here three years. My grandchildren attend Royal Bishop's College, and my youngest may be head girl of Bridget Thomas Academy next year. It is a much better life than we had in Colombo or Jaffna or in exile in London, and I will be sad when it is over, which it undoubtedly will be when I tap my touch screen and enter seven digits.

* * *

The fledgling nation is not without its teething problems.

For the past few years, the Sri Lankan government has rattled their sabres and threatened air strikes. They may have the firepower and the muscle to seize 45 archipelagos, but they cannot cross the Indian ocean without facing the US navy. The Ceylon Islands have hired frigates from the Diego Garcia base to protect the waters from Somali pirates, Yemeni mercenaries and rogue rockets from Pakistan.

There is also the thorny question of immigration. The scattered indigenous population are granted citizenship, but the non-Lankan expats are not. Governor De Kretzer maintains that priority will be given to those cursed with a

Sri Lankan passport. In the first year, they receive five million applications of which only 40,000 are granted passage. Minister of the interior, Sir Christopher Peripanayagam, is an open social darwinist and has publicly stated that he only accepts 'useful' immigrants and will shun 'uneducated freeloaders'. The unskilled, the lazy and the politically inclined are not granted residency.

Sir Christopher Peripanayagam is a divisive figure in the islands. He is not a great modernizer like Governor de Kretzer or Raviraj Balasingham. Like Foreign Minister Samarawickrema, Sir Christopher was seen as a details man in the pay of foreign powers. His ministry published the six most wanted criminals in The Ceylon Islands. Two were Muslim jihadists, two were Tamil separatists, one was a serial killer, one was a Marxist agitator. I am the most dangerous criminal in the island, and none of the names belonged to me.

Slowly, class tensions, ideological tensions and religious tensions begin to surface on the streets and in the workplaces, though nothing to rival the paradise back home. The *Economist* hints that The Ceylon Islands will devolve into capitalist fascism, not unlike Singapore or Dubai. Policymakers within the islands take this as a compliment.

If you haven't visited The Ceylon Islands, I cannot tell you what you are missing out on. Eleven months of sunshine and one month of snow. An island of wild animals where predators are kept on a leash. Landscaped hills, aquamarine lakes, cities of steel, and citizens of fixed smiles. And an air of controlled freedom that is the envy of the uncivilized world.

* * *

A good night's sleep can turn a good idea into a great one or a bad one into a terrible one. I didn't get much sleep, and now it is 8 a.m. as I stare at a brown box, knowing that the phone will ring, and the caller will be impatient. If the Muslims are blamed for the blast, the Ceylonese will storm their mosques and the Arab nations will withhold their oil, and release their savages.

Last night, I stared at our ebony ceiling fan, while my wife snored out her morphine and Xanax cocktail, and thought of dead nations and crimes that live on. I think of ideals I once had, and of children that I would kill. You can take the Lankan out of Lanka, but not the Lanka out of the Lankan.

I could tell you I am doing this under duress, but that is untrue. I could tell you I am doing it to forward my position, and that is partially true. I could tell you that I used to gamble compulsively and that I haven't visited a casino in 30 years. I could tell you that sometimes the biggest gamble is to do nothing and wait.

In the next decade, 500,000 Maldivians will drown when their islands are swallowed by the Indian Ocean. The Sri Lankan and Indian governments have granted citizenship to most of them, but why go to the third world when you can have the highest GDP in the uncivilized world?

I could tell you that I didn't expect to enjoy the gift of life as much as I had when I took the assignment and moved to this place.

From my office, I see the statue of Chamara Jayawardena, holding his cricket bat aloft, as if he has scored a quadruple century on the fifth day to win the unwinnable test. It is the first thing immigrants coming to the main island see. It is our Statue of Liberty, founded on a statute of limitations. I stare at it while my phone rings.

The caller is not from The Maldives, but the neighbouring building. It is the great Raviraj Balasingham himself, founder of the nation, a man who has taken decades to wash the blood off his paws.

'Chris, is that you?'

Ravi is the only person on the planet, aside from my family, not to address me as Sir Christopher.

'Ah, Ravi, how?'

'Have you heard anything about a terrorist plot?'

'Can't say I have.'

'The Israelis are agitated.'

'When are they not?'

'That's true. They think the Maldivians are behind it.'

'The islanders are too busy jailing each other.'

'Keep your eyes open, Chris.'

'Always, brother. Always.'

It is 8.29 a.m. History is a zero-sum game. The law that governs the universe is the one that binds the stars. The strong must devour the weak. My father was a schoolteacher in Jaffna during the height of the troubles, and he was eaten alive.

Did I believe in The Ceylon Islands when I took this assignment? Why not? If you can cherry pick the best Lankans and put them to work, and keep them doped on fantasy, you can have something resembling paradise. What made me change my mind? The Maldivians have a lot of sinking treasure chests. That's it, really. I'm an economist, I only make rational decisions.

The next call will not be from the Maldives, but from Diego Garcia, and I may have no more excuses left to give.

I call my youngest daughter, and we chat about cricket, about her speech to the girl guides and about the three boys who think they like her. I hear the beep of call waiting, but I do not hang up. I have dragged this out for ten long years. A few more won't hurt anyone.

The 1969 Game

THIS GAME WILL RID YOU OF YOUR DELUSIONS. THIS GAME will cure your fear of death. Shall we begin?

Where were you in 1969? Where were you when Woodstock played, Stonewall rioted, Mai Lai was massacred, and man stepped on the moon? Where were you during the Manson killings, when the Pope went to Africa and John and Yoko stayed in bed? Where?

Now the date 1969 is not universal. It works well for those born in 1975. For you to play this game, you need to pick a date before you were born, but not too long ago. A date that you have a memory of, even though you weren't around. A date where you know the world existed, even though you didn't. Got it? Ok let's go.

Where were you in <insert date here>? Where were you? Were you a cherub in heaven awaiting the date of your conception? Were you an unfertilized ovum in your mother's womb, or an itch in your dad's testes? Were you stranded in a previous birth, unaware you were living out the last years? Where?

Ok. Now where were you in 1869? Unborn cherub, unfertilized cell, or living out previous birth in Victorian Ceylon?

Repeat same for 1769. Where were you? Were you somewhere or nowhere? Then do it for 1069, then for 569, then for 69 BC. Cherub or cell? Where were you?

Now fast forward. Where will you be in 2069? Hopefully if you stay off the sugar, get in the exercise, and lay off the stress, you'll be in an armchair with a good book, surrounded by the fruits of a well-lived life. Good for you!

Where will you be in 2169? Not sure the quantity of mallum or quinoa required to be breathing then. Soon there will be software that preserves your consciousness. And cures for old age. But until then, let us, for argument's sake, assume your skeleton would be swimming in soil.

Where will you then go? Somewhere or nowhere? What's the likely scenario? How about 2269? Somewhere? Or nowhere? Where will you be? Ask your heart. If you listen, it will tell. 2469? Quiet your mind and ask. 3369? What does it say?

Play this till your mind melts. Or until it becomes silly. Then take a long breath. And tell yourself that you are here. And it may be certain that once you weren't, and likely that one day you will not be, here you are. Holding the page, reading the sentence. You are here. And it is now.

All that's left to do is smile and thank the sun. And find things to laugh about and care about, while your cells slowly and inevitably unscramble.

The Birth Lottery

1

I see light and blue, and breathe water and salt. I make poetry with things that shine and magic with things that do not. I kill every three days – sometimes for survival, sometimes for love but never for pleasure. What was I before I was I? I neither know nor care. I only know the things I need to. And over the centuries I forget.

2

I am born to the Naama tribe. I drink the earth's sap and sire children on both banks of the Aruvi Canal. All my wives leave me for lesser men. So I bash the yak drum and call on demons. One arrives and says I suffer because I injured him in a former life. I say I do not remember. Dolphins rarely do, he replies.

3

I live at the foot of the mountain and have climbed it every full moon. My sisters and I, we hide in trees and rob those who pass. I steal three children and sell them for more than they are worth. I live off the spoils before I am caught and taken to the mountain temple. I work as a water carrier for

188 years. It is a sour life, and I am not sure why any of it chose me.

4

I am born in the Sinharaja forest and surrounded by things that wish to eat me. These include my parents and my closer relatives. I survive with scars, sharpen my teeth, grow claws, and avoid all predators. The sickness wipes out thirteen tribes, and I am one of the few it does not take. I realize that brute strength can sometimes be overcome by blind luck.

5

Every creature has its code. Black leopards never hunt the young. The garudas never massacre the same school of fish twice. The lions only copulate on the full moon, which is why they will be gone from this island in two generations. I, too, honour a code. Just because I am born a viper doesn't mean I have to become one.

6

I am born to the river people. The Maduru Oya gives us everything we need, and the forest gives us the rest. I spend my life listening to winds and watching suns. I marry the chief's son, and we have seven children. I live long enough to bury three of them. Sometimes, I am grateful for the four that survived. But mostly, I am not. Any mother telling you she has no favourites is a liar.

7

I specialize in the shaving of heads. Some for priesthood, some for execution. As the years go by, one number outweighs the other. In my 30th year, I see visions in the curls that I cut. Stories of lives not yet lived. In one, a demon kills the three sons of a matriarch. In another, a mentally ill prince arrives in Thambapanni and births generations of chaos.

8

It is the time of King Pandukabhaya. It is he whom I work for. It is he whom everyone works for. I lift bricks, pound mortar, tear rock and break my back on my 30th birthday. The days are endless, and sleep is the only thing I allow myself to crave. Every one of my children become slaves like me, and so, I suspect, do each of theirs.

9

A bald couple in robes brings a tree sapling to the capital, and the end begins for me. The island bows to the teachings of the Buddha, and revenue at my taverns and brothels go south. I take business underground, and there are enough and more hypocrites to sustain me. I donate half my money to the temple and hope someone up there keeps accounts.

10

The war comes to our village, and no one knows which flag to fly. My father's side supports the Prince because he defeated 37 chieftains. My mother's side backs the Old King because he is kind and just. I follow my mother and live out my days in a dungeon. I have nightmares featuring rivers and haircuts and broken rocks.

11

I am Ahmed Dinaam, bastard of an Arab trader and a Yaksha seamstress. I spend my days on Nilaveli's coast, fixing ships and gazing at stars. I've seen pirate vessels burning on Trinco's sands and mermaids dancing at the lips of China bay. I've seen the face of God in every sunrise, and I die a century before he sends us his prophet.

12

I am the Queen's lover, though not the only. The Queen's appetite is vast, and we are legion. Some are promised riches to commit crimes. Some are offered the throne to do murder. A few get poisoned, and many get jailed. My greatest achievement is never becoming the favourite. I perform perverse acts at various times of the month and still manage to retain my head.

13

I speak out against the Lord of Ruhuna. They place me in a cell and burn me and beat me for 15 years until the Lord's cousin's army releases me. I spend the rest of my days hunting down the families of my tormentors. I make a necklace from 147 severed fingers, and it fills me with unpardonable joy. I am not born human for another three centuries.

14

I am the koha that plants eggs in nests and keeps villages awake during Avurudu. I've informed on parrots, had squirrels killed and crows assassinated. A baby sparrow from a stolen egg once asked why I treat others with such cruelty. I told her it was because there was no one fast enough to catch me. I let her enjoy a warm worm from my beak. And then I ate her.

15

I feast on the flesh of someone's child. I liquefy their organs. I devour their brains. I pick out viscera from between my canines while my molars grind the cartilage. I live on a giant grave with my hundred wives and thousand children. I am a connoisseur of meat and morality and decay. And nothing tastes more succulent than a carcass marinated in sin.

16

My clan have patrolled these valleys for centuries. Though my nest is atop the snowcaps of Pidurutalagala, I feel warm all the time. The creatures of the Mahaweli feed us their firstborns in return for protection. If we keep our wings strong, our scales dry, and sacrifice to the Sun God, we may be able to keep this mountain from melting. As long as our children and their children believe in the Sun God, we will all be safe.

17

I make a living spying for the enemy. And everyone is someone's enemy. I sell forest weeds as cures for the plague. I make swords for kings to use on innocents. There are many wars, and I support every side. I amass my treasure from the coffers of Anuradhapura, Angkor and Siam. I live in a palace of rock, fearing a knock on the door. When it comes, I answer with a smile and thank the knock for taking its time.

18

I am a travelling musician. I have been to thirty-nine kingdoms, played at three hundred festivals and ravished a thousand nymphs. I have performed for Marco Polo, Ibn Battuta, Chen do, and Kublai Khan. I have seen three wonders, sailed four seas, eaten curried dragon, and run from a giant squid. I have done everything under every sun. Except give my heart to anyone.

19

Both of us go from slave to cook and learn the culinary arts from the great Xiao Wan. We end up on the same trade route, but on different vessels. We leave each other love notes. Carved into rocks at Nicobar, etched on trees in the

Andamans and hidden in the dunes at Lakadiv. After 27 years, we buy our freedom, chain ourselves to each other, and spend our days cooking feasts for our children.

20

I am the King's love poet. He rules a small district and runs a tiny court. He wishes to be immortal, which is difficult with a name like Abhaya the third. He hires poets to write for him, then kills them and steals their words. He keeps me alive because my work is a hit with his concubines. Most kings like to see themselves as seducers, even while they rape.

21

My father is General Namalingham of the Great Chola Empire. I grow up in a fortress in occupied Polonnaruwa under siege from local rebels. I fall in love with a rebel girl, and we flee the city to live in the forests of the south. When we are caught, my father's soldiers try to behead her before my eyes. The forest folk who save us, let the soldiers go free, despite my objections. We sit with them in the trees and listen to the war until it finally stops.

22

I am an irrigation engineer, and I counsel the kingdoms of Ruhunu, Maya and Pihiti. They do not let noblemen travel between kingdoms, but I am respected across the land. In 1320, I give up three wives and five palaces to move to the jungle with a rodiya boy. I build huts, wear loin cloths, swim in lakes and tell stories. We live a life of beauty and truth. Dreaming of sins that I do not remember committing.

23

I am a schoolteacher in Dambadeniya. I do it because there is a vacancy, and I have nothing else I am good at. My life unfolds likewise. My husband is chosen by my brother. My home is run by his mother. I teach arithmetic because no one else would. In my 83rd year, I lay my fingers on a Persian lute and finally find out what I am meant to do. I die of a stroke three years later.

24

I raise livestock and breed horses. While I am working, my country splinters into too many kingdoms to count. As does my family. One son fights for Sithawaka, one for Kotte, another for Kandy. My daughter marries a Portuguese. I write a song about unity called *Eka Mavakage Daruwo* on the day that I bury my eldest. We are all descended from Kuveni. Anyone telling you otherwise just wants your vote.

25

My wife runs away with a hunter. His abandoned lover says she knows where they are. We gather our fury, plot our revenge and cast our spells. We unify our rage to wound our former loves and maim our once beloveds. We plan to do the deed and step off Lovers' Leap hand in hand. It is while rehearsing this that we discover what the other's touch feels like. We abandon our revenge and I move into her hut.

26

I drive a bullock cart from Mathugama to Kotte. A man from Lisbon offers me gold to smuggle goods and people into Colombo. I take the money and feed my family, build my walauwwa and grow my teak. It is a terrible time for the country, but it is an okay time for me. I am born Mudiyanselage Katunaminda, but the name chiselled on my gravestone in 1588 is Don De Silva Fonseka Pieris.

27

It is the first alliance between the Tamils, Cholas, Moors, Malays and Sinhalese, and I, the Great Arasaratnam, am charged with leading it. With an army of four thousand, we rout the Portuguese and hold the Sithawaka kingdom for three hundred moons. Then they return with bigger cannons, eviscerate us all, and erase our names from history.

28

All the things that shape my life are decided before I can speak. I am born a Moor in a time of great persecution when everyone is converting to the faith of the conqueror. I become Catholic and am disowned by my parents, my siblings and my community. Then I watch them flee their burning homes from the balcony of my wife's villa.

29

I am the justice who signs as a witness the agreement between Wimaladharmasuriya and Joris Van Spillbergen. The one that hands the coast to the Dutch and the kingdom to Ceylon. A treaty that both parties break. I never marry, never amass wealth, never create. Never do anything aside from putting my name on a document that will outlast anything you have ever touched.

30

The field is big enough to feed all the neighbours but too small to be divided amongst four. The brothers share profits from the paddy, fruits from the farm, and they share me. Each claims to be the father of our only son and dismiss the daughters as another brother's burden. The youngest brother, the one who loves me truly, is the only one who touches me never. He listens to me play the Persian lute and never asks how I learned it.

31

As the second-born, he is betrothed to me. As my reward for looking after his grandparents, he is promised. Then they marry him to Nangi and she bears him no sons, and they shout at each other, and I know what to do. It takes all my strength, and when I do it, he comes not to my arms but to grief – to a cloud that no one can chase. I then do another terrible thing that cannot be undone. It, too, does not yield the expected results.

32

I am brought to the hill country as a slave and made to pluck the sweet leaf. I am imprisoned with coolies from South India, even though my family has lived here for centuries. I bear children for five different masters, and each are taken from me. I take my life before my ovaries dry up. I am not unhappy to go.

33

Born on a coffee plantation, I learn everything there is to know about climbing trees, catching frogs and swimming up streams. I grow surrounded by family, servants, dogs and goats who love me with all they have. The plague that kills the crops, snuffs out the old people and murders the livestock, enters my lungs, and asphyxiates me before my ninth birthday.

34

I am ordained at the age of six and become an expert in Pali, Sanskrit, Mahayana, Theravada, the cosmos, and the human heart. I advise lovers on emotions I am unlikely to ever feel. I keep families together and loins content. I keep love alive, but rarely do I receive it. The only way I contain my envy is by seeing the world in its magnificent pointlessness.

35

I am a concubine of a nobleman. I am not one of his favourites even though I can play the lute and sing. When the English storm the castle, I am ravaged but not ravished. My face is cut, but my maidenhood undefiled. I play for local stage productions and die a spinster in 1834. I once asked a priest how many sleeps before Nibbana, and he replied, many.

36

For neither the first nor last time, I take my own life. The details are myriad and ultimately singular, and I have neither space nor time to share. I ask myself the same question in each of my 27 years. Is it better never to have been born? Is this not what the Buddha teaches? I address this to all the gods but receive no answer. So after some deliberation, I decide to give them mine.

37

I am an elephant in the Kandyan kingdom, and every few months, to celebrate being conquered by foreign invaders, they parade me in chains and walk me miles carrying burning objects that scald. I don't mind, because I get to go home to Ravani, who lives with me all my life and bears me many calves.

38

My name is Namali Abeysundre. I play the church organ and perform abortions for girls in need. I never marry, and

I won't tell you why. I learn much later that the soul only enters the body at birth. If I had access to that information, I wouldn't have wasted every Sunday for 50 years on my knees at Kotahena Church.

39

I am born to a good family in a glorious city by a lagoon. While there are bitter wars down south, our kingdom enjoys peace and prosperity. I am a town planner, a family man, and a fortunate man. Yet a great sorrow plagues me whenever I walk Jaffna's streets. I am unsure if it is a tragedy of its past or of a great horror yet to come.

40

I am born to a family of Burgher musicians. Among my many feats on the sitar is composing an anthem for the government. The government changes my words, my meter, my melody and my meaning and uses it at rallies that I do not believe in. I speak out against them loudly and sing in tune. And escape the country with all my relatives before they decide to shut us up.

41

I am born to two activists before the end of a long war. I am the reason they stay in Lanka, sift through the mess, and try to quell the darkness. I am the reason they go to the front lines, the reason they get killed there. My mother thought they would fail. My father believed that one day someone will not. I cannot tell the future, but I can recall the past. And as soon as I learn to speak, I will forget all of the above.

42

Is it better to be a rich man's pampered dog or a poor man's abused child? Is human birth superior without exception to being born a beast? Is beast birth superior to plant or microbe birth? Does every creature think of itself as the centre of the universe? These areas are grey, and while I was being fed wild boar steak, let off my leash at the beach, and given every neighbourhood pooch to frolic with, I did not think of them once.

Baby Monitor

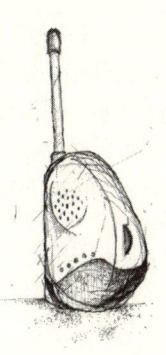

HE BETS ON STOCKS AND GAMBLES ON OPTIONS AT 3 A.M. On his desk: a computer, a mug of tea and a baby monitor. He works in solitude while his petulant wife snores in her room.

He plays jazz at low volumes and listens for the baby's cry.

When his wife was in labour, he scrolled through her phone and learned of a departed lover. Conceivably, the father of the baby, the same child for whom he was spending the witching hour staring at spreadsheets. The lover that gave his wife the one thing he couldn't. Just like in that song.

Sound comes over the monitor, the creaking fan, the slurping dog, the gurgling wife, and then a hiss. He turns off the jazz, and listens to the air, to the squeak of the fan's metronome. To another hiss. *The child. Is not yours.* Who said that? He wants to sprint but he cannot move.

He rushes to the bedroom, feels the draught, and sees the open window. The fluttering curtain, and the hooded figure leaning over the cot. The figure, wrapped in a cloak, reaches in and grabs the baby. Our man screams, but no sound comes. He tries to move, but has forgotten how to.

The hooded figure picks up the baby and dangles it, not without affection. The figure shuts the window with a familiarity that is unsettling. What is it darling, asks the wife pulling on a t-shirt. The figure lets the hood fall from his face. I don't know love, says the stranger holding the child. I think your dead husband's back in the study. I thought I heard jazz.

My Name is Not Malini

'WHEN THE BABA LIKES YOU MORE THAN THE MAMA, IT becomes a big problem. Much worse than when the husband starts giving you the look.'

The housemaid in salwar kameez speaks in the patronizing tone of a schoolteacher. The other three maids are reluctant students of this lecture. One wears jeans, one a frock, the other a glittering gown. Gown, the only one without children in her care, is asleep on the couch by the window. The window overlooks a desert filled with lights.

'How's your family?' Salwar asks Jeans. 'They must be decent, no?'

It isn't the first question to be greeted with a silence that evening. But that doesn't deter Salwar from her monologue. She is a cook, babysitter, and part-time gardener in her fifties, making her the oldest in the room by two decades.

'Don't know if this one understands,' she points her head to the Filipino maid in a frock. The Filipino wears headphones and has sleeping twins on her lap, one head per thigh. Salwar turns her face to the closed door and the music seeping through its corners. 'They shouldn't have parties like this, even in a compound. If neighbours call the holy police, everyone in trouble.'

'Go away, Jojo', says the toddler to Salwar. He knocks down the tower he's been building with his blocks and slaps her hand when she tries to clear the rubble.

'Okay, patiya. You play, okay?'

She chuckles and looks from Jeans to Frock to Gown.

'He jokes with me. Loves me. More than the A.M.M.I. Don't worry. He can't understand Sinhala. Father gives no attention. To him or the mother. Luckily, I'm not so pretty anymore. Or might become big problem. I'm sure your sir doesn't bother you?'

The maid in jeans sighs and removes the bottle from the toddler she is feeding. 'Please. Can you not talk? Baba needs to sleep.'

Four of them are squeezed into a children's room while outside a Sinhala and Tamil New Year party rages. The evening was presented to the compound owners as a cultural event, and the guests are mostly Lankans, with a smattering of locals. The apartment is large and crowded and smells of cardamom, cumin, perfume and sweat. The gathering has secured a liquor permit for traditional Sri Lankan wine, even though no such thing exists. The gathering is segregated along gender lines, as is everything on this side of the desert, and most guests have left their children and maids at home.

The room's décor also appears to be bisected by gender. One wall is ocean blue and features postcards of cars and superheroes. It faces a pink wall with pictures of ponies and Disney mice. The host children have been in bed since 8 p.m. and have left instructions that none of their toys be touched. This was conveyed to each maid via the host maid, a stern young European who preferred to be referred to as an au pair.

'Your family is Sri Lankan, no?' asks Salwar.

The maid in jeans eyes her and nods.

'Must be rich. To be working here and affording help. My family is from Lebanon. They take me all over. I've been on a yacht, been to Marrakesh, been to New York. Someone has to look after baba while husband and wife are fighting, no?'

She laughs and receives another glare from Jeans.

'Don't worry. Your baba won't wake. I know how children sleep. This one is my twelfth child.'

The boy is bored of the coloured blocks and is pulling toys that do not belong to him.

'Aney baba, please don't. That sudu aunty will scold. Shall we colour this nice picture?'

Jeans regards the older woman

'You call us "Help". That's a very nice word. Better than servant.'

'But not as nice as au pair.'

Salwar is pleased to finally get a response from her fellow Lankan.

Jeans points her nose at the sleeping maid in the gown and high heels. 'If that monkey keeps snoring, I swear I will throttle her.'

Jeans' voice is gruff and masculine unlike Salwar's ascending screech. Salwar is pleased with Jeans' contempt for the African maid. Nothing brings Lankans together like a spot of shared prejudice.

'What the hell is she wearing?' says Salwar. 'Thinks she's Cinderella?'

Jeans gives a half-smile and says nothing.

'I've been looking after this one since he came from his Ammi's bandi,' says Salwar picking up the blocks. Her toddler is now maiming a colouring book with crayons. 'How long have you been in the gulf?'

Jeans strokes the baby's head and says nothing.

'You are much better than the last one they had. Real number that one. Mad about men.'

'Shh!' says Jeans as her toddler stirs. 'Please, Akka. Better not to talk. Don't know who is listening. I just want to go home without anything bad happening.'

'Ah, you're fresh. You get used to this place. Three years now. Ask me anything. I can advise.'

Jeans greets the unsolicited offer with a shake of her head.

Outside is a blast of voices singing a familiar tune about legendary pescatarian Suranganie and her adventures in seafood delivery.

'My God. They're singing baila? Haven't heard Sri Lankan music in a long time,' says Salwar. 'Are you finding it hard here? It takes some time. But you get used to it.'

'I'm just here for a year.'

'What we all say.'

'What time do they give to eat?' Jeans places the infant in the cot and opens out a net.

'What's that gadget?'

'A food cover that we use as a mosquito net,' says Jeans. 'My madam is petrified of dengue and zika. And she's stingy.'

'Don't say bad things about your madam or your sir.'

'Why? Are you going to sneak?'

'Someone might,' says Salwar, looking from Frock to Gown. 'Anyway. You must be thankful to them.'

'For what? They use me. They call me Malini because…'

'That was the last one's name.'

'Saying their two-year-old will get confused.'

'Get over it. I got a different name at every house I worked.'

'That is very sad Akka. I'm only doing this for a year. Here. Pass this one to that one.'

Jeans picks up the plate by the cot, takes a cutlet and a kokis and hands it to Salwar. Salwar takes a cutlet and a kawum and clicks her fingers at Frock, who is stroking the hairs of her sleeping twins and nodding to music that only she can hear.

The Filipino in the frock sports her countryman's trademark grin and the two Lankan maids smile back as if starring in a commercial for the national carrier of Sri Lanka, responsible for flying 40,000 housemaids to these parts each year. Salwar passes the cutlets.

'Hungry?'

The Filipino takes off her headphones and smiles. 'Beg pardon?'

'You hungry?' asks Salwar in English.

Frock smiles and shakes her head.

'No, thank you!'

She plugs her ears.

'Spoiling the market,' says Salwar to Jeans 'These ones work for cheap, and they have English also. And even if you beat them, they smile.'

Jeans walks to window to take in the view. 'I miss home every day,' she says.

A bell rings, and laughter follows. When the door opens, noise fills the room. The conditioned air is cool, but the hot smell of the red desert is inescapable. The infant and the twins stir, while the maid in the gown continues her throaty snore. The toddler looks up from his blocks as the host family maid barges in. No one sees him put the tiny red brick in his mouth and spit it out.

A European au pair isn't seen often in these parts. Like many Caucasian women, the host maid wears a sari badly. She also wears an expression as blank as the one worn by the Sri Lankan Ambassador to this kingdom, when questioned by a journalist on the rate of suicides among Sri Lankan maids.

'You come serve now. One by one please. Looks like everything is getting delayed.'

'Can you close the door please. All the babas will wake,' says Jeans.

'This not my problem. Quick someone go. Go serve now.'

Salwar asks her toddler to play hide and seek as she looks in the direction of dinner. It has been two hours since she fed the boy and ten since she fed herself. The boy calls out. 'Where you going, Jojo?'

'Malini, can you watch my one?' says Salwar.

'That's not my name.'

'You think my passport says Jojo?'

'What happened to that other Malini?' asks the Host Maid, adjusting her sari pleat and patting her brown hair. Jeans shrugs as Salwar exits.

'She talks too much,' Jeans points her head at Salwar's retreating figure. 'I don't like to talk.'

'I heard she is jailed?' asks Host in a voice that sounds from a country that was invaded in the last world war.

'I don't know.'

'She was caught stealing?'

'Dunno.'

'What you know?'

'Can you watch this child? He's not mine. I need to go toilet.'

'I have three asleep upstairs. And a dinner to manage. You go toilet later,' says Host as she steps out of the room.

'I'll watch her. No problem. You go, if you like.' The Filipino in frock smiles and turns to the window overlooking the compound. Outside is a spiral road filled with two-storey-four-bedroom-swimming-pool homes identical to this one.

Salwar returns with a mound of yellow rice surrounded by curried dhal, masala chicken and devilled potato.

'This isn't Lankan food. They have got Pakistani caterers.'

Frock and Salwar sit in silence until Jeans returns from the toilet. Salwar mixes the flavours with her fingers while Frock stares into the lights from the compound. The Filipino takes off her headphones and gets up to serve. She asks them to watch over the sleeping twins. 'Thanks very much. Appreciate it.'

She rolls her Rs like an American and exits the room with a grin.

'So many Pinoys everywhere. Every Sunday the Al Hamra Mall is full of them, make-up and all. Hoping for white boyfriends. I can't stand these chinkies.'

'Pinoys are not chinkies,' says Jeans, just as the Filipino returns with a plate filled with meat and rice.

'All look the same to me,' says Salwar.

'You should get your food,' says Frock to Jeans. 'The sirs and madams are serving already.'

Jeans ignores her and looks from Salwar's plate to her face.

'Do you call her madam or miss?'

'Who?'

'That she-dog from Lebanon who employs you.'

Salwar gasps, while Frock takes her plate to the window and slips her headphones back on.

'Please don't insult my madam,' says Salwar.

'I saw how she talks to you. You shouldn't put up with it.'

Salwar stuffs her mouth and considers her reply.

'I travel around the world, play with children, and eat better than this. You kindly worry about your own madam, please.'

Jeans eyes her sleeping toddler, the Filipino in the Frock and the snoring African in the Gown. She lowers her voice.

'You know the first home I was at, we were put in a room like this. And then one of the girls, Sri Lankan, from Moratuwa. Said she'd been groped in the toilet by the host.'

'Where's this? Here?'

'I was damn wild. I said call cops. But they said to shut up and cleaned her and next day made her take the pill.'

'That was wise,' says Salwar.

'She still got pregnant and lost her job.'

'Where was this?'

'Kuwait.'

'She's lucky. If that was here, they would've flogged and stoned and beheaded her.'

'They don't stone pregnant women.'

Jeans goes off to get her food.

'Excuse me. You think we should wake her?' Frock points to the African maid in the gown.

Salwar shrugs, and Frock smiles but this time it is only the mouth that moves, not the eyes. They sit in silence until Jeans returns. The noise outside is of dishes clanking and tongues, loosened by booze and baila, wagging without caution. Outside the compound, there is no booze or baila but plenty of wagging tongues. Outside the compound there is an abundance of oil and religion and greed.

'Where else have you worked?' Salwar asks Jeans.

'I worked for a family in Kandy, then Kuwait, now here.'

'I like Kuwait. Not as nice as Jordan though. My best places are Nigeria, Singapore and London.'

'London? Don't tell lies.'

'Why should I lie to you? Ambassador's home. Madam was jealous of me, so they cancelled my visa.'

'Jealous of what?'

'I wasn't always fat like this,' says Salwar.

'Why is everyone asking about the last Malini?'

'There was some scandal. That's why I asked about your sir.'

'What scandal?'

'Said she was caught stealing. But must be more than that.'
'They sent her home?'
'She was arrested.'
'She was fucking the driver,' says Frock in perfectly accented Sinhala. 'She is fucked.'

Jeans and Salwar stare at her, then at each other, then back at the maid from The Philippines.

'She's in jail,' says Frock and this time there is no smile. 'The driver got transferred. She got jail. He got transferred. She's getting stoned. So much bloody bullshit.'

'Shh!' says Salwar. 'There are children here. Where you learn Sinhala?'

'I pick up. I know Arabic, Mandarin and your language. I want to learn Spanish, then can go to America.'

'I thought your people were Spanish.'

'Nope. We just let the Spanish rape us. Then let the Americans screw us.'

Frock gets up, walks over and stirs Gown. Gown wakes with a shudder. She lifts an arm in front of her face as if expecting a blow. She adjusts her gown straps and yawns.

'Go and eat. The food is finishing.'

Salwar has not stopped staring at Frock. Gown stumbles off in heels too high and disappears down the corridor. At full height, she is bigger than the rest of them, and her skin is better equipped to hide bruises than theirs.

'Damn sin. That's the problem if you're pretty.'

'She's not pretty,' says Frock, whose Sinhala is much less friendly than her English.

'Most houses are good and decent. Even here,' says Salwar. 'But there are bad places as well. Maybe not at our level. But some of these low-class families…'

'Don't give me that. Groping happens in any class of family,' says Frock. 'You of all people should know.'

'What do you mean by that?'

Jeans plays blocks with Salwar's toddler, keeps her ears peeled and hopes for a fight. The food was mediocre, and the room is stuffy. Any entertainment would be welcome.

'The last Malini is in jail. Somebody sneaked to their employer about the affair with the driver. They say it was another maid.'

'Are you serious?'

'They will stone her for adultery. You know how? They will tie her arms and bury her to her chest so she can't even flinch. Then they throw rocks at her face.'

'Why can't they just send her home?'

'Shh!' Says Jeans. 'You'll wake the babies.'

'They sell oil and bullshit to the US. They can do whatever they want,' says Frock with a smile.

'Please! Your language in front of the child.' says Salwar.

'I even knew the girl who was beheaded.'

'The young one?'

'From your country.'

'The one who killed the baby?' asks Jeans.

'Official charge was witchcraft. It was an accident,' says Frock. 'No proper inquiry. Straight to Chop-Chop Square. She was 17. This is a horrible fucking place.' She turns to Jeans. 'Good luck if you think you can leave after a year.'

The door opens once more. The sound of baila and frolic are replaced by dessert spoons and chatter. The men are in their corners talking of the wealth they have amassed, and the land they will buy back home. The women are around a table swapping tales of those not present and speaking of their boredom. Gown walks in and sits on the bed, the rice and curry forming a mosque-like dome on her plate.

'Built an appetite in your sleep?' asks Salwar.

'They don't give me eat,' says Gown.

'Who gave that dress?'

'Master's eldest son.'

'Why did they bring you?' asks Jeans. 'You don't even have kids.'

'They think I run away.'

Gown starts wolfing down the buffet. The Filipino forms a barrier of pillows around her sleeping twins. Salwar's toddler is distracted with a phone screen.

Jeans' infant stirs in her cot.

'When my madam was in Dubai and stayed at a friend's, she got notes with her coffee from their maid, one of your people,' she nods at Frock, 'Saying "Help me". Apparently, the madam was beating her with a cricket bat.'

'So, what happened?' asks Frock.

'My madam introduced her to a social worker.'

'That means nothing happened.'

'It happens,' says Salwar. 'I know girls who sleep outside on the floor. Some are chained. Some have to eat nails if the food's too salty.'

'You have to make sure you get a good family,' says Frock.

'How?' asks Jeans. 'As if we get to pick.'

'Get details before you sign,' says Frock.

'I have a polytechnic degree in bioscience,' says Jeans.

'Those social workers are spies,' says Salwar. 'Talk to them and they talk to your madam. I found that out in Nigeria.'

'We are worse than their pets,' says Jeans. 'They take our passport, they take our name. I have a degree and have to clean drains while that stupid woman watches cartoons.'

'Don't disrespect your madam. You are here through God's grace.'

'What is God's grace? It's all just shit luck. Where we are born. Which houses we get. Nothing is planned. Everything is a sweep ticket.'

Frock plugs in her earphones. Gown polishes the last grain from her plate. Beneath her makeup there are bruises, the same marks that trail up her arms and reach her neck.

The door opens and the host maid enters looking frazzled. She brings in a little girl and a smaller boy, both in pyjamas, both half asleep. Outside is the sound of a guitar being raked and voices croaking.

'Can you watch these two please? I have to serve desserts.'

The kids wail and Salwar brings out the playing blocks. The host maid grabs Gown's empty plate and slams the door. Each child wakes and exercises their lungs. Some call for Mummy, some call for Malini. It is a good twenty minutes before all are docile again. The twins and the infants fall back to sleep. The host children play with the blocks. The little girl nibbles on them, while the boy throws them at the window.

'I know many. Held like slaves for years. Then sent home in a coffin,' says Frock.

'I'm done in a year,' says Jeans.

'Can you stop talking?' says Frock. 'You sound stupid.'

'You stay if you want. I have my plan.'

'If you hate it so much, why did you come?' asks Salwar.

'Because I am a girl from Ratnapura with a polytech degree and no English.'

'You have children?'

'I have parents. And a useless husband.'

'I wanted children at your age. Might even have put up with marriage. There was a man once. Took all my savings. Then the tsunami took him. That's the story anyway.'

The door opens and Salwar's madam from Lebanon, who some think looks like a she-dog, storms in.

'Jo! Why isn't he in his pyjamas? Have you changed his diaper?'

'Madam. He sleepy. I change before.'

'You fool. His rash will get worse.'

'No rash madam.'

'Really? Where's your brain?'

'Sorry madam.'

'See! He has wet himself. Aiyo. No use saying sorry now.'

'Go get the bag from the car. Now!'

The other maids occupy themselves with the children and avert their eyes as Salwar scampers out of the room and her madam drags the boy to the toilet. Gown attempts to play blocks with the host kids and gets punched by the boy for her efforts. After her madam has gone, Salwar sits in the corner and says nothing for a long time.

Frock takes out her headphones and shakes her head.

'You know, if I studied like you, I wouldn't be here. All I got was Sunday school. They don't let me pray at home. Tell me Jesus was Arab. Santa Claus is black. Tell me I am a fool to believe false gods.'

'We're all fools,' says Jeans. She turns to Gown. 'Does master's son hurt you?'

'Leave her alone,' says Salwar. 'You think this is a Ratnapura Polytech?'

'Who asked you? Just because you're happy to be treated like a dog.'

Salwar stands up. 'What did you say?'

And that's when the little girl from the host family starts choking. They are unsure which of the blocks she has swallowed but when her face starts turning blue, they all start screaming. Jeans hits her spine as the girl struggles for breath. The door opens and women flood the room. Some of them join the screams, others go silent.

Outside on the balcony, the men blow smoke into the Middle Eastern air and talk of investments and opportunities and about how life in the desert isn't as bad as everyone makes out. They are interrupted by a doorbell, and men in blue outfits carrying first aid kits, who apologize for having gone to the wrong compound. An apology they later recant.

The tale has a happy ending. At least for the girl child, who spends a night in hospital and suffers bruising to the throat but no brain damage. Not so happy for one of the maids. Almost having a child die on your watch is as stonable an offence as witchcraft.

Ceylon Teas

WHAT GOES INTO YOUR TEA, ASKS THE YOUNG JOURNALIST charmed by the debonair tea maker. He is twice her age but wears white suits and owns the hills that surround them.

The sweat, passion and pride of my planters and pluckers, he says, pouring her a cup. The spice of this isle, the songs in the air, the blood in the soil, all go into my tea, he says, nostrils sipping aroma from his teapot. She giggles and has a taste.

The secrets of the wind, the perfume of the forests, the valour of our kings, it's all here, he says, taking her hand in his. She breathes deeply and places her cup down. If you weren't a tea magnate, you'd be a poet, she says, fingering her wedding ring. Though there is one key ingredient that accounts for the success of you, and your wonderful tea, that you have not mentioned.

She bats an eyelid. He smiles as he always does when a deal is about to be sealed. And what may that be, he asks. She takes a last sip and raises an eyebrow. Your wife's money, she replies as she shuts the notebook.

Small Miracles

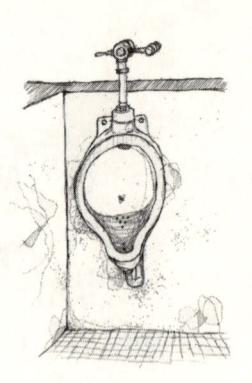

PARINDA KNEW HE WAS SMALL WHEN SOMEONE LEFT A picture of his penis on the office noticeboard. It was in a collage of eight others and his was, by far, the darkest and the teeniest.

They became known as the Urin8 and ignited a ruckus around the offices of DDBO Colombo, an advertising agency that had grown as most businesses grow, by acquiring clients and discarding standards. The penis collage couldn't have come at a less opportune time.

It was that time of the decade again. Sri Lanka Tourist Board had called for a pitch and the ad agencies were clamouring for scraps. Sri Lanka tourism wasn't a profitable business, but it was a government account, which meant it had a large budget that had to be spent.

'I don't know why we pitch for this shit,' said Hasitha Walpola, senior copywriter, who dressed as if the grunge era was still in full swing.

'Money. Why else?' said his partner Peter David, an art director of few words and fewer images.

Right then Sonal Kalpage, the new recruit, sauntered through the creative department in her shortest skirt yet. The eyes and tongues of every male followed her swinging buttocks as did the disdain of every female.

'Sonal. Did you post those dick pics on the board?' called out Hasitha.

'No,' she said, 'Did you?'

The picture was immediately taken down by Mr Amarajothy, the office admin. An investigation was launched. The source needed to be identified and the IT manager Ahamed Indikhab was called into the MD's office.

'Disgusting, Indi,' said the managing director in her hyperbolic lilt. 'I am disgusted and dismayed. Especially at a time like this. Who's responsible?'

'Madam, I checked all computers. It wasn't printed from office.'

'But the device. Surely you can trace.'

'Device?'

'The hidden camera gadget you told me about. What men, Indi?'

'You can't buy in Sri Lanka. Must've been purchased online,' stammered the IT guy.

'So trace it, Indi. How hard is that?'

'I don't have access to everyone's home computer.'

'So, get access. I want names by this afternoon. Seriously men. I am too busy for this nonsense. If Singapore hears about this, that's my training budget gone. Yes come, Hasitha, Peter. Cracked it, have you?'

The creative team passed Indi in the corridor and hid their smirks as they entered the office.

'Okay boys, what have you got? Apparently at Grey, they've already finished working.'

The MD's door closed as Indi stumbled towards his corner office. It was on the fourth floor next to the canteen. Squeezed next to unused offices, where longstanding employees that management couldn't legally fire sat all day and did nothing.

Here were the bromide printers, the paste-up specialists, the Sinhala lettering artists, and a half-dozen others whose duties were rendered obsolete by Mr Jobs and Mr Gates. They sat and drank tea and read the newspapers and cursed the management who continued to pay their salary while waiting for them to leave.

'You saw the picture?' said Ranapala the manual typesetter. 'They have photographed people's cocks in the toilet and posted it.'

'How did they do that?' asked Palitha, the Sinhala hand-letterer.

The longstanding employees were playing draughts and waiting for the peon to bring them tea and a letter granting them a year's severance pay. They had been waiting three years.

'You know that fly on the urinals downstairs?' said Ranapala.

'That's just a sticker you fool,' said Kiri malli, the paste-up artist. He was called malli despite being two years away from pension. All three had been offered computer classes and a chance to upgrade their skills. All three had declined.

'No. No. That's a hidden camera. I'm never pissing in this place again. I'll go choo in the carpark. Or better, on the MD's face!'

They all laughed.

'Your choo is so chooti, you'll need a micro-lens to shoot it,' said Palitha and they all laughed some more.

***

'I bet it was that slut from finance,' said Sonal Kalpage in the canteen.

She was sharing banis and plain tea with the rest of the account servicing team. Most of them were too young and fresh to be working on the Sri Lanka tourism pitch.

'Which slut?' asked Nisal Muneer, the AE on Lankem, a glorified peon who did everyone's shitty jobs with a smile.

'The ugly one,' said Sonal.

'Aren't all of finance ugly?' said Andrea Thiyagarajah.

'The one who Parinda banged,' said Sonal.

'She's pretty tasty,' said Nisal. 'Who said he banged her?'

'I saw them in the car park last night,' said Andrea, leaving breadcrumbs over her mouth.

'So?'

'At 9 p.m.'

'Ah,' said Nisal.

'I bet that tiny black shrivelled one was his.'

'Did anyone make a copy of the poster before it was taken down?'

'Hasitha and Peter have it on their mac.'

'That was a sorry collection, I must say,' said Sonal, wiggling her little finger in the air.

'Except that big one. That looked like mine,' said Nisal.

'You slept with the slut, as well?'

'You shouldn't call her that.'

They all hushed when Parinda Abeytunge, account director in charge of the Sri Lanka tourism pitch, walked into the canteen.

'I need help. Who is free?'

Nisal raised his hand though he was the busiest of the lot. The two girls averted their eyes and covered their smiles. Parinda frowned.

'What are you two on?'

'I'm on Cotton Collection,' stammered Andrea.

'I'm waiting for briefing,' said Sonal.

'So basically nothing. I want both of you on this as well. Collect all tourism print ads for countries in Asia. Here's a list. Find the ads. Burn a CD. I'd like 5 ads per country please.'

'Yes, sure,' said Andrea, avoiding his eye.

'Nisal. I'd like you to research tourism taglines.'

'No problem, boss.'

'And specifically, whether a line has ever been used before.'

'Which line Sir?'

'Small miracle.'

The girls giggled and got a glare from Parinda.

***

Sri Lanka. Small miracle. It wasn't the worst tagline. Bit pretentious, but containing a bona fide product truth, which was a rarity in an industry that lived off lies and damn lies. They hired marketing graduates and gave them offices and titles and allowances to unearth these nuggets of gold, hidden amidst the vast acreage of bovine manure that surrounded the marketing industry.

'Sri Lanka is small. That's our unique selling point,' says Ravi Samsudeen, the strategic planning guru.

'People still use that term?' asks Hasitha Walpola.

'Nothing's unique anymore,' says Peter David dolefully. 'It's all been done.'

'Okay, creative can perfect the words. But Sri Lanka is small. That's good for tourists. They can see so many miracles in a small space.'

For the next 2 hours, the four men argued over synonyms for small, while the three AEs tried to look serious. 'Compact. Diminutive. Tiny.' Nisal was taking notes on his laptop, Sonal was doodling on a notebook while Andrea typed the names of men in the agency. She paused when her list reached 11. 'Little. Mini. Chooti.' The best thing about a laptop is that it's impossible to distinguish between someone working hard and someone stalking co-workers.

'Can you ask the peon for coffee?' said Ravi to Nisal. Nisal popped his head out the door and barked an order at a man in scruffy slacks. The man in scruffy slacks turned out to be Ranapala, bromide artist, hired when the MD's father started the company in the 60s, before Nisal's father had reached puberty. Ranapala said something unrepeatable to Nisal who went the colour of pic number five of the Urin8. He went to get the coffee himself.

Ravi Samsudeen was a typical strategy guy, which meant he took 38 slides and a few leaves from the thesaurus to come to the startling discovery that 'Mothers like to give their children the best.' He would later tell everyone that Small Miracle was his tagline and no one would believe him.

While the team talked over each other, stuck pieces of paper to the wall and convinced themselves that they were doing something of actual value, Andrea trimmed her list of names down to eight.

'What's that?' whispered Sonal.

'All the guys the slut has slept with.'

The list is copied, pasted and then emailed.

* * *

Janela Fernando didn't care if other girls called her a slut, especially someone with a horse face like Andrea Thiyagarajah. She even had a sticker on her cubicle.

'A slut is a woman with the morals of a man.'

She also had pictures of Audrey Hepburn, Jane Fonda and James Dean pinned to her walls along with quotations from the bible and phone numbers for every production house, caterer, courier, recording studio and casting agent in Colombo. She started in finance, but now worked as a runner for AV head Danila Guneratne. She had no love for advertising and only took a job to get out of looking after her grandmother, a crotchety cow plagued with arthritis and a disdain for those who straighten their hair.

She dated only a few boys since finding out that her school sweetheart of five years had been cheating on her. But those boys had big mouths and bigger powers of making stuff up. Some of them happened to work for DDBO Colombo and one of them called her.

'Did you hear about the picture?'
'I'm busy. Which one?'
'The one with the dicks.'
'Heard about that.'
'You know who did it?'
'Must be one of the creative boys. Always watching porn and jerking off.'
'You don't know anything about it?'
'That dustbin near the paste-up room reeks of cum.'
'One of them isn't me, is it?'
'Listen I'm busy.'
'Did you photograph me when I was sleeping?'
Click.

* * *

The rumour was that M&C Saatchi Colombo had the pitch in the bag. Their chairman was a classmate of the newly appointed tourism minister and had helped with his election campaign.

'So why are we even pitching?' groaned Hasitha for neither the first nor the last time. He was staring at a list of potential 'miracles' of Sri Lanka, which ranged from the

Buddha's tooth to the Buddha's foot and from elephant gatherings to dolphin schools. His art director was thumbing through award annuals looking for a layout to crib.

'Why is the internet so damn slow?' grumbled Peter waiting for his desi porn to arrive. The internet in the office was as noisy as a modem and as swift as dial-up.

'Because madam thinks we have a chance. Husband plays golf with Tourist Board CEO.'

For the past five years, the tourist board campaign had been outsourced to an ad agency in Dubai. The anonymous agency had yielded the line, 'Land like no other' and busted two year's marketing budgets on a TV commercial that had only been scheduled 5 times in the past 60 months.

'It's window dressing,' said Hasitha, scribbling more synonyms for small on an A3 pad. 'No one's gonna come here with the war on. No matter how we advertise.'

'That's it!' exclaims Peter. 'War tourism. Ammataudu! That's it. Instead of hiding the war behind shots of elephants and tea pluckers, we advertise it. Appeal to adventurers in Europe! Gun nuts in America!'

When Peter David got excited, he spoke in exclamation marks.

'You haven't eaten, have you? Let's go get some hoppers. You always come up with dumb shit when you're hungry.'

'Jesus!' shouted Peter, staring at his screen.

'Don't blaspheme,' said Hasitha, putting his sweaty feet back in their sneakers.

'Buddhu ammo!'

Instead of his usual weekly download of Bollywood starlet heads cropped onto naked Hispanic chicks, Peter's foggy screen began crowding with an assortment of male appendages.

***

It was a jpg of the printout that had graced the notice board earlier that day. Sent from the studio server, which everyone in the agency had access to. The server was used to send artworks to clients, costings to marketing, invoices to vendors and Sinhala Buddhist propaganda from the studio manager to everyone@ddbocolombo.lk

Eight penises, taken close-up. The first was dark, hairy and shrivelled. The second fair and thick. The third was lopsided and shaped like a kolikuttu. The fourth was thick like an eggplant. The fifth was modest and damp. The sixth tiny and chubby. The seventh was the longest and looked semi-erect. The eighth had one thing in common with every other penis on the planet: it was ugly.

There were a few differences between this digital representation and the hard copy of the soft tissue that was previously corked to the board. Unlike the pixelated printout, the jpg was high res, warts and all, as evidenced by the birthmarks on numbers 5, 3 and 2.

The other key difference was that this one came with captions. Eight names. Bultjens. Anuradha. Kristo. Hasitha. Mumtaz. Rilla. Parinda. Stuart.

* * *

The post-mortem took place at Khans, the dive bar on Marine Drive, two lanes down from DDBO Colombo and a javelin throw from at least three other ad agencies. The bar was rumoured to be a front for whatever went on upstairs, speculation ranged from gambling to whores to kasippu to gangster stuff. All that was observable and verifiable was that arrack and chasers were sold at wholesale rates and this attracted boozers from the offices nearby.

They came not for the dust-caked chairs, the smell of carcinogens, or the croaks of uncles fresh from the betting. They came because in Khans no one could hear you bitch.

Female patrons were rare, as it wouldn't do for respectable women to be darkening such doors. Andrea and Sonal were straight out of high school and yet to be schooled in the need to be respectable. They sat at a veranda table with Nisal and Mumtaz, a junior art director whose name was one of the eight on the offending all-staff email, the subject of that evening's discussion.

The email had also been the reason for the emergency staff meeting that morning. The MD, flanked by the finance director and the executive creative director, had flailed and screamed for close upon half an hour. She had called upon admin manager, Mr Amarajothy, and head of IT, Ahamed Indikhab, to outline the new rules of conduct within the agency.

'This is disgraceful. I am disappointed and disillusioned. Indi has deleted the disgusting email from all computers. If it is seen on *any* computer at DDBO, there will be severe disciplinary action and possible expulsion.'

The MD knew it was nigh impossible to sack anyone with this country's labour laws unless they took a shit on her desk before witnesses. But she liked to pretend that she could fire people. Maybe if she could plant it on the servers of the bromide room, she could get rid of those freeloaders. She should have a discreet chat with that useless Indi.

Mr Amarajothy was called upon to translate for the non-English speakers, which was around 40% of the agency. So the MD's frenzied rant was tempered by a mild-mannered bureaucrat reading a translation scribbled by the Sinhala creative director 30 minutes earlier. The MD announced that all non-work-related emails would be screened and there would be a ban on all pornographic material in the workplace.

Eyes darted back and forth. Eyebrows were raised and smirks hidden. Many thought of the cardboard boxes stashed under Peter David's desk.

'We will be launching a thorough investigation into where the email originated from and how it was spread. If you know of anything, please come forward. Your identity will be kept secret. Indi, please put up that email address.'

Back at Khans, the AEs ordered more white rum and kept on chuckling.

'Mumtaz, is this one yours?' asks Andrea placing the printout on the table.

'Eh put that away. You'll get us all fired.'

'This is after hours, away from office. If you guys watch porn, why can't we check out some carrots? Even these baby ones.' Sonal leans in and grins.

Nisal shakes his head and lights a cigarette, hoping the waiter doesn't pop by.

'I'm off, we have a meeting on the tourism pitch at 8 a.m.'

'Stop being a suck up, Nisal. That pitch is lost already. After all the money they busted, as if they will ever change "Land like no other?"' says Sonal.

'Only numbers 4 and 7 look circumcised. Judging from your skin Mumtaz, I'd say you were 4,' says Andrea sipping from her clear glass.

'This is an invasion of privacy.' Mumtaz blushes, but only in a way that looks like he's pleased.

'You stare at our boobs every day,' says Andrea looking down at her modest cleavage. 'Now that everyone knows how small you are, you think it's an invasion?' Andrea makes notes on Sonal's doodle pad while Sonal's eyes glaze over.

'Big or small. Sri Lanka tourism screws us all,' she slurs.

'How do we know they belong to agency people?'

'We don't. So there's flimsy deniability,' says Andrea. 'The paste-up guys think there's a hidden camera in the urinal. But number 4 is wet. Maybe there's one in the shower.'

'Who takes showers in office?'

'Kristo and Rilla, after their morning badminton game. Both on the list.'

'So Parinda the boss man has the smallest. Big surprise. I want to know who number 7 is.'

'Here be careful with Parinda,' says Sonal. 'He sneaks to MD.'

'I told you number 7 is mine,' says Nisal.

'I called your ex. Apparently you're more kolikuttu than plantain.'

'You called who?'

'Whatserface. Mumtaz, we all know about you and the slut. It was on the workshop trip right?'

'Man we were all drunk that trip.'

'So you let her photograph your ladies finger?'

'We fooled around. I don't remember man.'

'You think she's collecting trophies from all the guys she's seen?' asks Sonal.

'That's twisted,' says Mumtaz. 'And that's not mine. I have a birthmark right...'

Everyone screams as he lowers his belt. Nisal pays the bill and gets up.

'Do girls always do this stuff?'

'What stuff?' asks Andrea.

'Sit around and talk about our size and all.'

Andrea and Sonal share a smirk and glare at Mumtaz.

'As if there's nothing better to talk!'

***

Nineteen people used the studio server on the day the email was sent. The message left at 20.47, an hour after the racist studio manager says he locked up for the evening. The spare key was with the security guard, who claims he never left his post, but was seen having roti at the Beaumond Kade down the road around 8.

All this was gleaned by amateur sleuth Andrea Thiyagarajah, while the pitch squad argued the merits of the current round of creatives. It was a high-powered meeting featuring the MD, the ECD, Ravi, Parinda, Hasitha, Peter, and the new girl from media. While Nisal took notes on his laptop, and Sonal pretended to on her doodle pad, Andrea slipped out to do some sleuthing.

She learned that Janela the slut used to get rides home with Kamal Bultjens, the finance executive and then with Anuradha the media buyer. She hadn't dated anyone since Stuart the copywriter, her high school boyfriend of 5 years was caught making out with an intern in the car park.

Andrea then snuck into the men's toilet where she was greeted with the stench of unwashed body parts and the sight of hairs on the sink. While holding her breath, she managed to snap photos of the three urinals and the underused shower. She was caught by Kiri malli the Sinhala lettering artist who, on his daily rounds of badmouthing the MD and cursing her children, had unexpectedly got a bog tight. He saw her, zipped up and sprinted to the car park.

She ascertained that a urinal camera would require noisy drilling, whereas a shower cam could be clipped to the wall unit but the angle would be difficult to shoot at. Most of the Urin8 penises were erect or semi erect, which would suggest they were taken pre-coitus. Like the men who owned them, most penises shrivel and pass out right after ejaculation. She knew this from her limited fumbles in the dark with her two and only boyfriends.

When she made it back to the boardroom, all the Small Miracle ideas had been rejected, except the one with the collage of photographs in the shape of a Sri Lanka map. Peter had the horrified look of a man who would spend his weekend doing image searches. Ravi and Hasitha were embroiled in a heated discussion. The strategist was writing the headlines, while the copywriter was changing the strategy. And the MD was droning on at the media girl and warning Indikhab of IT that if the projector failed this time, he would get his salary cut.

Andrea took her seat next to Sonal and gasped. Janela was right there, sitting before her, getting briefed on models and locations for the TV script.

'Will Danila not be presenting TV costings?'

It was the first thing Andrea had ever said in the last month of sitting in meetings.

Parinda looked up from his file and frowned.

'Janela is the producer on this project,' he says. 'She's more than capable.'

* * *

The day after the pitch presentation, Andrea Thiyagarajah was sacked for incompetence, poor attendance and for circulating a banned pornographic image via the office email. While Andrea couldn't dispute her attendance record, she vehemently denied emailing the 8 dicks to Sonal and Nisal after the porn embargo was imposed.

The pitch had been a disaster and Andrea told anyone with a pair of ears that she had been the scapegoat for lame creative, useless strategy and an account director with a 'teeny-weeny choo-choo'. She did the rounds saying goodbye and telling everyone that advertising was a bunch of posers and bullshitters and that women were treated like shit despite the company being owned by one. 'I wish my daddy gave me a company,' she said loudly outside the MD's office, knowing full well that the lady in question was enjoying a week's R&R in Portugal to get over the failed pitch.

Her last stop was at the desk of Janela Fernando, whose boss Danila Guneratne was also in Lisbon, 'sourcing new business.' The department comprised three desks, some cameras and walls filled with compact discs.

'Heard they're not confirming you?' said Janela, raising her eyebrows and stirring her tea.

'Did you bang them in this room?' asked Andrea, sitting on Danila's famous couch.

'Yep. One of them squirted right where you're sitting,' said Janela and laughed as Andrea moved from the couch to the stool.

'You're disgusting!'

'Am I?'

'Everyone knows they were your photos.'

'All everyone knows is that you spread vicious gossip. Maybe if you focused on your job, you might still have one.'

'And what do you spread?'

'Singapore office has a handbook on harassment. If you weren't already fired, I could complain about this.'

'Did you take the photos before you sucked them? Or after?'

'They never fire anyone at DDBO. You must've really pissed off madam.'

'How did you hack my machine?'

'I'm not the enemy, little Andi. We both fight the same bullshit. Ravi the planner can joke about rape and brag about cheating on his wife. All while he's pitching wedding rings for Swarna Mahal.'

'Someone's prepared their defence.'

'I'm single. I have a career. What I do is no one's business.'
'We all know about your career.'
'You know less than nothing about anything.'
'I know about your rides home.'
'How do you get home, little Andi?'
'Don't need to sit on laps.'
'Because Dada sends the driver. How can you mock MD? Didn't you both go to the same stupid school? Do you have to walk every day to the bus stop? And get whistles from every baboon in a sarong? Then get on the bus so a pervert can rub you? Or take a tuk at night, hoping the driver won't detour to an empty lane?'
'I don't exchange rides for hand jobs?'
'Has anyone, even one person, in this agency or anywhere… mentioned… even once, that they've slept with me?'
'Everyone knows.'
'You didn't find anyone, no? Not one dickhead.'
'As if I care.'
'You think I need to install cameras to snap cocks? Lankan men think it's charming to send photos of their mallis to girls they think are fast because of what other girls say about them.'
'Ah. So you've been blackmailing? That makes sense.'
'Most times, withholding a complaint is more effective than complaining.'
'And that's how we get promoted.'
'You know less than nothing about anything.'
'How did you hack my machine? I just had a firewall installed.'
'By whom?'
There was no knock. The door opened, and IT manager Ahamed Indikhab popped his head in.
'Need a ride?'

'Only if it's on your way? I'll get my bag.'

Janela hopped out of her chair and dropped her business card on Andrea's lap. It read 'Janela Fernando. Head of Production.'

'Thanks for your good wishes. Call me if you need anything. I'm looking for qualified junior execs with intelligence. Tell if you know anyone.'

* * *

The Tourism Board account stayed with the Dubai agency, though the Tourist Board adopted the line, Small Miracle as its tagline, claiming that while several agencies had used it, it had in fact been developed internally and shared on the original brief. It was later scrapped by a President of Sri Lanka, a man like many of our leaders, who liked to project big, while thinking small.

'How dare they!' he said to his youngest son. 'As if we are small. Nonsense!'

If You're Sad and You Know It

(Suicide prevention rhyme for
children aged 35 and over)

If you're sad and you know it, slit your veins.
If you're sad and you know it, slit your veins.
If you're sad and you know it,
and you want to nice-and-slow it.
If you're sad and you know it, slit your veins.

>If you're sad and you know it, take a leap.
>If you're sad and you know it,
>and this life you want to throw it.
>If you're sad and you know it, take a leap.

If you're sad and you know it, eat a gun.
If you're sad and you know it,
you can Hemingway or Van Gogh it.
If you're sad and you know it, eat a gun.

If you're sad and you know it, swallow pills.
If you're sad and you know it,
and this line you cannot toe it.
If you're sad and you know it, swallow pills.

If you're sad and you know it, tie a noose.
If you're sad and you know it,
and the whole world has to know it.
If you're sad and you know it, tie a noose.

If you're sad and you know it, tell a friend.
If you're sad and you know it,
and you need someone to say it.

Say what?
I dunno.
Something like this maybe.

'Stop weeping
even in the worst,
there is stuff worth keeping.
One bad month doesn't make a bad decade.
Put down the pills;
stop being a dickhead.

Disappointment, despair, disillusion
are natural.
But those are just the ailments,
none of them are terminal.

In the end, we are all just dust.
Here for brief sparkle
and eternal rust.

Breath is precious,
and air is too,
and you are more than a gift
though you see it not,
but I do.
You are a blessing.
Though you see it not.
I do.'

If you're sad and you know it, tell a friend.

Time Machine.
I Have Built A
(Part One)

OF COURSE, THE TITLE IS STOLEN. EVERYTHING IN THIS damn world is stolen. The land that you stand on is stolen, the ideas in your head are stolen, the government steals the money you make, and then your very breath is stolen, and most thieves are never caught.

I stole the title of this tale from a 6-word short story I saw on the world wide web. Inspired by Papa Hemingway's 8-syllable baby clothes epic, which apparently, he'd never written. This was penned by some guy who wrote comics and had a name like Roger Moore. I tried to source the author but all reference to him had disappeared from the web.

I also stole the time machine, or the deux ex machina as the more unkind among you will no doubt call it. I was not the one who built it. That credit belongs to Professor Cyril Ponnambalam, Dr Kumar Thiruchelvam and Chancellor Sivaram Duraiappah. Though some would say not.

Ponnambalam headed NASA's department of particle physics, Thiruchelvam worked as a lab technician in the Kremlin and Duraiappah ran a technology college in Tel Aviv. All three resigned from their posts in 2004 to return to Sri Lanka, though not with their families. Two were executed by the Tiger leadership a week before the end of the war, five years later. One was reported missing in action.

They weren't the only scientists, engineers, financiers and logisticians from the diaspora to return to Sri Lanka following the 2002 ceasefire. Many came on humanitarian missions or for peace conferences, most to assist with reconstructing the north and the east, fractured from decades of war and about to be pounded by a tsunami. A majority were recruited by the LTTE, some by force, some by extortion, some by the memory of wrongs.

While the ceasefire dragged, while leaders sat at desks in Switzerland and traded insults, these men of science were busy, using obsolete technology from forgotten wars in Albania, Fiji and Malvinas, to fashion weapons to bludgeon the Sri Lankan state into giving the Tigers one of their own. While peace talks floundered, while elections were boycotted, while wars reignited, while one side was annihilated, these men worked 18-hour days without leave. Uninterrupted by family or finance, housed in agreeable cottages south of Kilinochchi, with a tight budget, fixed materials and a defined goal. Perfect conditions for ingenuity and invention, necessity being the mother and all that.

I was put in charge of inventory – perhaps because my background was in accounting, perhaps because my wife's sister was married to the President's brother, perhaps because I was a colonel during '89 and saw things that I have kept my mouth shut about all these years.

I had a team of 15 weapons inspectors, mostly young officers, and was given less than 3 weeks to clear warehouses. To catalogue and classify 'conventional' weaponry and to destroy 'unusual and unorthodox' weaponry. My boys were young, honest and wet. There were essentially clerks assigned with bagging and tagging. The quieter ones had come in from processing the bodies.

What happens to the bullets left over from wars? Melted down and turned into schools and hospitals. Yeah right.

They are used to start fresh wars. Mine was not to reason why, mine was to do the best with not much. The might of the military was busy cleaning coastlines, mopping up mines and mass burying corpses, and thus my team was skeletal and third rate. Warehouses of weapons don't pose threats, only the idiots operating them.

'Men. We have 14 warehouses to clear in as many days. Stick to procedure, file daily reports, move fast and we will finish this. Dismissed.'

I wasn't one for pep talks. I was a good marksman, a decent infantryman and an excellent pen pusher. I then spent 15 years counting money for a garment manufacturer, before the President's brother called me. You couldn't say I was overly prepared for this mission.

Among the weapons captured were gravel guns or Kalashnikovs that fired pebbles to pinpoint accuracy, night binoculars with 100x zoom, boots that left no footprints, canisters that turned air moisture to drinkable water. There were boomerang daggers, elephant repellent, encryption wires and fire rocks.

The tone amidst the officers, in both their reports and their backchat, grew from respectful reportage to excited incredulity.

'Sir, we can make money sir. We can market these fully sir, can export. Why sir must we destroy?'

A pack of them got together and wrote me a letter.

'The Sri Lankan government, glory to the motherland, may assume ownership of these innovations and share them with the world as such.'

I pondered whether this government would want to share examples of Tamil brilliance, when they were trying to convince the world of the enemy's savagery. Not a good idea to ponder when work needed to be done. Two warehouses were filled with grenades and landmines built from coconut husks, jak splinters and banana stems. These dead geniuses had brought warfare into the organic era.

I assigned my best men, a corporal and a sergeant, to scour the grounds for logbooks or files or evidence of a bonfire. The last phase of the war was quick and left the rebels with little time to scorch the earth. The camp was surrounded by scraggy forest and the warehouses had survived government shelling, though the neighbouring villages had not.

The government would argue that the Tigers' decision to hide amongst villagers meant that civilian casualties would be on them. There was talk that the military top brass would claim zero civilian casualties. I wondered how they would sell that, when I, and all others with eyes, could count thousands.

If a commercial airliner is taken hostage, can a government blow it out of the sky and blame the hijackers for passenger deaths? Is the human shield argument even worth entertaining? Big wars are won by carpet-bombing civilians. Why? Because it works. The spider web of Tiger camps and strongholds were flattened, its survivors gunned down, its leaders turned to corpses.

Known for its organizational meticulousness and fondness for bureaucracy, it is tough to imagine the Tigers had no method to their wizardry. Three warehouses were filled with armoured vehicles without wheels, clearly designed to hover and sadly unfinished. And then there was Warehouse No. 13.

We completed the inventory report with three days to spare. I rewarded the men by confining them to individual cells and serving them Chinese takeaway. Since the collective letter writing, I was ordered to prevent them from 'engaging in any discourse with one another'.

I explained to each man that I agreed with them in principle, but this outranked us all and was controlled by giants and would soon be over. I did not have to do this, but

I am a human first and a military man second. Yes, that is possible, though not advisable.

Some of the men were proud that even with such advanced weaponry, the bloodthirsty rebels were no match for the might of the Sri Lankan lion. I did nothing to dispel this youthful delusion. The war was won, as all wars are won, by stooping to the barbarism of the enemy, and then stooping lower.

Some thought it was sorcery and we were right to destroy it, especially the gadget in Warehouse No. 13. The ones who had been on mass grave duty, said very little, just ate their Chinese as if it were gruel and slop.

I received the reply with a swiftness uncharacteristic of the Sri Lankan state. Discharge each soldier to separate platoons, make each sign a gagging order. Then deploy Special Task Force. Incinerate. Without delay.

I faxed my report once more, highlighting the importance of preserving these scientific marvels, my mistake was letting the idealism of the men infect my tone. The call was from the President's brother.

'Algama. Why?'

I tried to explain that we spin it as Sri Lankan army inventions. Or we sell them to China at a huge margin.

'Who is this we?'

I told him that the destruction of these weapons would be picked up on satellite, that he should come and see for himself. He laughed loudly through the phone.

'The UN are coming in two weeks. They see this, they'll think we are hiding more.'

I began to describe the weaponry that I had seen, but he didn't bite. That's when I laid my final trump.

'Sir. Did you read the dossier on Warehouse No. 13?'

'Algama. I hired you because you don't waste time. I am surrounded by time wasters. Are you also one of them?'

'I think you will find I am the opposite,' I said. 'I delay because of time. Prabhakaran's scientists seem to have invented a machine that can travel through it.'

He laughed loudly. I emailed him my latest photos and he stopped laughing. He would helicopter in on Friday. I instructed the STF to box all the merchandise and to warehouse them until the arrival of the President's brother. Then I took my notepad, my flask of highland tea and let myself into Warehouse No. 13.

* * *

Guess who dropped in to share my tea? Thilakan, hard at work in the eastern province, decided to hop a chopper and pay me a visit. The first knock on the door was tentative. I had told them no visitors and while I didn't inspire fear like many Lankan COs, an order, even from an accountant, is to be obeyed. The second knock was firmer, the third rude. I shoved the door open, prepared to deliver expletives, when I saw the face of the jackal.

Captain Thilakan had been a Tiger commander of the eastern province. His defection to the government, along with his bosses, had tipped the balance of the war. He had survived numerous assassination attempts and was now set to reap the rewards of his treachery, or loyalty, depending on which way you spin it.

A thickset man with a slow gaze, he looked tired. While his superior turncoats marked out bunkers and arms cachets, not unlike this one, he had been entrusted with clearing mines. It was high-pressure work and by the furrows on his brow, it looked like his deadline was tighter than mine.

'I came to help you close some boxes, Major.'

His salute was deferential, though his gaze was not. He left his flankers behind and accepted a sip of my tea,

Ceylon Uva pekoe with ginger and honey, though this brute appreciated none of it. Warehouse No. 13 was empty, except for one large crate in the middle under two spotlights. I had it opened and its contents placed on gunnysacks. Thilakan refused to look.

We stayed on our feet while he told me a tale very different to the one given to me by the brigadiers who briefed me.

Before the R&D wing of the Tigers had set up shop south of Kilinochchi, it had existed as a diaspora. The leader of the Liberation Tigers of Tamil Eelam had an army of scientists developing weapons for him across five continents. The Sinhala bullies had over the decades chased some of the brightest Tamil minds from the island and Prabhakaran had electoral rolls in 75 countries and conscripts to track down long names ending in consonants.

The scientists gathered in undisclosed locations, usually places where meetings of dark men with moustaches didn't arouse suspicion, mainly Singapore, Dubai and Mumbai. They were given problems to solve and used available resources to do so. They even managed to rent laboratory space in Canada.

From the Tamil diaspora, some willingly lent their knowledge, time and bank balance to help the LTTE bomb and maim their way to a Tamil homeland. Others had their sons and daughters conscripted if they didn't comply. Many believed in a separate state, though not as many as you think. It was a mixture of machan talk and mafia methods.

The problem was not with the funding or with the talent. The logistics of flying 35 scientists from 17 countries to a central location once a year was taking time to yield results. By the early 2000s, they had built bunkers and submarines and suicide belts, but their experimental weapons programme had yielded little.

'The three stooges, Ponnambalam, Thiruchelvam and Duraiappah didn't invent it,' said Thilakan, looking for the first time at the chair in the centre of the room. It was a recliner, fortified with Formica, studded with crystal and doused with a mineral called miridium, only found in the mountains of Toppigala. It had an armrest, a backrest and no cushions. Eight analogue dials that looked like reincarnated water meters, and a manual of laminated pages strapped to its handles. It was lined with plastic that resembled steel.

Rumour had it that Melbourne University's Dr Selvarajah Nalliah, while experimenting with stealth technology for the Australian military, had inadvertently invented a device that could pierce frequencies. A prototype was shipped to Trincomalee along with its creator. Both were driven to Akaraipattu and detained until suitable facilities were arranged. Dr Nalliah died in a blast, which the Tigers blamed on the army and the army blamed on the Tigers. Many Tamil murders went unsolved, not for dearth of suspects, in fact, for reasons quite the opposite.

'The stooges didn't invent the technology. They just messed it up,' said Thilakan, sipping my tea and avoiding the chair's gaze.

'Why you call them stooges?'

'Aiya! Their weapons were hopeless. Gravel guns jammed, fire rocks took hours to burn, elephant repellent brought snakes to camp.'

I met many Tiger turncoats since Karuna defected in 2004 and none of them slipped into informality as easily as Thilakan.

'Captain. Please do not call me Aiya.'

'Sorry, sorry Major. Ask anyone. Too many young cadets were turned into kheema in that chair.'

The three stooges attempted to create a teleportation device from Nalliah's technology. Thilakan had to recommend test subjects with degrees in physics. The device, now cased in a cylinder, looked like a polling booth, and could move wherever a radio was tuned to its frequency. It managed to travel over 700 metres to a neighbouring chena cultivation where a Sanyo transistor was tuned and waiting. What was left of the boy driving it was smeared on the inside of the booth.

'Waste of university talent. They killed seven fellows like rats. Thalaiver cancelled project after that.'

'Why did they need physics degrees?'

'Major. This isn't a bumper car in Satutu Uyana. Have you seen those controls?'

We wandered across to the chair that looked less like a joyride for six-year-olds and more like an airline seat from the Palaeolithic or Balangoda Man period. Perhaps it had been stolen from the Tiger bombing of Air Lanka in 1986. It looked cheap but for some reason made my stomach hollow. The meters were digital in the way a Casio watch from 1983 was. The sheen was sandpapered, the rivets looked duct-taped. There were three seatbelts along the chair's frame and below the seat was the device.

'Major, we destroy it tonight.' He picked up the object chained to the footrest. It was a book made of transparent slides, and had been hidden under the seat. 'If America sees this, they'll think we have nuclear. Last thing any country, dictatorship or democracy, needs, is America interested in its wars.'

I had the compound searched and re-searched and came to conclude that the book written on translucent formica may have been the only copy in existence. The writing was in neat Tamil, which we both could read – I who had sat foreign service exams and only passed languages, and he who had spoken it since he could walk.

The book outlined Selvarajah Nalliah's time fabric theory and came with a repeated warning that the device not be used for travelling within the same time zone. 'Miridium will combust and scramble the traveller's molecules if time fabric is not crossed.'

It is hard to believe that the three stooges had not read this, easier to believe that they chose to ignore it. The rest of the book was filled with what looked like tables of logarithms. Thilakan shook his head. 'Let us incinerate this now. My men will help you.'

The tea was over, and I could neither win the argument nor deliver the sales pitch. So I told him a story and won my stay of execution. I told him that the President's brother would be arriving by helicopter the next day to inspect the weapon. Thilakan was tired and confused and decided to sleep. Incineration would be first priority tomorrow. While it could be argued that I outranked him, both he and I knew the height from which these orders came. I realized that a change of mind was unlikely. Or about as likely as Prabhakaran inventing a time machine and never using it.

* * *

It was 1 a.m. and I had visited the bathroom seven times since Thilakan's departure. He had commandeered the general's quarters and had six guards on the door. Muscular lads who could do nothing to prevent the Captain's snores from escaping the fortified suite.

I had switched from tea to thambili and soon would receive a pot of ranawara juice. I retained a staff of one for this mission, a young corporal from Wellawaya skilled in the art of making drinks. I may not exercise, and I may eat too much rice, but I never neglect the fluids. I could not imagine that my body, fattened on 15 years of corporate service, would hold up for too many more sunsets.

The outhouse was for officers only. A hole over a drain with a steel chair without seat above it to spare decorated soldiers the indignity of squatting. A frog occupied the ceiling and conducted a conference call with a pair of geckos on the jak tree outside. It punctuated my never-ending stream of piss, which I delivered from seated position.

Minutes later I found myself on a very different throne, one that smelt better than the first and did not feel as brittle, despite appearances. The armrest was wide enough to house eight separate dials, each stolen from a different clock. The dials had diagrams dedicated to them on pages 7–12 of the journal. Engraved on formica in Nalliah's neat hand, they were the only things in the document in English, though they may as well have been Greek.

THz, Ly, Savart, Foe, ParSec, Glk, Erlang, and MicroMort were the units of measurement on each of the eight dials. The log tables at the end featured range values for each of these next to four digits. It was assumed that the reader would understand what these units measured.

The column of 4-digits began 0208, the sequence went down in increments of 100 before rising by 1000 every twelve entries. The first seven entries were as follows. 0208, 0108, 1207, 1107, 1007, 0907, 0807. After 0107 it jumped again to 1206.

I skimmed ahead to see 0101 being followed by 1299 and 1199 and that's when my accountant's brain caught the pattern. Month and year and a parade of coordinates. The last entry was 0308 and in over 1000 entries not one number was duplicated.

I don't know too much about physics, but I did know something about spreadsheets. I have been staring at them most of my life and that is a skill you never lose, the ability to stare at numbers for periods without suicidal thoughts. I had an old classmate who was a sports journalist. 'I don't envy you suit and tie, Mercedes-BMW, banker-stockbroker, live-in-mansion types.' He told me once at an old boys' get-together. He was drunk and like most drunks, could not tell when his audience was tired of him. 'Because you wear your ties, load your briefcases and stare at spreadsheets all day, sometimes at night.'

He proceeded to go on about how all he stares at are sports games and books and his wife, the things he loves. I was going to say that I would rather look at digits in boxes than his wife. But instead, I shook his hand and let him take home a tuk-tuk while I slid into my Mercedes.

My number was 0366 and I ran my finger down the values for THz, Ly, Savart, Foe, ParSec, Glk, Erlang and MicroMort before my attention was stolen by the forks on either end of the seat. They looked old, antique in fact, and had the date 1792 engraved on their end.

'The key to crossing time fabric lies not in frequencies but in solid matter,' read the more coherent of sentences in Nalliah's journal. 'The conduit must be an object that has retained its coordinates for sufficient period.' This was followed by 70 rows of equations.

I didn't need to know how the bullet exits the gun, how the mortar rips through flesh or how the bomb produces fire. I just needed to know which button to press. Why choose March '66? Why an uneventful month in a forgettable year? It is because of where the conduit was and where I was at the time.

Even if you have a precise date and a solid plan, is it really possible to alter history for the better? Could I have gone to 1983 to warn the Tamils and thwart the mobs? Could I have floated to '75, killed Velupillai Prabhakaran before he tasted blood and stopped a 30-year war? Could I have nipped Sinhala chauvinism in the bud and gone to the 50s to shoot SWRD, wait someone already did that.

I could've used it to jump a trend, to pre-empt a spike on a spreadsheet and make fortunes as wide as Mahasen's sea. Invested in computers in the 80s, bet on Sri Lanka in '96, started a reconstruction company 6 months before this carnage ended. I could've taken penicillin to first world war trenches, assassinated Hitler, Pol Pot and Bush when they were toddlers, warned a coastline of oncoming tsunamis, told planes not to take off. Or could I?

If I am to stare at numbers I do not understand, risk being turned into mung seed, I had better make sure there was a reason sounder than boredom. Changing history is complex business. Which button do you press at what time, and is it always just the one button? If I am to operate elaborate logistics, I must choose a plan that will not fail.

Nalliah's time fabric theory strongly advised against travelling beyond one's lifetime. 'Matter cannot exist where it never was. Only where it has left its prints.' So that narrowed the search. What could I alter since 1945 that would have a significant impact on today? What do I regret about the world, what would I undo if I could?

There is of course the very real fear of getting fried. Nalliah's journal is clear on the perils of dialing inaccurate frequencies. Was my life really bad enough to try for a refund? Was the present that unbearable? Wasn't I enjoying a cushy ride? New era of peace, married into the first family, why would I want to leave and risk getting smeared across an old Air Lanka seat?

I have a tiresome wife and vacant children, but who doesn't? I may be past my prime and may never have a memorable sexual encounter again, but is that really such a problem? I'm afraid it may be.

I have no clue how time or history moves. If I assassinate a Milosevic, a Pinochet or a Cheney, how sure am I that another butcher would not rise in their stead? Maybe certain destinies are made to play out as written and it is not our place to meddle. Maybe the only thing I can affect and take responsibility for is my own could-have-been-better life.

March 1966 it is. There is one hour of darkness before Thilakan arrives to incinerate. I strap in and turn the dials. 11.33, 5534, 93889, 2.3434, 473, -19, 000998. Nalliah's journal warns on the importance of precision. I finish the ranawara juice, which tastes like soil and water. I press the button. I do not expect it to be so silent and I do not expect it to hurt so much.

***

Staring at Sunsets

AROUND THESE PARTS, PEOPLE GO MISSING ALL THE TIME, though few of them make the front pages. It helped that his family owned the papers, and his uncle ran the country. The jealous spoke of his private jet, his tea business in Asia, and his boutique hotels out east. The gossips spoke of his taste for gin, gambling and married women.

When his jet went missing in '93, there was much talk and many theories. The government, who owed him favours, did it. The mobsters, whom he slandered, did it. His wife, tired of his roving eye, did it. His plane was hijacked by aliens, swallowed by the Bengal triangle, or borrowed by the CIA.

After a year, people stopped talking about theories. After another, they stopped talking about him. After a few more, those suspected of his vanishing were snuffed out by that prolific assassin, nature herself.

While he sat alone, free of noise, on an island not far from here, writing his story in a yellowing journal… Staring at sunsets through large binoculars, surrounded by books and fruit and no one.

Time Machine. I Have Built A
(Part Deux)

THE HISTORY OF SRI LANKA SINCE 1945 IS A CATALOGUE OF me missing out on sex. In 1958, when SWRD was sprouting the vitriol that would divide a nation, I was going to Aunty Sumana's piano class. She used to put her hand on my shoulder as I played Chopin. In my night-time fantasies, she wore a floral sari without a blouse and her hands ran down the front of my chest. In my soggy dreams, I was always playing C.T. Fernando's 'Handa Paane' while her head disappeared between my thighs.

When the 1962 military coup was taken down with whimper and without bang, I was also whimpering and not getting banged in my first year of cadetting. I heard Aunty Sumana ran away with a prefect from my school, who played in my chess team, was uglier than me and couldn't play Chopin and for neither the first nor the last time I thought that could've been me.

When the 1971 insurrection happened, I had a girlfriend in Polonnaruwa who only let me touch them under the umbrella. When the island changed from Ceylon to Sri Lanka in '72, I fell into a whorehouse in Nikaweratiya along with nine other cadets and even though I ended up with the prettiest I was unable to spark the flame. By the time the '83 riots came along, I was married with three, transformed into my wife's peon and unable to raise a flag nor fire a gun.

On an accounting conference in Texas 1998, while yet another Jaffna mayor, Sarojini Yogeswaran, was being murdered by Tamil Tigers, I was the one of few in a crowd of 40, who did not end up in someone else's bed, despite paying for the drinks that loosened up the ladies and brazened up the gents.

I may pretend that this does not rancour. That my moderate wealth and meagre successes make up for my misfortunes in the sack and lack of hard tissue in the trouser area. But quite frankly it is poor consolation. And all can be back traced to March 1966.

* * *

The time machine had two conduits that came in the shape of two dessert forks made in the year 1792, the year the English stole the Ceylonese coast from the Dutch. The forks had lain in a stately home in Jaffna since 1838, the year the Kandyan king gave up the ghost and the future Sri Lanka became another conveyor belt in the great factory of Britannia.

The forks belonged to Mary Wellesley Frost, wife of an English cartographer, and was sold in an auction, after Sir Sargeson Frost and his family migrated to the hills around Bambarakanda where malaria took his youngest and exiled the Frosts and their grief back to Hampshire, leaving behind the cutlery. The forks were bought by a landowning Tamil family, the Mylavaganams, and hid in an almirah in their ancestral house on a Kanakesanthurai flatland until 1987, when the Mylavaganams fled, and the house was shelled and the almirahs were looted. The shiny unused forks ended up in a warehouse run by the Tigers amongst unsellable kitsch stolen from Tamils whose rights they were fighting for.

Nalliah's journal stressed the importance of using a conduit which had maintained its position in space, across 'swathes of time'. He claims to have contacted the Mylavaganam family, then exiled in Denmark, who verified that the forks stayed untouched in an almirah behind glass for the past century because someone's grandmother had misplaced the key.

When I landed, my clothes stayed intact but felt starchy and smelt of heavy mothballs. The chair looked untarnished, the silver forks looked shinier or perhaps that was my imagining. There was a smell of petroleum, which I did not expect to be a by-product of being squeezed through frequencies.

The machine attached to the chair was silent, there was no engine revving, no 80s keyboard ripples, no rumble, not even static. The chair was steady and steadfast. I only knew it had moved by the pain that bent me. It began with cramps, contorting the fingers and toes, tying knots in the stomach, and rippling through random muscles. They switched from acute to numbing and several frequencies between. I writhed against three seatbelts leaving burns on my skinny ankles and wrists and my bloated belly.

I had lofty ambitions of not crying out for fear of waking Thilakan but I squealed like a slaughtered pig after the second stomach spasm and no one came running. Then came the diarrhoea vomit feeling, though the retches were dry and as painful as the heaving farts. And then it stopped, and I looked around and saw the forks on the handle shining like little stars and found myself in a room with a pettagama and an almirah.

It smelt of dust and must. Inside the almirah were dinner sets, tea sets, girayas and padlocks, speckled with mildew and protected by glass. At the corner of the cupboard, in glass box, the doppelgangers of the forks, glistened as bright as the conduits on the chair. I wondered if I would glisten when I met my younger self.

The pain left no grogginess, no hangover, it merely left. I tiptoed downstairs and contemplated what the household would say to a man wandering their rooms dressed as a soldier from 40 years later. It was a reasonable and pointless worry, as most of them are. The door to the red veranda was open and I met no one as I slipped out.

The house was not enormous, but it had presence, the heft of an era bygone, encased in trees bearing jak, mango and kohomba. I walked outside but could not identify the street. It was mad dogs and Englishmen weather and the place bore little resemblance to the scarred land where I had spent the war's final days, serving at the pleasure of maniacs.

I passed people with wide collars and gelled hair who spared me not a glance. I wondered if a man in camouflage was a common sight in 1966. Especially when I got smiles and nods. Maybe Jaffna in those days had nothing to frown about. Boy would that change.

I stumbled down the road to Nallur Temple and got my bearings. In the city centre, the newspaper seller asked why I was dressed in an army outfit. I gave my name and rank and file and said I was helping with the governor-general's visit. 'We have a governor-general?' remarked the man, covered in grey stubble, and handing me a Veerakesari. The headlines spoke of Sir John's speech in parliament, of a plane crash in Tokyo, and a coup in Syria. And the date was two weeks early.

The currency in my wallet was as useless as my credit cards. He stared at the five-rupee coin minted in 2007 and said nothing.

'Oh, my apologies. That is military money.'

ID card design hasn't changed in 50 years. I showed him mine and he shrugged saying that he did not read Sinhala. I told him to run a tab for me and that I will repay it on the

28th when the governor-general comes, but to not mention this to anyone as it could be a security risk. He stared at the gun in my holster, which had also survived being squeezed between frequencies, and said zero.

I managed to get a room at the Tourist Board Rest house near town and secured three meals. I used the governor-general routine and it worked without me having to flash my holster. Perhaps it was the medals pinned to my camouflage that did the trick with the boy at reception. Jaffna was sunny and lazy and wide-eyed. What a lovely place Sri Lanka was before the savages broke loose. The girls on the road averted their eyes but kept their smiles. The men spoke slowly and precisely. I unravelled the city on a bicycle and found my way to the youth hostel.

I knew I would find them on the balcony. The Russian girl was leaning over it and laughing, her braless blouse fluttering in still air. The skinny boy next to her had his hands in his pockets and badly needed a haircut, a shave and a bath. I watched them talk, she giggled, he sniggered and grinned. That night she will kiss him on the cheek, and he will beat his stick in the bathtub. I knew because that wanker was me.

***

History is whatever but flesh is flesh. Reality is what you can eat and touch and swallow and hide yourself in, the rest are abstracts. In 1966, I was a 19-year-old virgin, who had read Gorky and Tolstoy, and of course Marx and Engels, had joined the youth volunteer peace corps organized by the LSSP and funded by the Russian Cultural Centre, where groups of young people were sent to up north to share modern agriculture techniques with paddy cultivators. There were ten of us, five locals, five Soviets; five guys, five girls. It was true cultural exchange, the Russian boys were trying to seduce the local lathas, while both of us natives were trying to bed the suddhis.

We called them all Russians, when only one of them was from a town anywhere near Vladivostok. The two girls were from Ukraine and Latvia, one was blonde and small, one was tall and dark. Both preferred me to Shelton, the bespectacled gamaya from Gampaha. The other boys were from Belarus and Georgia.

By day we photographed paddy fields and mended fences, and did farming workshops with Weragoda Sir and Lyudmilla Miss, who we suspected were rolling in the paddy together. At night we sat on the beach, drinking, and smoking and trying it on. The Burgher girl seemed close with the tall Russian, but we then saw her flirting with the stocky one. The village girls from Kelaniya spoke poor English as did the older Russian who kept plugging them with drinks.

We sat by bonfires and spoke of revolutions and what was fair and what was evil, and I snuck peeks at the rose white legs belonging to Sofia and Kristi, solid like tree trunks, not the brown twigs of our locals. I caught them both stealing looks at me at different times. I had no competition from Shelton the gamaya and the merry month of March lay spread-eagled before me. The gamaya, a poor seducer, was the loudest in discussions on capital, freedoms, land and property. But he was sweaty, and his lenses were bottle bottoms that magnified his beady eyes. The three Russian boys were lining up for the Burgher girl and trying to crack the village lathas, which meant my path was as open as the A9 highway.

Sofia, the small blonde was the prettier, easier to talk to, and enjoyed a morning swim, which I professed to as well, even though I cared little for sunrises or water. She wore a blue swimsuit that hugged her bones, I had baggy shorts that offered camouflage.

Kristi, the tall brunette was the sexier, freer with her hands, looser with her tongue, drunker after two beers, easier to grope, but didn't always laugh at my jokes. Over nights of change-the-world chatter, I got to sit close to both and have their heads on my shoulder, while watching the flame, and cooing at the half moon, I got to kiss Kristi before she passed out, comatose on Petrov Vodka, who feigned no recollection of my lips on hers the next day.

It was at the party on the island of Delft, a boat ride from where we were – as everything seemed to be those days. Weragoda Sir and Lyudmilla Miss were among thirteen chaperones, most of whom went missing as the night wore on and the smoke grew thicker.

It began as a belated Defender of the Fatherland celebration shared by the Ceylon-Soviet Youth Club (that was us) and the Soviet-Ceylon Volunteers Association, which was headquartered at Elephant Pass and specialized in fisheries development. Then the Lanka-Norway Youth Alliance made the trip from Trincomalee, and the Socialisme Française Jaffna Chapter also plugged, and so on a pre-poya moon day, Delft was a bonfire of young communists swaying in the moonlight and trying to get into each other's shorts.

Sofia and I had conversations about when we would give up our virginities. She was waiting for the right guy, and I said that I was waiting for the right girl, though I didn't add that the right girl would be anyone with breasts who was up for it. Speaking in the lexicon of capitalism, my saving myself had less to do with supply and more with demand.

Kristi had made love at 15 with her beatnik boyfriend and had had a few lovers. 'Few enough to not make me slut.' She was seen sharing beer with a burly Czech from the SCVA. That night under the pre-poya moon, to the perfume of spilt booze, to the static of Beatles, Seekers and Kinks, broadcast by Radio Ceylon on a Vega transistor, and inspired by the grassy cigarette we shared with the French hippie from Jaffna, Sofia and I agreed to be each other's first.

At 2 a.m., with the party still burning and our loins still smouldering, we chose to disagree over the hypocrisy of the west. She said the United States was building a colonial empire, stealing the wealth of Latin America, invading Asian democracies and funding Middle Eastern despots. I reminded her that the US never had a Stalin. Chaperones circled the beer shack, eying the noise and watching the locals. Ours was not the only argument on that beach that night.

I said that New York would eclipse Moscow and that China's cruelty would hold it back from greatness. She said the CIA didn't give a shit about my shitty country. Who knows why we chose to contradict each other, when neither of us felt passionately over the positions we claimed to hold. For some, anger is an aphrodisiac, with us, it was a shower of Siberian temperatures. She turned away and downed her gin. I stormed off to the waves.

I thought of banging the Burgher girl, or picking up a loose lass on the beach, and there were plenty, but after a walk and a cigarette that wasn't green and after seeing Shelton groping the saucy supervisor from Belarus, the minx from Minsk as he later called her, I came to the conclusion that dick trumps politics, the same conclusion that led me to turn that machine's dials. I returned to concede, to agree to disagree, to celebrate our cerebral passion with fire further south. To find my princess in the arms of the chaperone from the Norwegian group. The man with the white beard and the cowboy hat. The man she was kissing.

The Russian boys said she had gone to his room and returned only at morning. The Lankan girls said she was drunk, and the pervert had taken advantage of her. We didn't speak for the remainder of the volunteer month. Kristi tried to fondle me as a cheer up, but I recoiled from her charity and from communism and from attending parties with bonfires. I spent the next decade couched in loathing and I dropped every catch that came my way. Even the sitters.

In the end I got to hold some hands, shoulder some heads, dance slow and swim with a hard on, and daydream of promises to fuck. I did not put my flesh in other flesh for a good six years. All because of a disagreement on Fidel, Cuba, and a bay full of pigs.

In the 1990s, I met the Burgher girl, by then a buxom mother of four and wife of three. She recalled that night with a cackle. 'What happened with you and the Latvian chickie? She was fully in love with you. And you treated her like shit.' That was after she fucked the pervert in the cowboy hat, I felt like saying, but instead my rejoinder was, 'What Latvian chickie? There were so many.'

* * *

The aches returned whenever I sat on the machine. As if the air above, it was jagged with pierced frequencies. I managed to trade in my medals, my shoes and my exotic currency at the pawnbrokers on the road to Kayts. The gun I kept holstered under lock at the rest house. I spent two weeks stalking the boy and the girl in my civvies, and it amazed me what children they were. I stopped eavesdropping on their infantile Marxist talk, for it curved my insides much like the machine that had brought me here. Neither noticed me hanging around their meeting rooms, strolling beside them on the beach, or hopping the same bus. When not in uniform, I was just like everyone else.

I picked up my chair from the Mylavaganam residence one morning. It was lighter than I thought, but still required me to bend my back and lose my breath when I took it down the steps. I was confronted by their servant, as domestics were called in those days. I said I was from Ponmalai Furnishings and that this chair was wrongly delivered last week. She even helped me find a three-wheeler large enough to transport it.

I parked it back in my room at the Rest house, smiled with all my teeth at every staff member, and kept reminding them that on the 28th I would pay not only for the last month, but for two more months in advance.

I was served rice and curry for all three meals and did not complain. I sat in my standard rate room staring at a chair I could not sit on. While counting my limited funds and scheming against a bearded man in a cowboy hat, I noticed indentations on the side of the seat. The grooves were oval and rough, and I realized that they fit my fingers as if carved to measure. The match was perfect. Had I gripped the armrest during the stomach spasms, and embedded my prints in the wood?

I noticed something else. Lower on the handle were thicker indentations, also finger impressions, stubbier and shapelier. Index, ring, and middle dug into front of armrest. I leaned forward and planted my digits; the fit was far from snug. A shudder began at my lower back and crawled its way up my spine. It would appear that someone, with stubby fingers suited to piano playing and trigger pulling, had used this chair before me.

* * *

Do I wish that I made more money, rose higher in these made-up ranks, married someone who didn't make me yawn, had children that didn't inspire violence in me? Not particularly. I did no better or worse than any other animal. Notwithstanding what they made me do in 1989, I didn't harm or hurt all that much. Though I do wish I had a few more screws.

I know not what is out there to greet us when we croak, perhaps answers, quite likely nothing. If I do wish for more of something, it would be notches on belts, orgasms in organisms, the taste of strange women's tongues. My wife and I, before she was my wife, rented out rooms in places strange, and drunk with passion, fell into each other's bodies and stayed locked in there.

Ah, the taste of new flesh, of being welcomed into someone's sweat for the first time, there really is nothing to compare. Even the forgettable encounters enthral when recalled, harden whatever softness. But too few, too far between.

The hostel was on the same road as St. John's College, well tendered by the volunteers, the fence had been painted by Shelton, two of the Russians, and me. I remembered the hot day and the shoddy job I had done and how the Russians had to paint over my crap while swearing and how I was too busy staring at the girls sweeping the balcony to care.

I rang the bell and asked for him from one of the Kelaniya lathas. He looked slovenly in his slippers and slacks, his facial hair was sporadic and had the texture of parched grass. His shirt hung like a stained rag.

'Hello putha. I am Seevali Mama. Your mother told I was coming?'

The boy looked confused. Then I saw her a staircase away. What a child she was, the face of a nymph, the body of an air stewardess. She peeked through the banister, her straw hair falling over her face, I turned to him and smiled.

'You have grown ah. Amma didn't say I was coming to pick you?'

I walked back to the gate, and he followed like I knew he would. Uncle Seevali was my mother's second cousin who lived in Trincomalee and never visited. He would die in the early 70s, though his legend would waft through every family gathering. I would hear anecdotes of his follies though we would never meet.

'Let's have some lunch. There is a Muslim kebab place I know you will like.'

On the way I mentioned playing cricket in Gampaha with him when he was 8 and how the servant boys used to chuck faster than Lindwall. I told him how his mother met his father, a story he hadn't yet heard. I shared tales of his grandma, which I knew he would recognize. I made him stub out the cigarette, I told him how pointless a habit it was. He grinned and lit up another.

Teenage boys are the easiest demographic to manipulate. Pander to their narcissism and inflate their self-worth, get them drunk and talk about sex. I resisted reciting lines from Kipling and Newbolt. Instead, I told him not to be afraid, because the things that scared him would never happen.

We sat on the rest house veranda, and I filled him with arrack and tales of my sexual prowess, not all of them made up. He was a willing listener as I always was and then he told me about Sofia and how tonight was going to be the night.

'Do not assume anything putha, until your dick is in the snatch.' I cadenced my wisdom, as if it were written by Shakespeare. I told him about posture, about eye contact, about speaking slowly, about touch, about confidence. Lessons I learned after nature rendered me celibate.

'I saw her. She is tasty. But are you sure about this party? There will be vultures everywhere.'

I advised him not to leave her with strangers, not to get too drunk and not to get into arguments, especially over politics. 'Sex and economic theory go together like a ponnaya and a lesbian.'

I wanted to keep him there all afternoon and tell him how to make friends and influence people, how to stop worrying and start living and how to be effective in seven habits. I wanted to tell him to take that stock analysis job in Germany, to place bets on England winning the world cup that year and never ever consider joining the armed forces.

I wanted to tell him that communism will lose, that apartheid will end, that walls will fall, that wars will drag for 30 years. But I knew he would do nothing of use with this information.

It is too late for lectures or too early perhaps. The boy was eager to please, but not so eager to learn and that was why he would struggle to attract females. Every word he said to my refined knowledge is 'I know, I know', when I with some reliability knew that he did not. I gave him a clean shirt that I bought in the market, knowing he would never wear it, but hoping he might. I wished him luck for the night not mentioning that I planned on being there.

My next task was to track the man in the cowboy hat. This proved less than simple. I stood outside the Soviet-Ceylon Volunteers Centre and watched the troops coming in from the fishing seminar. There was a mix of young and middle-aged, but none resembling the man from snowy beard. It is hard to pick a man in a hat when he is not wearing one.

I stood at the train station awaiting the Norwegian friends and the French leftists. They came in two bunches, but no Santa beard, no John Wayne.

Impatient and feeling ill, I decided to take an early ferry to Delft Island and scope out the hunting ground. I picked a cove by a hillock where he could whisk her away from the madding crowd, where the path wound down and the shadows touched the waves. I prepared bottles of water to give our hero to replenish his chi. I even brought a pill from the future, one that never worked for me, one that I found in my wallet next to an unused condom.

As the sun grew dim and the boats came in, as the youngsters gathered with their candles and their radios, I sat in the corner sipping rum. It was an hour before midnight when I saw the hat. It was brown leather like the side of a cow and riding the head of a Scandinavian woman. It took me a while to digest this. Did memory obscure things that an undeveloped mind could not process? Could it have been a lesbian that stole my bonnie away?

* * *

If Prabhakaran had used this machine, where would he have gone and why did he use it only once? Did he go back to 1983 to stop the death of his friend Seelan? If Seelan hadn't perished, neither would 13 Sinhala soldiers, or thousands of Tamils, or hundreds of thousands of Lankans. Did Velu end up believing that the war shouldn't have happened, or that it shouldn't have been lost?

Did he go to take back some of his hits? Back to 1975 to unkill Mayor Alfred of Jaffna, back to the 90s to unassassinate Gandhi and Premadasa, back to 2002 to keep the ceasefire.

Back, back, back.

Back to 2006 to unfix the election between the warmonger and the appeaser. Unslaughter civilians in Jaffna, Mannar, Muthur, Sampur, Vanni and Batti. Did he go to plant new bombs and to unbotch killings? Or like me, did he go back to catch the one that got away? Did he go back to simply get his soldier tickled?

* * *

Half an hour later, the hat was flicked by one of the local boys and passed around the Norwegian group in glee. The original owner appeared annoyed, but then got distracted by beer and a conversation on international finance. I watched the hat go from hand to head-to-head to hand. Until finally it found its home.

The local boy from the Socialisme Française passed it to the Korean girl from the Soviet institute who dropped it while dancing, where it was picked up by the bartender who gave it to Lyudmilla Miss who was not sleeping with Weragoda Sir that night, but with a ripped fisher boy who had invited himself to the party.

The radio stopped broadcasting at midnight precise and the crowd groaned at the static. While the chatter escalated and the waves crashed, fisher boy left with Lyudmilla Miss and handed his hat to the vermin. He was younger than I remember but had that smarmy gait. And though his facial fluff was really just stubble, it was unmistakably white.

I followed him to the bar and watched him try his luck with the underage. His opening gambit was 'howdy pardner' in an accent that was a mix between Hungarian and Scandinavian. The girls got to try on his hat while he tried on his pickup moves. I blocked a few of his chats, mocked his one-liners, lampooned his accent and pointed out that cowboys were genocidal imperialists, land thieves who murdered innocent natives. I managed to scare away both him and the girls he was chatting up. And a nearby

French teacher who had stopped by to smoke something not quite legal.

Somewhere after midnight, the idiot boy who had worn my clean shirt sparked a discussion on the Bay of Pigs, which concluded with him walking off and her sobbing by the bar. I looked around for cowboy man as I took the stool next to her. Until the boy returned, I would serve as a buffer against lotharios in dodgy head gear. I offered her my handkerchief, assured her that young Algama would be back, that he was a passionate young man, simmering with greatness. I told her some jokes to lighten the mood and prepared her for our hero's return.

It is when she leaned into me, that I realized how drunk she was and that it is her I should've shared my bottles of water with rather than him. At least the cowboy was nowhere in sight. I also became aware of blood running through veins previously too parched for even the world's finest pharmaceuticals. By the time I noticed how her rosy skin shone in the poya moon, her lips were brushing mine and I was as hard as the rock by Palaly that lovers threw themselves off.

I opened my eyes and looked into a mirror, into eyes that were my own. Across a barroom, as the stare pierced me, I realized two things. In two weeks, my lazy stubble had grown to an itchy beard. And for some inexplicable reason, the cowboy hat had found its way onto my head.

The Losing Bet

HE SAYS HE WILL SHAVE HIS HEAD AND MARRY HER IF Bangladesh beat Pakistan. He likes to place decisions in the hands of gods, in the gloves of batsmen, or in the paws of match fixers.

He knows Bangla will never beat the country that once owned it, especially in a World Cup. But if it did, he would shave his mane, give up art, take a 9 to 5, and marry her.

However, if Pakistan won, he would go to a place where artists can have multiple women. He would ask her to come, knowing she would not. Win-win. He announces it to the folk huddled around his TV. He mentions only the head-shaving bit.

'If you want to be bald, be bald. If you want to go to Amsterdam, go,' said his beloved, tired of holding teacups and smiling. When the match ends in a tie, he realizes there are things more important than cricket and hair. He gets on his knees before all present. She exits the room and returns ten minutes later with a pair of clippers.

Second Person

YOU START TALKING TO HER BECAUSE YOU'RE BORED. YOU'RE at Ranil's house drinking and he gets her on line for you. He tells you she's fourteen and has big tits and talks like a nympho. You give her your hand phone number. She starts calling you.

Her name is Suba, and she's actually sixteen. You're actually thirty-two. You should have outgrown this years ago. Every other day, she calls you after school and you sit in meetings while she talks filthy.

You've come to a curious time in your life. You've lost faith in love affairs and pornography pleases you more than the prospect of a partner. You honestly prefer masturbation to sex, and it begins to scare you.

The computer at the office is flooded with porn and you're the only one who knows where it is. The juniors are afraid of the machine and so is your boss, though he pretends he isn't.

In Sri Lanka, sex is distributed unevenly. You get it in abundance if you're rich or powerful or beautiful, or any cruel combination of the three. You don't get it if you're ordinary, pleasant or good-natured. You don't get it if you're rolling in self-doubt and it shows on your face. You don't get it if you're someone like you.

Obviously, things aren't happening these days. You're trying to convince yourself that it's just a lean patch and you're done with relationships. But weeks are turning to months and the months threaten to turn into years. You count the women you've screwed and compare them with the women in FHM. You count how many women you haven't screwed, and it drives you nuts. Or drives you to grope for your nuts gazing at FHM.

Everyone else is getting it. Even Mohan in accounts. He's shacking up with his secretary who is as gorgeous as he is fat and ugly. Sathi, the promotions director, claims he screws all the foreigners who visit the hotel, and the sad thing is he's probably telling the truth. He eats raw pig fat, and his belly stays flat. He spends fortnights in the sun and his skin stays olive.

So, you call Suba and start flattering her. You use words like 'princess' and 'sexy' and 'sweetheart'. They all work. She bores you with her family. She tells you she's going to be a pop star and that she's already written songs that are sure hits. She could even write a song for you.

You cut to the chase. When can I see you, you ask? My father won't let me, she murmurs. You debate for a while. You hang up.

Later that night she calls you. Right after Baywatch. You sit out in the garden and feel yourself under your batik sarong.

You haven't kissed a boy?

You tell first. Have you kissed?

Mad? Of course, I haven't kissed a boy.

No...o...ha...he...he...You're silly. I mean girl!!!

Her inane drawl excites you even more. You drop your voice to a whisper.

I can kiss you. All parts of you. Even soft parts.

Chee... what are you asking?

Let me feel you.

And so on. Your words like *kithul* honey on fresh curd. You hope your desire will stick and lure her to you. After 2 weeks of banter all that sticks is your foreskin to your Y-fronts.

Yet the sensation is enthralling. She has carved a niche in your fantasies. She looks like the girl off the teledramas, or so you convince yourself. Now you can use words like *polla* and *chichchi* in your conversations without blushing. She purrs without shame. Knowing that you know she is faking.

And so, on it continues. She is the first thing you wake up to and last thing you fall asleep to. It's freaky because you've always hated the way phones invade your privacy and hijack your time. Your last 3 relationships broke down because you couldn't notch up the required telecom points. And now the cellular phone is the nucleus of your existence. You hang it next to your car CD player and poke in your hands-free set as you drive to work. You eat, sleep, and urinate with it.

And you listen. To her talk about her school sports meet. To how she hates her big sister. To how she loves Enrique.

You know it's pitiful, but the heaviness of her breathing and the image of her teledrama legs wrapped around your scrawny butt spurs you on. You ask her if she's keen to hook up. Finally, she says yes.

* * *

You call Ranil. He's who introduced you to Suba. He says he got it from a friend of his who was a DJ at Achcharu FM. You feel a pang of something and suppress it, aware that it could well be jealousy.

Bitches call those buggers all the time, he says. *Gata Badu*... Can't screw but can have some fun. Why can't screw, you inquire. These are small bitches. They can't get out of the house, all you can do is talk and jerk.

You are very pleased with yourself.

* * *

You agree to meet at the Dehiwela Zoo. It is close to her tuition class. She will have her father's mobile, and you can call her on that. You construct your picture as you drive. Short. Possibly plump. Big tits and milk coffee skin. Like that teledrama actress whose name you can't remember.

She will be carrying a yellow umbrella and you will be wearing a red t-shirt and a gold chain. She may bring a friend. Initially you are reluctant, but then you figure what the hell. If her friend is a babe, you can ignore Suba and do the swap.

Today you will chat and impress them with your wealth and your good looks. You'll take them for a ride in the boss's Benz and drive them to Wellawatte for an ice cream. Remember to pick a place where no one you know will be.

You will then start picking them up from school. They go to St. Paul's Milagiriya, which is walking distance from where you work. Once you have built up trust you can take one to a hotel. First a cheap one, and maybe later outstation. If, as your friend says, they won't let you screw, then no problem. There is plenty of stuff you can teach them. You can preserve their virginity but still turn them into nymphs.

You wait for three hours but no yellow umbrella appears. Young girls pass by the dozen, but none of them pay any attention to your red t-shirt. Except for one. She is tall and fair, with an underdeveloped body and malnourished breasts. Good, as they say, for a screw.

You follow her around the zoo. Probably, as usual, because you're bored. You pass the flamingos and move towards the big cats. You follow the meagre flesh of her butt as it sways in harmony to her footsteps. She is with a group of girls and an elderly lady, a grown-up.

You dial the number and an old man answers. Suba has given a traditional d-rope, a *lanuwa*. You call her home, but there is no answer. After one hour at the zoo, you grow weary. The place stinks and the animals look as shabby as the people staring at them. You make your way to the entrance and lick an ice cream, an oral cold shower. You finally get to Suba. She says her father picked her up from tuition and wouldn't let her use the phone. You fail to hide your bitterness. You mention that if you can't meet her, you might start looking for another girl. So leths just talk, she lisps. You make me horny, no, please don't go. Her moans no longer sound sexy to you. They sound like what they are. The whinings of an infant.

The fair girl walks to the entrance with her gang of four plus chaperone. You see goodbyes being exchanged and you hang up on Suba and get in your car. The girl is walking towards Karagampitiya. Alone. She stops at a bus stand. You stop ten metres before it. The bus she mounts is yellow and has Pitakotuwa written on its back. Following a bus doesn't require skill. It just requires infinite patience, which at that moment you have in abundance.

She gets down near a housing scheme. You park and follow her on foot. So, this is what it has come to. You, stalking a young girl. You tell yourself you are one sick *paraya* dog but continue following. She weaves down Anderson Road into the housing scheme.

You walk past her, pretending that you are also an occupant. You feel her eyes upon you as you pass. It makes you tingle. You linger at the end of the corridor and watch her enter flat number 19/7.

You scamper down to the mailbox at the front. Nineteen upon seven. The box is blue, and the paint is peeling. It is filled with leaflets for the upcoming elections. There is an overdue electricity bill for a Mr Naganathan. And a current phone bill. You enter the number into your mobile and are on your way.

***

Hello. Mr Naganathan, please. Right. I'm calling from the department of Census and Statistics. We're gathering information for the Municipal Elections. Are you the head of household? Right. And your occupation. I see. Do you own your own bakery? Very good. How many in your household? Your daughters' names and ages? How do you spell that? A-N-A-S-U. 20. Right and A-N-J-U is 13. Right. And your wife's name…

***

You work for the Sigiriya Hotel. Your time is spent in a sweaty Colombo office, working deals, drafting leaflets, and downloading porn. You work with three others. Ranil, Namini and Shereen.

Shereen is a lovely person but a repulsive lay. Namini's not bad, though a bit *goday*. Plus she talks too much. The whole of Colombo *and* Sigiriya would know if you tried anything with her.

You're sick of chatting with Suba. She babbles on about her exams and her sister and helps rekindle your aversion to the cellular phone. You've just discovered celebrity.com and it supplies you with enough jpegged snaps of Cameron Diaz, Salma Hayek and the chick from *Survivor* to get you through the day. You've also discovered a new face and a new number that you can use at your earliest convenience.

Then in the evening, Ranil comes to your cubicle. He spies a middle-aged woman striking a pose in a box on your monitor. Hey, isn't that Queen Elizabeth? You smell his BO. Fool, you say, her name's Helen Mirren and this is some b-grade flick she did in the 60s.

Enough jacking, he says. Come, let's put a booze. I'm going with my old advertising buddies. Why not, you think, and tag along.

The venue is the Jubilee Bar in Colpetty. The arrack is sold at cost. The place is just 3 fans, seventeen tables and one florescent bulb. A whale of a woman who everyone calls *Akka* serves drink and dishes out attitude.

You know there are rooms upstairs, says Ranil. That is how they make money. This is just a front.

You are drinking with three of Ranil's former work associates. They are so-called creative people who use that as an excuse to dress like beggars. You have met them before and don't particularly care for any of them.

Monro is a skinny young man who has prematurely grown middle-aged. Some of these women, not bad you know, he says, pouring a shot of gal. Me and Prasan went for a massage. Good scene, no machan? Can put a talk and get a screw.

You sip your gin and ponder. Ranil drinks stout and Monro, Prasan and the fat fellow drink gal. Both drinks you cannot stand. One tastes like liquid marmite and the other smells like urine mixed with paint thinner.

Shall we put a massage, machan? The question is directed at you. You've never done a whore in your life and don't intend on doing it with these pricks. I'm happy with my gin, you reply. Pious fucker, Ranil grins.

There haven't been too many women in your life. Just one that mattered and a few more that didn't. To you they are unattainable objects. They disarm you with their beauty and you see your imperfections mirrored in their lack of interest. And it consumes your every waking thought.

You change the subject. Tomorrow Poya, no? No more booze. The table erupts in groans. Outside it is raining and inside it is dry. Monro comes up with the challenge. Free booze for the person who goes to get it. You put down five hundred bucks and watch the fat bugger get to his feet. You can't remember his name but you're sure it starts with L.

Prasan, the baseball-capped-gangsta-wannabe, brings up an interesting point. How many bitches before you settle down? He asks. All of them, replies Ranil and you and Monro slap hands. You inwardly calculate your lifetime conquests and realize to your dismay that you've only just made double figures. You could probably stretch it to twenty if you exaggerate it to yourself. Still, that's a few short of all of them.

Never stop screwing, advises Monro. Even if you find the perfect girl, taste something different. You can't always eat the lunch packet you bring from home. Once in a while, a man needs a burger or a kottu. You know who said that, machan? Freud.

Tupac Shakur in the corner is the unlikely voice of morality. I aint down with that shit. In my book, you fuck sluts till you're 25, then you find a chick and you give her love. You give her different kinds of love and you'll never get sick. You know what I'm saying?

So machan, give her love. Monro's voice goes high. I'm not saying no. But also, machan share your love around a bit. Then your wife will also enjoy.

You join the discussion. Does your wife know you cheat? Monro is horrified. Are you mad? I'm not married machan, but I say a different cunt makes you appreciate what's at home. Then you can stay married for 50 years.

Ranil brings his opinion to the table. You can't chase after girls after marriage. That's pathetic bullshit. Be with your wife, but if some tart like Pamela Anderson, or...or...

Helen Mirren comes and opens her legs don't be a ponnaya. Do her and go home. If it comes your way, don't kick it away.

Prasan is not convinced. I hope I aint like you old fucks when I hit thirty. I can screw any bitch I want – but if I get Sara, man…I am gonna stay true.

The old fucks howl with delight and rip into the boy. Defiling his virginal Sara with lewd fantasies. One involving a *spit roast*, the other a *swordfight*. Prasan storms off in a sulk. The others giggle. He'll be back. You briefly talk about cricket and then Prasan returns, and the case is reopened. Statistics reveal that Sri Lankans consume more hard liquor and talk more about sex than any nationality in the uncivilized world. Unfortunately, neither of these activities translate into any real action. In that department, Sri Lankans trail somewhere around the bottom.

When the bottles run out at half past nine, Prasan is still unconvinced. But, for some reason that you can't quite fathom, you are.

***

You drop them off at Hotel Devaki. Ranil reimburses you your five hundred bucks. The fat bugger hasn't turned up and probably won't. They urge you to come in, but you have had enough of their company. You feign an excuse and put the car into gear.

Outside Hotel Devaki, two women patrol opposite sides of the road. You keep the car in first, step off the gas and let the clutch guide you at 15 kph. She's standing on the corner and wearing a blue sari. You slow right down hoping that she isn't a ghost.

'Sir. We can go to room for thousand five.'

Vana Mohini, Colombo's most famous apparition, carries a dead child and throws it at horny drivers like yourself. This woman smiles and you're glad to see she has a semi-full set of teeth. Betel and spousal abuse rob most whores of their pearls before the age of forty.

'Too much.'

'Give thousand.'

'Five hundred in the car.'

Apparitions don't bargain. You scrutinize what you're paying for. Body looks slim, but that could just be tightening of the sari. No pot belly and decent sized breasts. Face is pleasant, though a tad worn with wrinkles.

'Car can't.'

'Why?'

'Scared, *mahattaya*.'

'See ya.'

You have four options now that you have refused the most obvious one. Pornography or Karaoke lounge or Suba or Anasu Naganathan. Pornography is the staple diet of every Sri Lankan male. It is preferred to the prospect of an actual relationship. Video shops are stacked with copies of copies. Each passed from hand to hand with lines of static from too many hurried fast forwards and excited rewinds.

You playback the last few blue films you have committed to memory. *Anal Rampage* had brown vixens with big asses faking orgasms with blonde Scandinavians with big dicks. *Animal Action* had two overweight German girls raping an underfed pig. The pig had a circumcised cock, which struck you as kind of ironic. Neither movie did much for your libido.

You park outside the Princess Palace and dial Suba. Rain pelts your windscreen and bonnet. Her line is engaged. Then you dial Anasu. Her father answers.

'Who's this?'

'Mr Perera. I am Roshini's father. She is a classmate of Anasu.'

The lie comes easily, and you are proud of yourself.

'Hello.'

The voice is sweet. You can see her long ponytail dangling like a pendulum from buttock to buttock.

'Anasu. I've been in love with you for so long. I had to call you. But if you want me to stop calling just say.'

'Who is this?'

The sweetness fades and is replaced with a guttural accent.

'My name is Enrico. You don't know me. I'd like to talk to you and get to know you. I think you're sexy.'

Before long you are talking, and you realize it is a lot more stimulating to talk to a twenty-year-old with a brain than a fourteen-year-old without one. She is cautious at first, but you know this type of girl well. Probably kept under house arrest by overzealous parents. Probably never had a boyfriend. Probably has a picture of Ricky Martin on her wall.

If you tell her she is beautiful and display good manners, she will be yours. She tells you she is studying accounts and wants to go to New Zealand. She doesn't bitch about her family like Suba but tells you about the lodger they have who gives her the creeps. She says she thinks he is a terrorist, and you laugh at her and make it sound like you are laughing with her.

'Do you have internet? *Appa* doesn't like me on the phone too long.'

'Doesn't the internet block up your phone bill as well?'

She giggles.

'*Appa* doesn't know nothing.'

She gives you the name of a chat group: www.viharamahadevi.lk.

Her handle is suzie. Yours is to be cupid. You find yourself driving to a 24-hour cybercafé in Bamba and not worrying about the consequences.

You could blame it on alcohol, but you choose not to. You could blame it on ticking biology; on the fact that you are thirty and closer to death. Early in life, you asked yourself the same question that Prasan posed at Jubilee. How many women before you die or get married. After much deliberation you settled on one hundred, which is a compromise from 'all of them'.

Your car stereo doesn't work, so you have to put up with radio. The DJ has a makeshift Australian accent and a working ignorance of the English language. 'Here's good one, love your enemies, in case your friends turn out to be completely bastards. Achcharu FM. We play everything. This is Marc Anthony.'

The same station is playing in the cybercafé. The place is almost full. Mostly boys in their twenties playing Quake. A few foreigners punching emails and next to you a ten-year-old nonchalantly downloading hardcore porn. You are no prude by a long shot, but the sight of Anal Fisting Fuck Sluts and Trannies Raping Homos before the eyes of a baby manages to shock you. The owner walks to you to deliver a steaming tea.

He spies the boy and your uncomfortable expression. '*Chuti*. Get out! Go sleep! I'll tell your father!'

The boy receives a palm to the back of the head and exits from right of the server. You guess that this performance was more for your benefit than for the child's.

Getting online proves tiresome. The virtual highway is as congested as the actual one. It takes you fifteen minutes to get to viharamahadevi.lk.

Yo suzie. Enrico here… I mean cupid.
How are ya
bit tired… bit excited.
Why
Cos I'm talklinhg to you.

Same old routine. Different medium. The DJ keeps rotating crappy boy band songs which you've sometimes admitted to liking. You keep spinning shit.

So, I know u do I
Maybee.
I don't think so.
Do you want to meet?
I don't mind.
Don't mind only
No, I would anything
Yu would aanything?
Give anything to see u

The DJ suspecting no one is actually listening decides to read stuff from a magazine. A magazine with more pictures than words.

'They're calling this the vanity matrix. Aye, do you look good and know it? Bee, you believe you are beautiful even if you're not. Cee, are you one of those who aren't pretty and don't pretend to be? Or Dee, are you beautiful and don't know it?'

The station is changed at the request of the gameboys, but the monologue continues in your head. Everyone wants to be A. Most people are B and C. Who hope they are a D. You return your attention to the dialogue.

I love ur hair and the way u walk.
How do you look
I'm not bullshittting. But I have a good body and girls like my face.
How old
21
ooh baby. R u studying

no working with children
can't be earning
no no unicef they pay in dollars

    In your younger days, you'd like to think that you sowed your wild oats, but you didn't really. A girlfriend a year, some maybe longer. And then at 24, Fiona Mowlana.

If you had one night, one week, and a lifetime with anyone, who?
I don't know. You?
One night Madonna, One week my ex, Fiona, and lifetime, Meg Ryan.
Fiona who?
Mowlana
Fiona Mowlana is that model, no?
She's been in few commercials.
She pretty
I know

You visited the same church as Fiona. You went on dates, and you presumed this was leading to something. Every weekend she'd fuck some guy in Cascades and let you know about it. Every day you would tell yourself that she would get sick of these arseholes and come to you. Eventually, she got sick of you and went to them.

You sex her?
U use dirty words
What u think I don't know
I make love I make good love
How big is you
Find out

That means it small
How many you seen
Only my daddy's

You are erect and the keyboard is smoking. Anasu is proving to be a worthy investment. But then again, that's how Suba had appeared at the beginning. She has obviously had experience. Either that, or she is naturally perverted. Either way, it is good.

You've made love before?
Sort of
did you sex
I'm virgin. I want like my Appa.
Disgusting. Appa is big?
Huge. U?
very big….very hard

You renew for another half hour. Time has lost its meaning and your wallet can support the indulgence. The annoying DJ has been replaced by Bon Jovi singing 'Livin' on a Prayer'. You would have preferred the DJ. She takes a long time to reply, and you distract yourself with celebrity porn. Finally, she returns.

Who is that?
Anasu, I want you
Whio is this
Sorry. Suzee right?
No suzi here
what's your name babe
Jebe Naganathan
Huh…
You're the bugger who's calling my daughter

Who are u
I will find you and thrash you
fuck off.. arsehol…
I know your number. Get out or I will call police

You shut down and walk out, giggling to yourself, though mildly repulsed. Is your erection valid if it is caused by a middle-aged father of two? You hate fake arousal. Britney Spears' head dropped on some hustler slut's body fails to elicit any response from your loins. But one blurred tabloid snatch of Anna Kournikova on the beach and you require a tissue.

As long as the nudity is real, so is the fantasy. That's your logic. Because if that is how Jerri from *Survivor* looks naked, that is how she will look in your dreams when on some unspecified day in some unspecified future yours and her paths will cross, and you will seduce her. But the truth is that they're just pieces of paper, and the images, real or authentic, will always be impossible for you.

* * *

You drive back to Hotel Devaki, Ranil's car is no longer there. The Poya moon is in its heavens and your night is still not over. You drive along at 15 kph looking for the whore in a blue sari with a semi perfect set of teeth.

You find a dark woman in a mini skirt who stumbles from the gate and looks upon you as an acquaintance.

'So, you want for the night.'
'How much for the night?'
'Five thousand.'
'I will give thousand five for a room.'
'That means only half hour.'
'You're an expensive *veysee*.'
'Don't call me *veysee*, sir.'

'OK.'

The pimp at the desk calls her Sivali akka. You don't call her anything. She is fatter than the whore in the blue sari. In your thirty-two-year history of owning a penis, this is the first time you have paid to have it entertained. You are more than a tad unsure of yourself.

The flower-patterned curtain that adorns the doorway flutters as you enter. The room is dusty and smells of sweat and other bodily fluids. There is no furniture except for a bed and a full-length mirror. The bed is stripped bare to its coconut husk stuffing. There are dulled stains on the walls and on the sheets. Dark brown. Like old scabs.

You take off your shirt and let your feet dangle off the side of the bed. You look in the mirror and watch the sweat drip across your belly. Your hair sticks to your scalp. Your eyes are sunken, and your neck is hunched. She kneels behind you and massages your shoulders.

'First time Sir is coming?'

You watch her fake smile in the mirror and realize that you have no hope of blaming this escapade on alcohol.

'How do you know?'

She runs a finger across your nipple.

'These things I know.'

You are aroused. That you cannot dispute. Even though Sivali akka straddles the parameters of what you would consider acceptable in the sober light of day.

'Why do you do this?'

This is evidently a common question. She brushes your hair with her fingernails and grins with all her teeth. You notice how unusually shiny they are.

'You don't want fuck?'

'I want to make love. Show me your breasts.'

The light-blue jacket and the black bra are flung to the floor. They lie liberated near your feet. You are more interested in these cheap articles than in the melon-shaped tits that brush against your hair. Brown balloons half blown. A nipple catches your ear and sends blood to your crotch.

'Mahattaya. Shall we start. I have to be out at half past one.'

You turn around and pin her to the bedposts. She pulls the rolls of sari to her waist and pushes her panty to her toes. You kiss her neck and begin thrusting.

'What would you like me to do?'
'First take off trouser.'
'I want you to enjoy.'

She laughs and you are hurt by her disdain. You repeat yourself and she repeats her laughter.

'I will enjoy if you enjoy. But Sir. Enjoy quickly. Please.'

You want to ask her about her life. Whether she is married. How much she makes. What she makes it for. You want to turn her into another Suba. Another Anasu. You refuse to accept that this is pure commerce. But it is. She is providing a service and you are relieving an urge. An urge that has been building up in your loins for months. Months which threaten to turn into years.

Her warmth penetrates the condom. Your tongue aims for her lips, but she turns and offers her cheek. She moans and you know she is faking. Her moans grow frantic in an attempt to force a climax. You continue to soldier on. You close your eyes and imagine. Anasu, Suba, the female cast of Friends, the woman newsreader on ITN, Dame Judi, Salma Hayek. The final image you hold is that of Fiona Mowlana dirty dancing with you at Cascades. Your hips let out a few spasms and you hold the position. Back taut. Stomach clenched.

You attempt conversation as you put your clothes back on. But she no longer has any interest in you. You ask about her family, and she ignores you. You feel satiated but weak.

You sit on the bed and watch her smooth the creases of her sari. She looks at you and frowns.

'Didn't enjoy? I can give good suck. Five hundred rupees. Just for you.'

She removes her dentures to reveal a lubricated set of gums. You are out the door and in your car in seconds.

* * *

There is nothing for you to think about on your way home. You stop at a Kottu joint and wash down your shame with egg roti and lime juice. Everyone you know fucks whores. Everyone you know watches porn and talks to underage sluts. Everyone you know cheats on their wives. Except for you.

Until now.

You wife is waiting up for you, reading a book by a Sri Lankan author you have never heard of and will never read. You jump into the shower and mumble your way into the bed. She has swapped the novel for that pamphlet from the clinic that she keeps shoving in your face. She lets you plant your kiss on her cheek but does not return your hug.

'I thought you were giving up drinking? What's the point trying if you're not interested?'

'I just had a few beers baba.'

'And how many cigarettes? If you don't want to do this, tell me without lying.'

You attempt a cuddle and put on your sweetest voice.

'Baba tired men. Tonight, let's sleep. Tomorrow promise we'll do.'

'You said that yesterday.'

Your mobile rings. You switch it off, hit the lights and go to sleep.

The Eyes Have It

JR LET 1983 HAPPEN ON HIS WATCH. HE LET HIS CITIZENS burn because he didn't have the brain or the compassion to save them. But bugger donated his eyes to science. Oh yes.

The ex-president's cornea was split and given to a Japanese lady. I did the surgery right here in Nawala. She didn't stop babbling. 'Jaffna library. I told them not to. If you burn books, you will soon burn people.'

After the procedure, she had jowls under her eyes and complained of nightmares. 'Let the robber barons come. If I starve the Tamils out, the Sinhala people will be happy.' Depression followed. 'I've done nothing. Why do they hate me? Are these the side effects?'

The sutures festered. They blamed my surgery, though it wasn't my fault. The headaches made her scream. Said she dreamed of people shouting at her. 'We could've been a righteous society. But nothing I did was right. They call me terrible names. But never to my face.'

I removed the cornea. And all symptoms vanished. There's a theory that the back of the eye holds memories, emotions, and dreams. No science journal has proven that. Though, none have disproven it either. She left for Kyoto smiling, though she was still blind in one eye. It's better sometimes not to see too much.

The Capital of Djibouti

THE PROBLEM WITH BEING A WIDOWED HEAD OF STATE IN a third-world country is that you cannot openly date. She thinks this as her taxi passes the pubs in Camden, where she observes grotesquely attired teenagers holding hands and rubbing lips. She is still not 50, but she is in her second term as Madam President. Although she is not an ugly woman, the beauty that won her a wealthy husband appears to have flung itself onto his funeral pyre.

She never wore this many saris, had this much paunch, or had those overripe banana splotches on her skin. It is true that a woman politician has to be tougher than a male one, she thinks, not for the first time. It is true you must suppress all that is feminine and still boss them like a mother. It is also exhausting.

That is why she sits in a taxi trawling through north London, wearing a winter coat, tinted glasses, more make-up than usual, and the key accessory – a wig of curls. After her husband's assassination, after her in-laws pushed her towards the podium, after they began clamouring to whisper in her ear, she stopped styling her hair or wearing trinkets.

They elected her on a wave of sympathy, by a majority jaded by violence and lame ducks. She banished the sycophants and pumped up her rhetoric. The little lady wasn't going to play and would be no one's mouthpiece. She had rumours spread that the author of her husband's quotable speeches was her, and then she exiled both rumour-spreader and speechwriter to embassies in the Balkans.

And though the severity of her budgets permitted her from looking like she frequented salons, she did miss the frolic of her youth, the abandon she once had. The taxi ploughs through Holloway, where she once went to boarding school, long before she met Ranjan, where she once kissed a boy, Viharamahadevi Park-style, under an umbrella in the rain. How silly she thought, and how very impossible today. If she were seen with a man under a brolly, the Colombo Stock Exchange would crash.

She remembers the film about Queen Elizabeth (no, not Diana's mother-in-law, the other one) and wonders if she could entertain poets at Temple Trees in Colombo, if she could sit at a bar in the Maldives and share wine with a stranger, if she could walk in a park without brutes with pistols following her.

If Ranjan's death had isolated her, becoming President had put her in chains. She loved the world as she once loved men and wine and poetry and now, she was kept from it all. This was true for most places her expense accounts took her, except, that is, for western Europe.

The summit in London on trade agreements between South Asia and East Africa had been tedious. Half the diplomats spent the symposium shopping for suits and ordering massages. She was sat next to the prime minister of Djibouti, who asked if she knew where he could pick up a cheap mink stole.

Woodberry Down passes by in the rain as the cab fare creeps past 30 quid. She doesn't think of taxpayers footing her bills, instead she thinks of all the sacrifices she's made that no salary could possibly compensate. That country stole my husband, my time, my privacy and my children's childhoods, she thinks. Surely, I could help myself to a taxi ride? I must propose a bill instructing all Colombo tuk-tuks to carry metres. Maybe Dr Lalith could source the tuk-tuk metres from East African factories.

Foreign Minister Dr Lalith Dissanayaka handled most of her deals, but not all. He was opposed to her annual European sojourn but kept his counsel for fear of being sent on a permanent one himself.

'Is this the best way to Epping?' she asks the driver. He is dark and bearded and he answers slowly.

'Best way is taking the train,' he smiles. 'It's faster. Less cost. But not as comfy, ah.'

'Isn't it faster through Walthamstow?'

'That way more traffic. Don't worry madam. This may not be a black cab, but I know London. I have the knowledge.'

'So do I,' she smiles, as she does when she denies someone a favour. 'And that motorway route is longer.'

'You want me to U-turn?'

'No, that's fine.'

When she met Ranjan, they were students at LSE. His father owned a tea factory in Haputale; hers was physician to the governor-general. He was popular among the Ceylonese in London, she avoided them and their trails of gossip. Their paths didn't cross until the final year, when they shared champagne at a dinner party for future bankers and ended up sharing a farmhouse in Epping and spending a few summers tramping across Europe.

Only her personal secretary knew where she was, and Fernando always covered up her post-tour tours, as he called them, and kept an eye on the children at home. Her eldest was applying for university, her youngest was failing maths and her middle one was becoming his father. They had been toddlers when the suicide-bomber girl hugged

Ranjan. Which wasn't the first time another woman had hugged him, she thinks, but let us not go there.

It had been another year of disasters. The war spreading to Kilinochchi, the power cuts extending to five hours, the bombs crippling Colombo, one almost maiming her sister, and the double-digit death count each day, for which she was supposed to take blame. Then there were calls for her to declare her assets and produce her university degree. Let us not go there either.

This weekend is about lunch in Epping Forest, a pint in the East End, a show in the West End, a gallery south of the river and a concert up north. She would relive her Sundays with Ranjan, she would do it without him and she would do it in a curly wig. She pulls out the red nail polish bought in Paris years before and never opened. It is a long way to Epping, and she isn't going to spend it thinking about Ranjan or the mess back home.

'Madam, you from where?' asks the driver as they turn onto the A110. His voice sounds gruff, and his accent sounds manufactured. She squints at his nametag on the dashboard, but without her glasses all she sees is a smudge that extends the length of the photograph.

In Sri Lanka, every stranger has an opinion on her. She sees it beneath each unctuous smile and behind each earnest nod. In Europe, no one knows nor cares, so she gets to be from wherever she chooses, which can be fun. For the past weeks she has had to brag about her country to distracted strangers. She had to feign interest in their lands and try to broker deals. For each trip, Fernando gave her colour-coded dossiers with large print.

'You from India?' asks the driver, eyeing her in the rear-view mirror. She puts on her glasses but still can't read. He looks Bengali or Keralan. This is important to gauge correctly. She once told a gentleman, who she thought was Arab, that she was from Honduras, only to endure an anthology of anecdotes from his native town Tegucigalpa. She believes it is too much smiling that has killed her cheekbones.

'I'm from Djibouti,' she says. 'But I live in London for 20 years.' She adopts the hard consonants and misshapen vowels of the African delegation with whom she shared a week and a conference room. 'You?'

'I'm from Sri Lanka,' says the driver. 'You know where that is?'

She looks at the grey day outside and the cars whizzing by at dangerous speeds, at the green sign overhead, saying Epping followed by a bent arrow in white.

'Of course,' she thinks of her sister who told her to join the theatre and not to marry the tea magnate's son. 'Used to be called Ceylon, yes?

'Yes. Yes. I've been in London seven years.'

She wipes her glasses and leans forward. Dhuruvasangary Joseph Soundararajan followed by a mix of numbers and capital letters.

'You live out east right? I've seen you before.'

The accent is more Whitechapel than Trincomalee.

'No, I live here in Epping,' she says, replacing her glasses with shades, turning towards the wasteland of chimneys in the distance. She uncaps her nail polish and adopts her meeting-is-adjourned posture.

'Djibouti is near Dubai?'

He wears tinted glasses, and his face is gaunt. He looks like a thousand other Tamil boys. Chuck a stone in Jaffna and you'll hit a hundred of them. She knew, she had.

'East Africa. Small country. Nice lakes, very peaceful.' She regrets having started on her nails. There is a phone she never uses that Fernando put in her handbag. She wonders if she should pretend to receive a call.

'No war there?'

'All our neighbours have war. Ethiopia, Eritrea, Somalia, Yemen. All are fighting. We had a war but all over now. Now Djibouti is peaceful.'

'You very lucky. My country has horrible war.'

'All wars are horrible.'

'Are you married?'

'Yes. After motorway, turn left please.'

'You have children?'

'No. I'm a bit late, can you speed up please?'

'I have a son.'

'I need to meet my husband in Epping now.'

She stops with the nails and attempts to open her bag with one hand.

'What was your war over?'

'It was between the Issas and the Afars,' she says, recalling page 3 of the dossier. 'Turn at the next exit please.'

'Issas. Afars. Like that other place, no? With the Hutus and Tutsis. Who was killing who?'

'In a war, everyone kills everyone.'

She opens her bag and realizes the phone she never uses is on her bedside tray at the Ritz. He has taken off his glasses. There is shading around his eyes and a scar on his nose.

'Is that why you left? Someone want to kill you?'

'Of course not. Djibouti is peaceful now.'

'Sri Lanka is not.'

'I heard Sri Lanka is beautiful.'

'It is not.'

'I see,' she says, picking at her nails again. She makes a point not to glance back at the mirror. Eye contact could be seen as provocation. Or worse, encouragement.

'We have war. They burned my home, killed my cousin. My younger brother fights, but I have family. I have to care for my mother.'

'They say Sri Lanka is getting better.'

'Who says?'

'Time magazine.'

'When they elected a woman, we thought there would be change. But things are worse now.'

She touches her wig to make sure it is in place and thinks of King Gajabahu, who used to disguise himself as a civilian and roam the populace listening to problems and taking notes. Walpola, professor of humanities and education minister in her first cabinet, wished to revise the way history was taught in schools. 'Madam, it is just a tedious harangue of kings and tanks and stupas and invasions. We glorify Sinhalese warmongers, airbrush noble Tamil rulers and forget everything pre-Vijaya.'

The clergy and the Sinhala nationalists opposed the proposal and after a while she did as well. After her first year, all the technocrats in her cabinet were replaced by those she owed favours to.

'All leaders same. Once they get power, they become pigs. Sorry for my language.'

She looks into the rear view to see if he is needling her, but he looks ahead with a fixed smile. On the radio, the DJ goes from posh accent to street, doing impressions of celebrities she has not heard of. She asks him to turn the radio up and he switches it off. He looks back at her in the mirror and considers his words.

'It's the leaders who mess up countries. Even here.'

'Your brother fights for whom?' she asks, knowing the answer.

'He fight for our people. You have Tamil people in Djibouti?'

She is certain this titbit of information was not on Walpola's dossier. She recalls a few facts that are.

'We are mainly Somali, Issa and Afar. There are some Arabs, Europeans, not many Tamils.'

'All Muslim?'

'Most. A few Christians.'

'Does your police harm Christians?'

'Not really.'

'In my country, they murder children for being Tamil.'

According to the bedtime story version of Ceylon history, King Gajabahu, on his eavesdropping mission, once heard a mother crying for her son, a royal soldier, taken prisoner of war by the Chola king in India. Moved, our King raised an army of giants, invaded the Chola kingdom, freed the POWs Rambo-style, and brought back 12,000 Tamil prisoners. If the Ceylon textbook version of history is to be believed, Gajabahu is either a hero who listened to his people, or the planter of seeds that spawned jungles of hate.

If I eavesdrop on my citizens, I'd be accused of spying, she thinks. Not that that ever stopped her. Telecom was deregulated on her watch and the mobile phone boom had given her ears in 33.4 per cent of voter-registered homes. If I held 12,000 POWs, the World Bank would cancel my credit and the UN would stop my post-tour tours.

'So your brother still fights?'

'They call him a terrorist. When a government sits by while animals destroy homes and burn people, who are the terrorists? Did the Djibouti government let its people kill each other?'

'I understand what you are saying,' she says with a diplomacy that she rarely takes on holiday. 'But governments can't take sides. They can't be responsible for what each and every citizen does.'

'That is their job.'

'Only in the communist countries.' She overdoes her accent, and realizes she is mimicking the Liberian defence secretary who had invited her to his balcony in Brussels the previous week.

'My country is called democratic socialist republic,' says the driver. 'But our so-called Madam President can't even spell those words. She has a fake degree from LSE. She slept her way to the top. Got into politics on the sympathy vote.'

'Is this the way to Epping Forest?' she asks, leaning forward and fingering the heel of her shoe.

'I'm taking you through another route. I have to show you something.'

'Men also sleep their way to the top. But no one notices.'

She had scolded the Liberian in filth. As if she would go to anyone's balcony under the gaze of snoopers and snipers. If she wanted to fraternize with war criminals, she had plenty back home to flirt with.

'Not like this bloody woman.'

She looks in the mirror. This time he glances at her and raises an eyebrow. It is unclear if he is apologizing for his language or emphasizing it.

'Don't say bloody woman. It shows bad upbringing.'

He pauses while negotiating a roundabout, as if any direction could take him where he needs to go. He opts for the narrow lane towards the woods.

'My cousin was beaten to death when I was eight. That is my upbringing.'

'I would prefer if we stayed on the main road.' She keeps her voice steady.

'No, this is shorter way. Trust me, I know Essex roads. This is not Djibouti.'

She imagines the papers tomorrow and the I-told-you-so-look on the faces of Fernando, Walpola, Dr Lalith and the Ghanaian who offered her a lift this morning. She thinks of her eldest son being pushed onto a podium.

'I'm sorry. I'm very late now. My husband is…'

'Just five minutes madam,' he snaps. 'I would like you to see this.' He tries to soften the snap with a giggle, which has the opposite effect.

She closes the cap of the polish and drops it in her lap. She blows on her nails and looks directly into the rear view. There is a long silence. He looks up and sees her staring. He catches himself.

'I'm sorry. I get upset with my country. With what it has done to us. I have seen you somewhere. You go to East End market?'

She watches as houses and shops disappear from view. She tells herself she can talk her way out of anything, the only real skill Ranjan taught her.

'Yes. Yes. I sometimes come east to buy vegetables.'

'That's where I have seen you.'

'In Djibouti, we trust in our government. Even when things go wrong. They are not perfect. But they know more than you and me.'

'If you're Tamil, Sri Lankan government don't care,' says the driver, pausing at a traffic light. 'They steal from us and make money. Our Madam President is in Brussels with arms dealers buying weapons to shoot my people.'

Ranjan had told her to always wear heels if she knew she'd be alone with men. And he had shown her how to use them. Back when he did martial arts training. Back when he pretended he wasn't fooling around with secretaries.

There is a memorial a few miles from Epping Forest done by the East London Tamil Association. It gets funding from the Epping Town Council and from Raviraj Balasingham, a Tamil businessman living in Manhattan. It is a tree trunk with a thousand photographs nailed to its bark.

He slows down and she looks at the faces. All white and black and laminated, eyes staring at camera, no smile. Young men with moustaches, young women with pottus, then the old people, then the children.

'That is my cousin.'

She has cried enough for the father of her own children, and she has cried for the children of other fathers. She has cried at the waste of it all and at the helplessness and pointlessness she feels most of the time when not on holiday. She has seen dossiers and dossiers of faces like these and has no more tears to shed.

As he drives past it at snail's pace, she realizes she has worn tennis shoes for her walk through the woods, a butter knife to a gunfight. He does three rounds before stopping the car by a photograph of a young boy in a tiger uniform holding a kalashnikov.

'That was my cousin. He was much better than me. Than anyone. You would've liked him. Everybody would've liked him. It's just a waste. It's just a waste.'

'I'm so sorry. I really am.'

He sighs and smiles.

'I'm sorry madam. I just wanted to show you, since we were close by. I like people to see his face. I hope your Djibouti never sees another war.'

He takes 10 pounds off the fare, and she does not object, even though it is not her money she is spending. She feels like being generous, but she does not know how much to give. He makes no eye contact when he drives off.

Her companion is waiting at the edge of the forest. He is dressed in an Armani suit and looks relieved to see her. She is only forty-five minutes late.

'I booked *Les Mis* and the Tate is half price today. Bad news is they're no longer serving the roast.'

He takes her hand but stops short of an embrace.

'You alright? How was the drive?'

She looks at the red on her fingernails, looks at his dark skin and asks him the question that's been bugging her all day. He laughs.

'The capital of Djibouti is Djibouti. Surely you knew that.'

The secret to being a happy leader, she thinks, is to accept that you will not remember everything. The secret to being a happy person, she thinks, is to know that someday everything will be forgotten.

She lets go of his hand. She shakes her head from side to side, like so many of her countrymen do. It is difficult to know if she is saying no or yes.

Black Jack

DESPITE HIS NAME, SOODU SAMPATH NEVER PLAYED THE cards. He only made pots of money from them. His casino had roulette tables, croupiers, slot machines and call girls, and when they found him slain at his desk, the gamblers placed bets on who did it. There were plenty of horses in that race.

The crime scene narrowed things down – somewhat. Japanese whisky was delivered to his office at 3 a.m., seal unbroken, as both bodyguards testify. Three glasses on the table, though only one with traces of cyanide.

Minister's son, the infamous hothead, dropped in to discuss investments at 4 a.m. Business partner, the notorious thug, came in for a meeting at 5 a.m. Brazilian call girl, Soodu's mistress, entered the room at 6 a.m. and screamed at the corpse. Nothing else on the desk except the glasses and a piece of paper with a scribbled number. Detectives were uncertain if the motive was blackmail, extortion or revenge.

The answer is all of the above. The brat, the thug, and the tart were guilty of many things, but not of Soodu's murder. The man himself put a capsule in his drink, thinking it would cure his limp prick. It was given to him by me, wrapped in a paper with that useless ayurvedic physician's number. I should've listened to my late mother and never married a casino man.

Assassin's Paradise

Preface to the First Edition

The book you are holding is, at the time of writing, banned in Sri Lanka. Along with the *Satanic Verses* by Salman Rushdie, *The Anarchist Cookbook* by William Powell and *Mango Friends* by T.B. Ilangaratne. The first because everyone else says it should be, the second because even the author thinks it ought to be, and the third because, well, politics.

Assassin's Paradise: Ceylon's Unsolved Political Killings is my third book and my second collaboration with Dr Anton Bultjens. It is a book that I could not have imagined without his extensive fieldwork. His team at Peradeniya conducted eyewitness interviews, while my team at Jaffna collated police reports. If nothing else, it proves that North and South can collaborate without violence.

I first worked with Dr Bultjens on my second book, *The Bureaucracy of Terror: Death Squads and Mercenaries in Sri Lanka's Free Market*. We interviewed dozens of contract killers, assassins, interrogators and army deserters, most of whom were willing to unburden themselves provided their names were withheld. The government censors rejected the initial manuscript, and Dr Bultjens and I were summoned to the Marakkada Police Station for questioning that lasted several days. The book was banned long before it hit the printers, though it was fortunate enough to find an audience in Eastern Europe and South America, and was longlisted for the Asian Reuters Award.

My first book, *Riot Police: The Role of the State in Communal Riots 1958-1983*, languished on the shelves for a good ten months before the UNP government found it offensive. That book contained many rare photographs from the riots of 1958, 1971, 1977 and of course, 1983. I wonder if the censors had even read the text. They would have found the book to be a balanced view and, like this one, to be motivated by patriotism, compassion and pacifism.

Criticizing your country is not an act of treason. It is an act of love.

But as academics who publish non-fiction often say, 'if it isn't being talked about, then let it be banned'. No one in Sri Lanka has read my years of scholarship or looks likely to ever do so. But they know my name, and that, like most things, is both a blessing and curse.

So why write *Assassin's Paradise*? Knowing in all likelihood that ordinary Sri Lankans, those affected by the rule of the armed thug, state-sponsored and otherwise, will never get to read about the appalling crimes committed a short walk from where they work, play and love. Dr Anton Bultjens and I have asked ourselves this many times over the past year.

Writing as a 50-year-old in 1989, I can say, without hyperbole, that Sri Lanka has entered its darkest hour. We are prolific in our slaughter and consistent in our indifference to it. To say that the conflict is between races is to see but a fraction of the problem. Sri Lanka's violence is multi-limbed and multi-lingual. Look no further than the assassinations analysed in this book.

These cases are many and varied. Suicide bombings, sniper attacks, drive-by murders, abduction, torture, even poisonings. Father Harold Bastian was hacked to death for speaking out on human rights issues, accusing both sides of carelessness and callousness. Amithalingham and Yogeswaran were shot at a meeting they called to make peace with the Tigers, and school principal Anandaraja was gunned for organizing a cricket match between Tamil students and Sinhala soldiers.

What they all have in common is that they are unsolved, though there is no shortage of suspects. Indeed, some cases suffer from an abundance of likely perpetrators. But no one has paid for these crimes, except those who have done so with their lives.

We began with the wave of murders in 1983 of moderate Tamil parliamentarians from assorted parties like TULF, EPRLF and PLOTE. Men like Dharmalingham, Ramachandran and Muttiah, to name but a very few. These are widely blamed on the LTTE, who did not like people other than them speaking for the Tamils. The LTTE blamed the government, even though victims like Pulendran, Gopalpillai and Master came from the ruling UNP party.

The killings of film star politician Vijaya Kumaratunga and media personalities Premakeerthi de Alwis and Sagarika Gomes were placed at the feet of the JVP Marxists during their reign of terror, not so long ago. And the killings of clergyman like Jeyarajasingham and Fernando point fingers at the armed forces and an impotent government.

What prompted Anton and I to publish were two recent killings, close to us both. My dear colleague in Jaffna, Dr Rajani Thiranagama and my friend of many years, dramatist and activist, Richard de Zoysa. In present day Sri Lanka, life has cheapened, and silence has deepened. Rajani and Richard were not venal politicians or ruthless revolutionaries. They were 'one of us'. Middle class Sri Lanka is no longer safe.

Both Rajani and Richard rallied against civilians being used as cannon fodder by government forces and armed terror groups. They mourned each village massacre, each suicide bombing, each government shelling. We share their disgust. If you are Sri Lankan, these are your brothers and these are your sisters, and you have failed them all.

We considered publishing anonymously. But no secret remains so in Sri Lanka, and we could not afford for an innocent to mistakenly pay for our 'crime', as has happened too often in our untidy past. We already know of collusions between our government and the enemy – taxpayers are arming the LTTE to chase out the Indians whom we cordially invited ourselves. Brother will kill brother, and sister will maim sister before we are done with this madness.

If anything, we hide behind our scientific rigour and academic integrity. We present the evidence as cogently and objectively as we are able. In various cases, the evidence may point to certain parties. We are not law enforcement officers or prosecutors. When it comes to pointing fingers, we are equal opportunity offenders. We follow the evidence, not the agenda. That is our best defence.

We write not for any party, but for the Sri Lankan citizen. The silent majority dragged into a war dreamed up by the myopic. As I write, there are 50,000 Indian troops stationed up north, while out east the Tigers slaughter villagers, and down south the government abducts suspected JVP Marxists and 'disappears' them. Before 1975, we had three assassinations in this fair isle. Since then, we have had 97.

Ninety-seven cases and no one arrested. Does this showcase government incompetence or complicity? Dr Anton Bultjens and I can only hope that in the midst of this lunacy, the stalwarts from the legal profession, currently warming seats in parliament, will bring back the rule of law. Perhaps in five years, this book will be available all over Sri Lanka. Though that is about as likely as apartheid falling or the Iron Curtain tearing.

More likely it appears, that Lanka's assassins, be they Sinhala or Tamil, Marxist or capitalist, are merely getting warmed up. And therefore, so must we, the civil and the peaceful of Sri Lanka. We must not be anonymous any longer. Instead, let us be brave.

Prof. Ranee Sridharan
Dept of Sociology
Jaffna University
1989

Foreword to the Revised Edition

I write today from some safety, but this was not always the case. For many years my phone was tapped, my children followed from school, strangers parked outside my home. This climate was foreseen by Prof. Ranee Sridharan in a book that has proved grimly prophetic.

The fact that *Assassin's Paradise* is available in Sri Lanka is cause for rejoicing. It wasn't the only prediction of Dr Ranee's preface, which has come to pass. She unwittingly foretold the fall of communism and apartheid, though whether it was sincerity or that famous Sridharan sarcasm is a point of debate. She did predict that assassinations would escalate. '…Lanka's assassins… are merely getting warmed up.' Regrettably, she was not mistaken on this.

Since the publication of *Assassin's Paradise*, just two months after Prof. Ranee's tragic murder, there have been 73 assassinations of high to low level public figures across Sri Lanka. Two heads of state have been taken out by suicide bombs. The UNP government's most formidable statesmen were neutralized in the span of three years. Cabinet Ministers Wijeratne, Athulathmudali and Dissanayake joined President Premadasa on the scrapyard of politics and the graveyard of leaders. Each cut down by person or persons unknown. Since then, the assassin's bullet has continued to hit Tamil moderates, Sinhala hardliners, and those with keys to kingdoms.

To read Prof. Ranee's preface, after so many years, is difficult. If only she were the last activist to be murdered on these bloody shores. Right after she was executed on Galle Road, in the presence of her daughter Samantha, I went into exile. I was offered a post at Humboldt University in Berlin, where I had a ringside seat to more of history's failed experiments. And there I could grieve for Prof. Ranee and for my failed country.

I returned in '94, when a new government of new faces promised inquiries into past crimes. I watched as lawyers obfuscated, until those accused in trials disappeared into peaceful obscurity. I watched the new government lie with thugs and thieves and employ those they should have been jailing.

Writing this at the turn of the millennium, I am aware that the days are not as dark as a decade ago. But neither does the killing look likely to abate. The intellectual climate in Sri Lanka has grown docile. Old school Marxists have died off, their credibility tainted by their actions and their bedfellows; their thunder stolen by a new generation of thugs who thought they were Che Guevara. The pacifist Woodstock generation, that spawned myself and Prof. Ranee, has grown old and weary. Some have paid with their lives while others have abandoned their quests.

The Tamil separatists are themselves divided, and in this arena, debates are won with bullets. Sinhalese moderates champion minority representation, while Sinhala hardliners bray about international conspiracies to rob their fractured kingdom. We are a nation of short memories and easy amnesia. Allies become enemies, nemeses become friends. In this climate, it is difficult to know who kills who. Do you shoot your enemy or your brother?

This expanded edition is for those who believe in Sri Lanka's future. And who pray for its present. It is more than a catalogue of unpunished crimes. It is a call for an end to silence. It is about unravelling who did what to whom. It is about making sure it never happens again.

I have added chapters that give an overview of the bloodbath that was the early 90s and the fallout from the third Eelam war. I have not rewritten any of the original text, even though it contains ideals I no longer believe in and causes that are no longer true.

This book is about the Sri Lankan tragedy, but it may still seek a happy ending. It is what happens when good people procrastinate. For Sri Lankans braver than me, who have stayed behind and stayed the course, whatever you do, for the sake of Ranee and Rajani and Richard and Neelan and me, please do not do nothing.

Prof. Anton Bultjens
Dept of South Asian Studies
University of South Dakota
1999

PROLOGUE TO THE THIRD EDITION

Assassins' Paradise: Ceylon's Unpunished Political Killings 1948-2005 is a masterwork of rhetoric and linguistic flair. The work of Sridharan and Bultjens was banned by the UNP government of the 90s and the PA government of the last decade. It also claimed to be without agenda, though that was clearly one of the many inaccuracies and half-truths contained within its pages.

The previous two editions were financed by France's Action Contre Le Faim, Norway's Policy Alternatives Centre and the US Fund for Peace. They sponsored Sridharan's research and Bultjen's fieldwork. And as those with a passing acquaintance of politics know, those who pay the piper will make him sing.

That is not to say that the work is without merit. It does an astounding job of cataloguing the ruthlessness of the LTTE in eliminating Tamil moderates and rival separatists, the bloodlust of the JVP as they slaughtered civilians, and the clinical barbarism of previous regimes in quelling both.

There are however many historical inaccuracies, especially with Bultjen's analysis of the wave of assassinations of the 1990s. Erudite historians employed by the ministry have obtained new evidence since the turn of the millennium, and have corrected mistakes in the text. Cases implicating the LTTE have been solved and archived. The text has been updated to include the latest atrocities caused by Tiger savagery.

We do not blame Sridharan and Bultjens for being misled by their sponsors. We have no quarrel with their academic credentials or moral integrity. But as these pages show, many have been conned into committing treason and tricked into murder.

This government believes in the freedom of speech and information. We are proud to be the first administration to allow *Assassins' Paradise* to be sold and discussed in our motherland. We will continue to uphold freedom in Sri Lanka as long as it does not compromise our war on terror.

While previous regimes have appeased and mollycoddled terrorists, the current leadership is on the brink of a historic victory, and nothing will keep us from our goal. There is a time for men of words and a time for men of action. This is the time for the latter.

Let us finally speak of the tusker in the room. Dr Anton Bultjens, found guilty of spreading pro-LTTE propaganda, has made unproven libellous allegations of human rights abuses by government forces. He is currently serving a five-year sentence, along with many other enemies of peace and friends of our enemy. For this the government has been criticized by those who know little of what they speak.

If we are to achieve peace, we must be united. We believe in freedom of information provided it is the right information; and in freedom of speech, provided it is not speech designed to divide and demoralize peace.

Today we publish Bultjens' words, even as we condemn his actions. When this war is won, we will need men like him to rebuild the new Sri Lanka. We trust he will repent, so that we may pardon him. Glory to Mother Lanka. May the triple gem bless us all.

        Bandula R. Somawardena, BA (Oxon) MA (Harvard)
                            Ministry of Publications
Government of the Democratic Socialist Republic
                                      of Sri Lanka
                                             2009

Introduction to the Restored Edition Audio Version.

Female Voice: Amma was scared of the dark. She slept with the lights on and hated going to the cinema. It was the only thing she was afraid of. So she stayed up nights with the lights on and read.

Male Voice: Once a month, my father would think the house was bugged. Which meant he'd come into my room and open all my drawers and break all my toys.

FV/MV: We've both had our homes broken.

We've both grown up with war, bombs, curfews, death threats, house arrests and nuisance calls.

We both had to flee the country we were born to.

And we both watched, as it destroyed our parents.

FV: In Melbourne, my sister and I changed our surname and pretended we didn't speak Tamil. We didn't want to be known as Ranee's children. My father stopped being an activist, stopped his academic work. He left us a year before Amma was killed. Then he came back. He stopped trying to be a husband and became a father.

MV: Our family moved from Berlin to South Dakota, from Beijing to Islamabad, and finally back to the country that spurned us. My father wasn't as famous as Samantha's mum. But he was angrier. We had to live with that anger when he came back from work. War has many victims, least of all the children of those who care.

FV/MV: For many years, none of us took an interest in Sri Lanka, in politics, or our parents' work.

The cowards who killed Samantha's mum were slaughtered along with thousands of innocents, right after the release of the government version of *Assassin's Paradise*.

Kamal's father was released after serving two-years for anti-democratic activities. He read the government's version and went into depression.

He just wouldn't get out of bed. The doctors said he had suffered a few minor strokes before the big one. And no one noticed. (Voice breaks)

FV: You could say a lot has happened between this edition and the first. Wars have been won and lost. Dictators have risen and fallen and risen again. The country has gone bankrupt and been sold to the lowest bidders. The people have spoken and then been silenced. I'm not sure we've learned much from it. But at least we're not shooting each other.

MV: My father lives in a wheelchair in Malabe and no longer speaks. He watches cricket on TV all day and luckily there's plenty of that. I played him the audiobook. It's hard to know what registers, but I can read his twitches and frowns. He looked pleased.

FV/MV: For the first time in our lives, Sri Lanka is safer than Europe and America. It's some sort of progress at least. Not much, but not nothing.

Samantha Sridharan and Kamal Bultjens
Port City, Colombo
2027

Title: Assassins' Paradise
Year: 1989
Serial: GH747892

All that remains of this title, written by two Sri Lankan sociologists of the late twentieth century, are its many introductions. The rest of the work was digitally erased, as were many texts, in the great purge of 2036.

Precious little evidence remains of the 30-year war and those who lived through it have contradictory memories. The thirty-year war has been shrouded in myth and folklore and it is hard to separate fantasy from fact. Many secrets have been buried and too many false legends have been unearthed.

Paradise has now been paved and most of Sri Lanka's libraries have burned or gathered moss. Whatever digital debris that survives, remains inconclusive. And unanswered questions abound. Was the war without purpose, was the dictatorship essential, and did the events of 2036 make all these machinations irrelevant?

This title will be shelved under fiction, until its claims can be corroborated by at least three or more sources.

Frances Peripanayagam
Executive Archivist
Ministry of History
Ceylon Islands
2049

Love Pentangle

AMALINI, AGED 22, STARTS SLEEPING WITH A MARRIED man named Bevaan.
Bevaan realizes he loves his wife Chandi, the day after Chandi leaves him for, among other crimes, bedding 22-year-olds.

Chandi has a crush on her boss Damith, who knows she is on the rebound, but still agrees to sleep with her.
Damith is obsessed with his gym instructor Erika, who after many bad relationships,
realizes the only one who gets her, is her best friend since school: Amalini.

Bevaan pleads with Chandi to take him back. Says he finds Amalini annoying.
Chandi brags to Damith that her ex is stalking her.
Damith tells Erika that Amalini is repulsive, according to Bevaan.
Erika serves this to Amalini with extra green chilli.

Amalini dumps Bevaan and stops talking to Erika.
Shooting the messenger, etc.

Heartbroken Erika lets Damith have her, which pisses off Chandi
who goes back to Bevaan.

Damith and Erika, and Chandi and Bevaan
end up at the same restaurant at different tables.
Both celebrating their couplings with expensive food on tiny plates.
Both dates are spent holding hands and glancing at phones.

Amalini puts on her most understated earrings and goes out looking for love.
And all she finds
for the next five years,
ten months,
and fifteen days
are pentangles.

No. One. Cares.

0348

Ranjana Wilatgamuwa posts a photo album featuring a younger him with an older her. Caption reads: *The dream that died. Ranjana Wilatgamuwa 1967-2014.*

Hey hey, U ok? comments **Tia Kumari**. Her profile is three girls posing at a nightclub called Amuseum. She's in the middle with bleached hair.

Ranjana adds 8 photos. His younger self at Kitulgala resthouse dated Jan 1988. Wearing a mullet and a leather jacket unsuited to sunshine. She wears a cap and an embarrassed smile.

Quite the pretty boy. Ade ela! Keep it up! comments **Martin Pinto**. MP's profile pic contains the Sri Lankan flag.

Ranjana tags **Fatima Yousuf** in 6 of the 8 pictures. *Goodbye Bunchy* he comments on one featuring a waterfall. *I will leave you alone now. Tonight I will kiss the sky.*

0357

Ranjana I am calling you now please pick up comments **Manique P**. Her profile reveals her to be the spouse of

Martin Pinto, a fan of Snoopy the cartoon dog, and residing in Melbourne.

Ranja, your Akki's worried comments **Saluka Ratnasena**, who lists *Sex and the City* as her favourite TV show and Fake Talk as her pet peeve.

Nine other comments follow which range from *Ranja chill man* from **JithTheGiant** to *U'll miss Lanka whacking the cup you foool* from **Ayman Ariyanayagam** to *Let Jesus into you and you will never stray* from **Disella Ramiah**.

Go to sleep Ranja says **Jacqui Medonza**, who works at It's Complicated. *You're drunk.*

Four messages are sent to **Ranjana Wilatgamuwa**'s inbox. Three are from **Manique P**.

Anyone know a Chinese that delivers at this time? asks **Somi Borelessa**.

Someone's got the munchees says **Devdun Malamuthuran**.

Lol replies **Somi**. *Just getting my popcorn.*

0412

Ranjana alters his favourite movies and books section. He adds 'The Last Emperor' and removes 'Rambo 3'. Deletes 'Charlotte's Web' and adds 'Crime and Punishment'.

You alrite man? Ado bugger don't be stupid. **Vasuki Nadesan** from Canada and Latvia.

Ranjana uploads more pictures of him and **Fatima Yousuf**. At a cricket match, wearing Lankan cricket tops. On Sigiriya's head, holding hands. Hugging at an Unawatuna sunset. Under each one he comments: *So long. Farewell. Auf wiedersehen. Good night.*

Ranjana, this is Aunty Padma. I suggest you call your sister right away. The number is +6137326372. From **Padmini Alahakoon** in Wales, whose photo albums mostly feature dogs and flowers.

Ranjana copy-and-pastes a private message. One sent at 0403 that day, 9 minutes earlier. The only one in his inbox that wasn't from his sister **Manique**.

Please stop this babi. We are what we are. You know this. I will never leave my boys. They don't deserve any of this. We can try and meet today, but only as friends. I will always love you. Bunchy.

Ranjana Wilatgamuwa comments *Too late bitch* and goes offline.

0453

Doz any1 know where he lives? asks **Pierre Chang** from Hong Kong. Their friendship began four years ago, with a group photo from a software sales conference in Male.

Kiribathgoda I think comments **Rodney Handunetti**, a fat man with a moustache and no hair, whose profile pic has him in swimming trunks.

Everyone's asleep in Lanka says **Tia Kumari** in Slave Island. She has just uploaded pics of her with two girls and two boys at a club called Sugar.

But you're up? says **Isuru Roy**, evidently stirred by **Tia**'s selfie in bikini taken last month and now used as profile pic.

I'm drunk. Lol says **Tia**. *Worried about Ranjana.*

He's drunk says **Martin Pinto**. *He'll be fine.*

Sure? says **Tia Kumari**.

We know him too well says **Martin P**. *He does this for attention.*

Just because you pretend to bang my sister, doesn't mean you know me. **Ranjana Wilatgamuwa** comes back online. *Arsehole.*

0455

Some people just need attention says **Martin Pinto** to his imaginary audience. He could not have imagined that this exchange would eventually appear on 97,466 walls.

I'm blocking you arsehole. Go perve at little boys says **Ranjana**.

Ranja, for your sister's sake I am tolerating says **Martin** before he loses access to the conversation.

Sorry for this drama says **Ranjana**. *Just saying bye in one go. Easier this way. 1,004 birds and one stoner. Ha ha.*

Ranja this is Martin says **Manique P**. *Your sister is sobbing here. What a cool guy you are.*

Ranjana you shud be ashamed. **Saluka Ratnasena** chimes in.

And like that **Ranjana** unfriends his sister and his cousin.

0510

Must be tough being Israeli. Must be tough being universally hated. First by bigots, then by those they oppress, and now by liberals posts **Rocky Nalawansa**. This prompts 29 different comments over the hour. Mostly Muslims applauding. The longest of which is 543 words.

Israel has a right to exist says **Dr David de Silva**. *And they are not going away.*

Ranjana Wilatgamuwa comments. *Israel is an apartheid imperialist state that uses smart bombs on children. Not as oppressive or barbaric as Saudi Arabia. Both Saudi and Zion are bankrolled by Uncle Sam. Are you* **Dr de Silva**?

I thought you were dead says **Ayman Ariyanayagam**. *Is this a ghost?*

Lol, not yet Aree is the reply. *Not yet.*

Tia Kumari posts more selfies from last night. 773 of her 1,034 photos contain her posing. They feature over 80 different haircuts. But the same smile. **Ranjana** likes 7 snaps from her weekend in Hikkaduwa. **Isuru Roy** likes 28.

Ranja, you were joking before right? Says **Tia**.

Was sad before. Still am says **Ranjana**.

I know girls who think you're cute says **Tia**.

Yeah right says **Ranjana**. *You wouldn't dance with me. And you've banged half of Colombo.*

Lol types **Rocky Nalawansa**. *Ouch.*

Boom goes the dynamite says **Chaminda Alles** who hasn't changed his profile in 10 years.

Not cool says **Shivani Kabeer** who changes hers each week.

Dislike says **Gillian Paramour** who has no pictures of herself, but many of sunsets.

If you don't apologize and erase that comment, I will report you says **Tia Kumari**.

What do I care? says **Ranjana**. *It's funny cos it's true.*

I am reporting you says **Tia**. *Your ugly. And you stink. Go kill yourself.*

Exactly my plan says **Ranjana**.

Hahah says **Khadaffi Joe**, whose profile picture is a boot stomping on a face. *That escalated fast.*

0545

I hope this is a joke, Ranjana Wilatgamuwa says **Harin Wewala**. *You're still hung up on that chubby bird.* **Harin**'s wall is filled with cricket articles and match highlights.

Sorry Harry, You have no right to insult this girl says **Bryan Thompson** of Tea Trails Bungalows.

She's a bitch says **Harin**. *Played him like a fiddle.*

You out of order Harry says **Ayman Ariyanayagam**.

I know Ranja since we were 6. I knew she was using him replies **Harin**.

Guys don't discuss this here says **Vasuki Nadesan** who lists Kamal Haasan and Rajinikanth as her favourite actors, and dead moderates Neelan Thiruchelvam and Lakshman Kadirgamar as her heroes.

Against the run of play, **Martin Pinto** posts a meme featuring former presidents and prime ministers of Sri Lanka.

Great Leaders. Two great schools reads the caption followed by the crests of Royal College and S. Thomas College. The photo gets 47 likes in 5 minutes.

Yo dickhead posts **Ranjana**. *I unblocked you just to make fun of this bullshit.*

Disce Aut Discede posts **Jagana Labrooy**.

Royal and S. Thomas produced all the fucktards that screwed this country comments **Ranjana**. *JR who sat on the '83 massacre, SWRD who passed Sinhala Only, Anagarika Dharmapala that racist prick, Lalith Kotelawala the crook, Ranjan Wijeratne the mass murderer, the pompous Senanayakes, the clueless Chelvanayagams. All the idiots that messed this island. Royalists and Thomians!!!*

Brothers, I urge you not to take this bait says **Ransith Adhihetty**. *Show that our fine schools are not easily ruffled.* He has a thomian crest as his profile.

Esto Perpetua says **Martin Pinto**.

The minister's sons who shoot at mirror balls in nightclubs? What schools? asks **Ranjana**. *The crooks that run the stock exchange. What schools?*

The question attracts 1,863 comments over the next 48 hours. From old boys of both schools. **Sambodi Polonnowita** leaves 37 comments even though he only spent one term at STC. **Ranjana** makes no further contribution to the thread.

0603

Ranjana updates his status.

So this is it. I have 1,004 friends and no one to talk to. Most of you are here because I worked with you or went to school with you or played music with you or because you followed my posts or I followed yours. I scrolled through all of you and looks like I've been collecting insecure, narcissistic, ignorant morons. Most of you I dislike. Some I despise.

This post attracts 17 likes in its first minute, then a few responses.

Go to sleep Ranja says **Belinda Cabraal**. *You're drunk.* Seven people like this.

U trying to c how many will unfriend you? asks **Pierre Chang**.

He's a troll says **Bang Bang Bala**. *Do a selfie song will you?*

Pierre Chang you boring prick replies **Ranjana**. *The only reason I keep you here is to laugh at your dull updates.*

Looks lyk someone needs 2 sleeeeepppp says **Rachna Dematagoda**.

Ranja, don't be an ass says **Deepika Asha**. Her feed is filled with her and her husband posing at different resorts.

Harsh says **Bang Bang**.

Ranjana Wilatgamuwa posts a picture clip. It is a compilation of **Pierre Chang**'s status updates compressed into a jpg.

Off to gym, then dinner.
Can't decide between ramen or pad thai.
Saw Avatar. Awesome.

You're a regular Oscar Wilde comments **Ranjana**.

No wonder you got dumped. Was because of your body odour? asks **Pierre**. *Everyone at that conference commented on it.* He unfriends **Ranjana** first.

0622

The montage of photos of **Ranjana** and **Fatima Yousuf** has been edited and placed on a red background. It attracts a second wave of comments.

Hang in there Ranja says **Jonathan Engelbrecht** who lists his birth date as 1 January 1901 and his religion as Buddhist Satanist.

Plenty more fish to eat machan says **Chaminda Alles**.

Don't be silly man. Let's put a shot today? says **Spencer Van Cuylenberg**. *After work?*

Don't ask him to drink!!! Are you madddd??? comments **Rachna Dematagoda**.

Better drunk than dead no? replies **Spencer**.

Ranjana dear boy says **Harin Wewala**. *This montage of you and Bunchy. The dream that died blah blah. Graphics are very cheesy I am sorry to say.*

Did you use Photoshop? asks **Khadaffi Joe**. *Or CorelDraw?*

Lol says **Devdun Malamuthuran**. *Burn.*

I'm just saying man. If you're gonna do it. Get a proper designer. And don't use comic sans. Shall I do a revision for you? Adds **Harin**.

The comment receives 5 likes and a flurry of abuse, mainly from mothers getting their kids ready for school. **Shivani Kabeer, Linda Gunasekera** and **Therese Maralassa** all urge Ranja's friends to get off their computers and see if he is ok.

0635

Chek out Ranja selfie raps says **JithTheGiant**. *#Ranjaselfies.*

Some were shit says **Khadaffi Joe**. *But some were da shit.*

The page features a series of videos, each recorded over the past year. Each on a Saturday morning at 6 or thereabouts. Each one featuring Ranja drunk and smoking a gold leaf. On some he strums an acoustic guitar and sings. The strumming is tight and the singing is flat. On some he rants about the government. None get more than 10 likes and always from the same people.

What a crazy day. Meeting 3 investors. Speaking at CIM. Netball game. Then Punchi's play. Need strength. Wish me luck. Says **Deepika Asha** unaware that she is in the wrong thread.

#humblebrag says **Laila Souraj**.

#hatersgonnahate replies **Deepika**.

0642

Ranjana posts a final picture of him and **Fatima Yousuf**. It's a blurred selfie taken at Mount Beach and dated the evening before.

Below Ranjana writes. *She was 23, I was 19. We loved. She left. Got married off. Had kids. Separated. Came back. Said she'd stay. Didn't.*

Ranjana then posts a video clip of him strumming acoustic. 'This is by a man who converted to Islam and lost his soul.' He sings 'Morning Has Broken' out of tune and ends with a nod. Then he says 'This is for you Bunchy.'

He gets up, pulls back the curtain behind the almirah and releases a rope from the ceiling. A noose dangles from where the mosquito net should be. He walks to it and places it around his neck. The clip stops.

0653

Malli pick up your phone you fool says **Saluka Ratnasena**. The privacy settings allow her to post, despite being unfriended.

Ranjana Chill man. Mahinda Aiya is come to your place says **JithTheGiant**. *Anyone else in Kiribathgoda to chek our boy?*

That's not a real noose says **Bernard Shanmugaratnam**.

If this moron is killing himself over that fatso he deserves to be hung says **Harin Wewala**.

I have called the Kiribathgoda Police says **Padmini Alahakoon** from Wales. *They will call soon as they get to you.*

Ranja b safe says **Mohammed Ameer**.

Can you even hang yourself from ground level? asks **Somi Borelessa**.

Here. He's standing on a stool says **Chaminda Alles** attaching a screenshot of the video paused at 5.47. *Can you see?*

You'll miss Arsenal getting relegated mate. Says **Rodney Hadunhetti**.

He's snoring probably. Bugger is all talk says **Suresh Koelmeyer**.

GROBR says **Gordon Baptist**, whose wall is filled with Sports Illustrated swimsuits.

Guys don't say things you'll regret says **Ayman Ariyanayagam**.

Devdun told me about you Ranjana. Hope you're ok says **Vihara Neyndorff**.

Fatima cares for you Ranjana. She's going through a lot says **Shakila Kawiratne**. Her photo album features pics from last year of her with **Fatima Yousuf**.

Ranjana Wilatgamuwa posts a clip.

0700

My Confession by **Ranjana Wilatgamuwa**. It is 3.48 minutes long. And like the rest of his videos, it contains an almirah behind his left shoulder and a curtain behind his right. He wears different clothes and this shot has no noose in it. He takes a swig of Lion Stout and grins.

'*If you are seeing this, I haven't entered my Death Switch password for three weeks. Which means I am incapacitated or dead or playing a sick joke.*

'*There are more videos that I have cued to post at fifteen-minute intervals.*

'*I have sent a personal note of goodbye to a few of my 1,004 friends. If you have not received one, it is because you are only an acquaintance or because I forgot to dump you. Now for a song.*'

He lights a cigarette and keeps it in his mouth as he fingerpicks Simon and Garfunkel's 'Only Living Boy in New York'.

Wtf?!? Says **Sulochana Keegal**.

I don't believe this. Says **Jagana Labrooy**.

Has anyone checked on Ranjana asks **Chaminda Alles**.

his phone no answer says **Spencer Van Cuylenburg**.

Guys those weren't real noose says **JithTheGiant**.

Bugger is full of shit says **Gordon Baptist**. *He is playing you all.*

Whoa just tuning into dis says **Venkat Sharma**. *Any one heard from Ranja?*

0715

The second video is titled *Calling BS*. Ranjana is seated with his usual props. Almirah, curtain, Lion Stout. He has a shorter haircut and a scraggy stubble not seen in recent videos.

'So this one is called Calling Bullshit. I'm calling bullshit on fuckers who annoy me. Wish I had me a Dislike button, an Eyeroll button, a Middle Finger button. A No One Cares button.

'Tia Kumari, the same dumb smile in every picture. Who are you fooling darling? We all know when you look like when the camera's off.

'Bang Bang Bala enough with the invites to see things I don't give a shit about. I'm not interested in seeing even a jpg of you. Why would I see your sister's crap exhibition? Pasting newspaper clippings on cardboard isn't art.

'JithTheGiant you illiterate. Learn some fucking grammar. And stop trying to be everyone's buddy. Maybe stop using the word buddy all the time.

'Deepika Asha, if you want to boast about your shitty life, then boast. Don't fish for likes with needy updates. "Guess whose hubby's taking her to the Maldives?" As if anyone cares. Clearly he has stopped screwing you.

'Linda Gunasekera's political brain farts. No One Cares. Jagana Labrooy's movie reviews? No One Cares. Spencer Van Cuylenburg's daughter's wit? No One Cares. And not that witty.'

The rant goes on, with **Ranjana** accusing **Isuru Roy** of being a stalker, **Belinda Cabraal** of stating the obvious, **Rocky Nalwansa** of liking everything and **Dr David de Silva** of being a clueless diaspora liberal.

0722

Wow, that was intense says **Dirk Lapan**.

He's not wrong though says **Chaminda Alles**.

The guy's mental says **Belinda Cabraal**.

Typical sympathy baiter. No friends, no hope. So now he's a keyboard commentator comments **Dr David de Silva**.

Spoken like a diaspora liberal. You must like MIA? Asks **Harin Wewala**.

MIA is da shit! says **Khaddaffi Joe**. *Greatest Lankan recording artist ever.*

She most certainly is not says **Harin Wewala**. *And she doesn't know what genocide means.*

FFS She's a rapper! Eelam gives her gangsta cred. Lanka's her Compton says **Sulochana Keegal**. *But the music is genius. Otherwise who is Lanka's greatest? Jothipala?*

She is not wrong about the genocide comments **Vasuki Nadesan**. *I was there in '09.*

Then you madam, are an idiot also says **Harin Wewala**.

Any word on Ranjana? asks **Ayman Ariyanayagam**.

Mahinda Aiya dropped at his house. His mom said he leaves for work early says **JithTheGiant**.

Noose was a hoax. Knew it says **Bernard Shanmugaratnam**.

Cracking up at all you idiots following this bullshit. Ranja's laughing his smelly ass off comments **Gordon Baptist**. **Gordon** has been friends with **Ranjana** for over 10 years, but has had no interaction with him till today.

0730

The third video is titled *Naming and Shaming*. This time Ranjana wears a cap and no shirt. He is more visibly drunk than on any previous clips.

'*OK buggers. This will only go out after my death. If the first video airs, I get beeps to all my devices. If I don't respond I have either lost all my chargers or am dead. And if I'm dead, you guys are so fucken screwed. Haha!*

'**Ransith Adhihetty**, *you are nothing but a government pimp. We know you got the tourism board account by providing Russian tarts to the minister. I hacked your email and sent it to the Sunday Leader. Esto Perpetua muthafucker.*

'**Belinda Cabraal** *does* **Sulochana Keegal** *know you are sleeping with her husband? Half of your office does.*

'**Vasuki Nadesan** *oh wise lady of Latvia. Do your students know that half your salary still goes to the LTTE?*

'**Manique** *my Akki. Your husband is a paedo. Sorry to break this to you, but I'm sure you always knew.*'

The video clocks in at 8.16 minutes and has him accuse 30 more of his friends of adultery, theft, drug abuse, hypocrisy, and, in one case, of vehicular manslaughter.

'*And* **Saleem Yousuf**, *loving husband of Fatima aka Bunchy. We have never met sir, but we have shared. I have lain with your wife on occasion over 18 years. Who knows, one or both of your loving sons may someday become guitarists. I have lovely pictures of her. But I will not upload, because I love her still. And always will.*'

He sings 'Always a Woman' over the wrong chords. All 1,004 of Ranjana's friends are tagged in the video.

0745

Can anyone confirm that Ranja is at work? asks **Rodney Handunetti**.

More importantly, can someone shut down his account? asks **Jacqui Medonza**.

If you don't like it, unfriend him. I of course have my popcorn. Says **Somi Borelessa**.

The fourth video hits right on the 15-minute mark. It is titled *Open Secrets*. This time Ranja is well dressed and sober. He smokes gold leaf and drinks from a teacup.

'*So finally I will tell the truth. Any IT guy worth his pen drive can hack into your machine and look through your web cam at you jerking off in your jungies. Anyone with coding skills can peep in on your life. Not just politicians and bankers.*

'*I have hacked every LMD Top 50 company. I could put a giant dickpic on the front of every banking website if I choose. I have a programme that scans emails. I have data on who is playing behind their spouse's back. Who is embezzling money. Who's being fired for bullshit reasons, and being replaced by someone who's better on the eye. And who every CEO gets his kickbacks from.*'

Guys. Just heard Ranja has been seen on a bus on baseline road says **Ayman Ariyanayagam**.

Colombo Police Cyber Crime division has been notified says **Bryan Thompson**.

I bet those clowns still use dial-up modems says **Suresh Koelmeyer**. *Colombo Cyber crimes. Ha!*

What is the crime here? says **Harin Wewala**.

On the video **Ranjana** reaches into a basket hanging from a familiar rope and picks a guava.

'*I've hacked the government censors website. If only you could see what you're not allowed to. I have unblocked TamilNet and Colombo Telegraph and 17 other sites that "criticize the regime, speak of human rights, push foreign agendas. Or report on Sri Lanka's statistics for drinking, suicide, child sex, domestic abuse and rape."*'

(Taken from SL censor guidelines)

He takes a bite of the guava and smiles.

'*I also have access to their recycle bins. 3,947 hours of incriminating filth. Wanna see?*'

0757

I have had enough of this. I'm deleting this arsehole. I advise you all to do the same. Don't give him the attention says **Bryan Thompson**.

He's unstable. He needs help says **Shakila Kawiratne**.

He needs to stop drinking says **Gordon Baptist**. 13 likes.

Must we have a live feed of his loneliness? asks **Jacqui Medonza**. 5 likes.

That's all this is. A live feed of everyone's loneliness. And their fake happiness says **Harin Wewala**. 9 likes.

I thought he was funny says **Rodney Handunetti**. *Hope the bugger's ok.*

It's sad. You try to be liked by hundreds. Then you try to be hated. Better than being ignored says **Dr David de Silva**.

The diaspora has spoken says **Harin Wewala**.

You are wrong Doc says **Vihara Neyndorff**. *Most of us just try to be loved by one. That's sometimes the hardest.* 15 likes.

Terrible news. Ranjana's body found in his bedroom says **Padmini Alahakoon**.

There is silence for one whole minute.

Then **Timothy Alles** says *Shit*.

I cannot even comments **Muhammed Amir**.

What happened? asks **Jonathan Engelbrecht**.

Omg says **Marie Fernando**.

Horrible Terrible says **Vihara Neyndorff**.

May the almighty Jesus have mercy on his soul says **Disella Ramiah**.

I thought he left for work? says **Nathan Chandrasena**. He has already entered RIP Ranjana as his status.

Are you sure? asks **Sambodi Polonnowita**.

He's gone. I suggest we show the family some respect says **Ayman Ariyanayagam**.

Anyone know how to shut down his profile? asks a resurgent **Martin Pinto**.

0815

The next video is titled *The Crooks*. This time Ranjana wears an Australian cricket t-shirt and a smirk.

'Hoo. You Silly Lunkets lost no? Anyway. You will never win a world cup again. If you do, I will hang myself. Haha.

'Over the years I have posted content about the ruling party and its family members. I have received threatening calls about this. Then over the past year, my clips stopped uploading. As if some government censor was watching my feed.

'This clip has been encrypted. If you get it, copy it immediately, for it will be taken down.'

Ranjana then names 32 journalists who have gone missing in the last 18 months. He quotes Human Rights stats on those abducted and tortured and imprisoned without trial. He gives detailed profiles of Buddhist monks who have shares in casinos, holds up photos of provincial councillors who murder tourists in Tangalle, and examines the curious case of a rugby player whose car caught fire.

'I cannot stop this. Maybe you can, but I can't. When things are this wrong, you either change them or you leave.

So I am off.'

41,643 download this clip before it is taken down.

1137

Martin Pinto confirms that Ranjana was found hanging in his bedroom.

'He was a highly intelligent, misguided and disappointed young man. But we loved him in our own way. His sisters and family thank all of you who have been his friends.' 3,457 likes.

RIP Ranja says **Ruwan Kotachchi**.

I don't understand says **Harin Wewala**.

Sleep sound sweet malli. I wish we had known you says **Saluka Ratnasena**.

My heart is breaking says **Linda Gunasekera**.

Thank god, they took down those disgusting clips. RIP Ranja says **Gordon Baptist**.

I don't care who hates me. But I loved him. I loved who he was and who he could have been. I also love my children and chose the best for them. I will never apologize for that. Rest well sad prince. I will miss you always.

And then **Fatima Yousuf** deactivates her account.

1143

When was the last time any of you spoke with Ranjana? asks **Harin Wewala**.

Apart from just nowww? says **Rachna Dematagoda**.

Not on here. In person says **Harin**.

I haven't seen him for years says **Timothy Alles**.

He hasn't been seen at his work for 6 months. His mother said he moved out and never visits. Even I haven't seen him in a year says **Harin Wewala**. *Who is saying his body was found?*

I met him with Fatima in Chilaw says **Shakila Kawiratne**.

When? asks **Harin**.

Must be June or July says **Shakila**.

Eight months ago? comments **Harin**.

At 11.47 **Martin Pinto**, **Saluka Ratnasena** and **Padmini Alahakoon** complain that their profiles have been hacked. No one is able to get through to the Kiribathgoda police. Meanwhile **Ranjana**'s clips are shared 12,465 times.

1155

A final video is titled *Strings* and has Ranjana smiling. He is in a well-ironed shirt. Judging from hair length it appears a recent clip.

'*Today is a rare day. Today I am happy. I met Bunchy and we talked. Things may never work out. But today I am happy.*'

He apologizes to anyone he has offended over the years. Says he sometimes feels very dark. He always has. But not today. Because today he has love.

This one's for you Bunchy he says.

He plucks strings and sings, and for once he is not out of tune. It is a song of his own composing and he sings it sweetly.

'You and me are connected.
Me and you are connected.
They and them are connected
You just don't see the strings.'

And he sings the song again. The clip is looped 3 times to fill 10 minutes. The film quality is grainy and the sound quality fuzzy. Still it gets 352,948 views. The truth rarely goes viral, but catchy songs often do.

Stale News

'TIS AN OLD TALE, OFT REPEATED. YEARS AGO, WHEN HE WAS ambassador, he visited a junior minister in an African tinpot dictatorship. It was to discuss the trade of tea, coconuts and arms, but all he remembered was his host's mansion and selection of vintage cars. How does a junior minister in the world's poorest nation live like this, he asks, not without jealousy.

My friend, see that 20-floor skyscraper? The Asian nodded. It was supposed to be 24 floors. See that six-lane highway. He nodded again. It was to be eight lanes. Development is a great thing, my friend. Always be around when it happens.

The decades pass. The African becomes chancellor. The Asian joins the cabinet. An invitation is sent. The African gawks at his palace, his jet, his private lake and the legs of his mistress. You have done well, my friend. But how, when your country is fighting wars?

You see that bridge that transports aid from the rich to the poor? No, says the African. The Asian smiles at him. Exactly.

'Tis an old tale, oft repeated, and never resolved.

The Prison Riot

THEY CALL ME POOSA. I DON'T CALL ME ANYTHING. I DON'T talk at all, not even to Milano. And I don't stay in the stinking pens with the rest of the animals. I sleep outside under the coconut tree where the guards can't see me, not even the Kicker or the Fucker. No one would sleep here cos its next to the kitchen drain that's clogged with rotten dhal and spoilt fish. To me, the smell is no worse that the stench of thirty bodies packed into a cell meant for ten.

There may be a rule against sleeping outside but no one has told me. The rules are written on the walls outside the Bamuna cells, but I cannot read or write so they must not apply to me. No one reads out my name from the register when the guards hand out that week's tasks. I end up at the Garment Factory watching Milano sew uniforms for civil servants, which is better than being assigned to electric work with Soodu Sampath or the bakery with the Cook. Sampath tried to fry me with a car battery and the Cook has poured oil on me on three occasions.

They don't try that stuff when Milano is around. Milano isn't a fighter, but everyone is scared of him. It is his curses that make others shake. And the bags of shit he seems to produce from nowhere. His curses are specific and personal, and not only does it seem like he means them, but it appears that he can make them come true.

Every prisoner shits in bags, paper or plastic, whatever can be found, except for me. It is better than walking over sleeping psychos at 4 a.m. and risking a hammering in the dark from the Kicker or the Fucker. During the day, the lines for the squatting pans are long and never orderly. I have my secret spot for shitting, and, as long as I keep my trap shut, no one will know.

The riot started at the end of a very good week. It was a pleasant few days, because the guards had stopped beating the prisoners, which usually happened when the Human Rights inspectors were due to visit. The riot broke out yesterday, two days before the scheduled visit, though no one can agree on how.

'That guard started it,' says the Prof. 'They are doing random searches and planting bottles in cells. That means they are looking for something or framing someone.'

'Which guard? The Kicker?' says Father Pieris.

'No no. The Fucker. It seems Soodhu's gang have tied him up and are hammering him.'

We are hiding in the Library, waiting for the yelling to subside. Which, of course, does not. Bad things don't stop just because you want them to, that is all I have learned from the cages outside this Library. Better, then, to wait for an explosion to arrive. Because eventually, it will.

The Library is next to the Kitchen which is across from C block. There are three cell blocks. A block has the psychos, the rapists, the gangsters, and the killers. B block is for terrorists, so most in there are Tamils and Islams. Some Sinhala rebels were first in B, but after the fist fights and toothbrush stabs, they were moved to A. As Father Pieris always says, A for arseholes, B for bombers.

Father Pieris was in C block with the rest of us, the harmless, the mad, the poor, the scared, the wrongly accused, the addicted, the screwed by courts. There are many words that start with C that could describe us all. The guards call us 'cocksuckers', though that is only true of the juveniles in the Garment Factory. Milano says we are 'cowards' though that may be true of every living thing. You won't catch me rioting for kinder guards or better lunches, or risking a bullet to make a statement when they send the army in. You won't catch me taking a beating for being in the wrong place. The Prof calls us 'cunts of misery' when he gets angry, though I do not know what that means.

The riot is in C block, and we are hoping it will end up moving along the corridor past the Kitchen and towards the Dispensary, where all the pills and powders are, past the Garment factory, where the juveniles pucker their lips, and onward to the Sick Room where the Lepers and the Dying are, and maybe end up at the Hilton where the Very Special Prisoners live.

We are holed up in the Library, donated by the State Minister of Education while serving 6 months for stealing from a fund meant for rural kids. The Deputy Minister for Fisheries served two years for manslaughter and funded the Kitchen renovation. Both ministers were released when the government changed. It was the prison's only renovation since it was built a hundred years ago by one of Queen Victoria's draughtsman, the Prof told us in one of his many library lectures.

'We have to wait for the Minister of Sewage to be caught smuggling septic tanks. Then maybe we will get proper toilets,' jokes the Activist. He makes this crack whenever someone was in the Library pretending to read.

Very Special Prisoners were all politicians or big businessmen and they stayed in cell 9 above the prison hospital, known as the Hilton. It was rumoured to be three times the size of a normal cell and housed only one prisoner. Some say it had a TV and an AC, though the only one to steal a glimpse was the Leper who was supposed to be sweeping the Sick Room. Lepers are usually hard to understand and after he was beaten and put in the Bamuna for a week, this one stopped talking altogether.

No one knew why the Prof was serving a life sentence. The Activist asked him once and was banned from the Library for a month. Some say it was for writing treasonous articles during the 1989 insurrection, others say that he chopped up his wife and served her as curry to her lover.

There is plenty of time for making up tales in C block, where there are no holidays or sick days, and the only medicine is Panadol, which you only get if you have boils on your skin or are dying. In C block, the days that are not exhausting and frightening, are filled with boredom and prisoners have to find ways to occupy their big mouths and small brains.

Some do not know why they are here, though for many it is for being poor. Why should you be punished, when being poor is punishment enough, Milano used to tell the Blue Meadow Killer, while they sewed uniforms for the police. There may be bad people in all three blocks, but there are worse people out there.

Twenty prisoners from C block are in the Library, and none of them are here to read. They fill up the floors and hide under tables and behind shelves and are crouched into bean shapes as if expecting a hammering. It is the most crowded the Library has ever been.

The Prof runs the Library and keeps track of who borrows what and which books are due and which are with Soodu's gang and not worth reclaiming. There weren't too many regular readers in the prison apart from Milano, the

Blue Meadow Killer, Father Pieris and some of the foreign prisoners. Sometimes the LTTE prisoners from B block would come, always in numbers, and always for quick visits. They would mostly borrow from the magazine and newspaper stack.

Constructed by the prisoners themselves, the Library had more shelves than books, with crooked lines of plank hanging off every wall and partition, making this tiny space feel more cramped than the sewer that I sleep in. The books are mostly second-hand donations from Colombo families who thought they were giving to rural schools. A jail sentence didn't stop the Minister of Education from robbing village kids.

Mostly the Library was a haven for druggies hiding from Soodu Sampath or a haunt for the Garment Factory youngsters, exchanging tongues for powders. When the carpentry prisoners sawed the planks, they hollowed out the insides of the shelves at the back, creating crevices small enough to store powders and large enough to conceal toothbrushes with teeth.

The Prof didn't mind what went on behind the shelves as long as the guards didn't catch anyone, and he was left to read in peace. He sometimes read aloud when I was in there, stories of the Boys Hardy, the Five Famous and by someone called Archer Jeffrey. I can't read, but I don't mind a yarn. Prof read for illiterate prisoners like me who came to sort books and stack shelves, though I'm sure the stories confused them as much as they did me.

'Oi Father!' Milano hisses from behind the Sinhala book section where Soodu Sampath's gang slapped juveniles who owed them. Milano was with me and a couple of the foreigner prisoners. Father Peiris was under the table with Prof.

'Father. Today is the day. We must carpe the diem.'

'Give a monkey some Latin and he's Steve McQueen.' says Prof, though he seemed pleased that his Latin lessons had stuck.

'Don't call me monkey, Prof. Monkeys have sharp teeth and big fists.'

'You are a crazy boy,' says Father Pieris, giving me a wink. Father liked me and sometimes let me eat from his plate while he stroked me. Milano didn't like me going to Father's cell. I only went to watch prisoners get blessed on a birthday or a sabbath even though, according to the courts of Ceylon, the priest had defied the fifth commandment twice.

'You and your Great Escape plan,' says Prof. 'Instead of a motorbike, you have a kunu truck? They will put you in the Bamuna for a year you fool. Then who will look after Poosa?'

'No one is guarding the Bamuna,' says Milano. 'The uniforms are ready. But I can't do it alone. Father, I need a driver for the truck.'

'Today of all days you pick?' Father Pieris turns away like a petulant lover and eyes the doorway and the corridors of cells. The shouting is finally moving from the Library. 'They will send in the army and the riot squad. They will come with guns.'

'That's the point,' says Milano. 'They will be guarding the prisoner in Cell 9. All the action will be near the Hilton and the Sick Room. The rioters, the guards, the army. No one will be guarding the wall near the Bamuna. It is perfect.'

'What Hilton? The riot is here.' There are five Tamils from B cell, huddling around the religion books that Father Pieris liked to read from. 'Those Sinhala pigs are thinking when to come and kill us.'

The Tall One reaches the top shelf near the magazine stack and pulls out three toothbrushes. He gives one to the Tamil with the scar, the other to the youngest and most innocent looking Tamil. The Innocent One looks down at the browned bristles and the sharpened point as if unsure about which end to use.

'No one wants to kill ya'll men,' the Activist isn't afraid of speaking out or of being beaten and engaged in both activities at regular intervals. He is engrossed in a book by that Archer Jeffrey fellow, the one with a cat on the cover.

'We heard them planning with the guards. That Hijacker said he would bash every LTTE's head on the Garment Factory wall. We are not even LTTE, as if that even matters.'

The Hijacker was a thug in Soodu Sampath's gang. He had hijacked an Italian plane to be with his son or something. Sometimes, Milano's stories about prisoners were hard to follow. The Hijacker has been here for 20 years and has spent his time doing push-ups and pulls-ups and squats and getting angrier and angrier. He always said it was the Tamils who betrayed him and stole his son.

'That Hijacker can't do jack,' says the Activist. 'Kathleen Burnett is coming tomorrow. I will report all this.'

'You report my arse,' says the Nigerian Barber. 'Human Rights bastards say they contact my Mama in Lagos. Now 10 months. Kathleen full of shit.'

Out of the Nigerians, Pakistanis, Venezuelans and Thais who lived on the bottom floor of C block, only the barber had learned to speak Sinhala.

'Kathleen can complain to international prison reforms. They can put pressure on the government. But we have to tell her what happens. Nothing changes if we keep shut.'

For some reason, the Activist looks at me.

'We have told her about the dangers facing Tamil prisoners,' says the oldest of the Tamils. 'What has she ever done?'

'I will talk to her,' says the Activist, bookmarking his page by folding its corner.

'Why are you reading those right-wing fairy tales?' asks Prof. We can no longer hear the shouting, so either the rioters have found the Dispensary and have swallowed every pill in sight. Or they have gone to loot the Hilton. Milano gets to his feet and gives Father Pieris a hard stare.

The Activist smiles. 'I'm writing a book about prisons. This Archer fellow was in prison they say. Trying to get ideas.'

'So, you're stealing from a criminal?'

'Who is not a criminal? Only fools like us get caught. The biggest crooks are the thugs who make laws. And the brutes who enforce them.'

'Didn't know socialists get ideas from Archer books?'

I could tell Milano was as bored with this conversation as me. He looked around at the armed Tamil boys and the silent foreign prisoners. And I knew the thought running through that beautiful brain. Can any of you fools drive a garbage truck?

'I only believe in zeros,' says the Activist, stroking his beard with his limp wrist. 'The world is a reflection of the number of zeros you think in.'

'I know I know. Property is theft. Competition is evil. Markets are cruel. War is peace,' the Prof and the Activist liked winding each other up. Milano began fidgeting and I realized it was time to go.

'The beggar thinks in zeros and tens. The day wager thinks in hundreds and thousands. The office guy thinks in ten thousands, and his boss thinks in lakhs. And then there are the owners of bosses. Who think in millions, but they too have masters. Who dream in numbers we cannot count to.'

'What's your point?' asks the Prof.

'They all envy the other. And they are all miserable.'

'Sounds like another fairy tale from your Archer.'

'Can I borrow this?' the Activist holds up the book as Milano squats in front of Father Pieris.

'As long as you don't steal.'

'If you steal from a thief, it doesn't really count. Kathleen Burnett from Human Rights showed me your file Prof. You have forged some bloody massive cheques, no?'

'Why don't you put that book down. Piss off from my library. And never come back.'

The Activist chuckles as the Prof snorts.

Father Pieris tries to avoid Milano's stare and fails to absolve himself. Milano squats before the priest and hisses.

'Father what if they hang you this year? You know the fires of hell await you, no?'

'Why don't you get lost Milano,' says Father, sitting up and peering through the doorway. I slink past him to see if the coast was clear. 'Ask that woman who crossed the road, when you mowed her down. You will burn long before me son.'

Outside the Library was dirty and dimly lit, there are stains on the concrete that weren't there before, which could've been blood or the remains of a burst shit bag. But I see no bleeders or shitters nearby.

'I was drunk, and I didn't know how to drive. You poisoned the mother of your children, while preaching from your pulpit. Let's see who will hang and who will fry.'

Milano gets up and walks to the shelf by the far wall. He reaches behind the picture books and instead of pulling out a toothbrush or a bag of shit as was customary, he extracts three orange t-shirts and three green shorts.

He addresses everyone in the Library, who lift their heads, emboldened by the silence outside. 'Can anyone drive a truck?'

He looks from the Activist to the Tamils from B block. From the Nigerians and the Pakistanis to the Prof. Outside the doorway are the filthy walls we all know and the familiar smells of bodies and tears. There is also a silence that we are used to but know enough about to fear. Milano settles his gaze on Father Pieris, the fallen angel who had agreed to the plan at the Garment Factory and was now posting bail.

'Fuck you all.' Milano pulls back his head and shows off the apple at his throat. 'They will beat you till your bones crack and pile you in the Dispensary like chickens. Come Poosa, let's go.'

* * *

The building was called Garment Factory not just because tailoring class took place there, but because that's where they incarcerated teenagers. The juveniles were mostly addicts and in need of currency and had young bodies to trade. In the outside world, garment factories are associated with nubile nymphs from the village who work the juki sewing machines and live in boarding houses and according to the Trishaw Thief are 'fully up for loving'.

I would never know anything without Milano or Prof or the Activist telling me. They don't seem to mind that I never reply. They all need an audience for the monologues in their heads. Milano ran his Great Escape plan by me until he had it memorized, then he shared it with Father and the Blue Meadow Killer.

The Colombo Municipal Council used prisoners to sew uniforms for the city police, the fire brigade and the garbage collectors. Every week Milano would pocket an orange t-shirt and a green short while I distracted everyone by vomiting at the door. I can vomit on command, regardless of what I have eaten. It is an underrated skill.

Outside the Bamuna cells is the garbage yard, where prisoners load the garbage truck each week, which stayed parked until it filled up. Then the prisoner would tell the head guard, who would report to the duty warden, who would call the municipal council. This could take weeks or months, by which time the yard around the truck began to fill with maggots and shit bags. Eventually, the council would send two garbage men to drive the truck to the dump, empty it and bring it back.

'My thatha was a mechanic, Poosa. You can start these old trucks without a key. If you know which wires to cross.'

Milano had crossed the wires of a car called Ford and hit a mother of two crossing the Avissawella road. He tells me that he is sorry more times than I can count. But he doesn't believe that he should forfeit his life when he can make amends.

'Poosa, I know where my grandmother keeps her gold chains. I will take them and pawn them and give money to those two children. Then I will get a job and pay them something for every year their mum was alive, which is 36. Then I will be free.'

The wall between the Bamuna cells and the garbage dump was high, but I could jump to it from the mango tree and Milano could if he climbed to the roof of the cell. I can climb better than any of the prisoners, but this is not something I boast about. I don't feel pride for things that just are.

The exit after the garbage yard is manned with a checkpoint and two guards, who change twice a day, with the rising and falling of the sun. Milano wouldn't be the first to attempt escape via garbage truck. The Trishaw Thief tried hiding under the chassis, and the Cricketer had hidden among the bags of filth, and both had been turned in by the garbage men in their orange and green outfits.

'The guards pay off those kunu buggers to sneak,' said the Activist. 'The poor are their own worst enemies.'

When we pass the toilets, we hear the shouting again, coming through the corridor from the Dispensery. I never like bathing or going to toilets. Too many bad things can happen around water. I have seen what the bullies can do in confined spaces. Even a bar of soap can kill when laced with razorblades.

'Don't be scared Poosa,' says Milano. 'We are not as fucked as you think. There is one guy who can drive us out of here.'

Before Milano rescued me, I used to get tied up in toilets and have water poured over me, and they all knew how much I hated water. Sometimes Soodu Sampath's gang would hold me down and piss on me. I have been beaten with pipes and sticks and had chilli powder thrown in my eyes. They tied things around my neck and made me deliver them to the Sick Room or Dispensary. I sometimes still do this for those whom I like.

Most of the guards pay me no heed. The new Head Guard seems like he has a heart and therefore he will not last here. Guards are not feared by prisoners as much as Soodu Sampath's gang, except for two. The Kicker has steel on his boots and the Fucker pours hot tea on prisoners for no reason.

'I know what you're thinking Poos,' says Milano, stopping to listen at the corridor.

'Why don't I drive? Especially since I know which wires to cross. You understand right? I cannot.'

I must have a face that appears to understand things that it does not. The silence is splintered by footsteps echoing towards the hall. We hear running and then screaming and then an army of psychos burst into the corridor. Milano grabs me and we duck into the toilet stall by the door. The stench is of dead things and soggy vomit. I try to wiggle out of Milano's grasp, but he is too strong.

The man screams as he runs with the mob at his tail. I peep under the stall door into the passageway and see the guard known as the Fucker hounded by the prisoner known as the Hijacker. The Fucker slips and the Hijacker mauls him and then the mob pile on and there is kicking and shouting and the sound of bodies cracking.

The Kicker is shirtless and in handcuffs and he is sobbing. Behind him is Soodu Sampath who holds a bamboo pole and wears the steel-capped boots. He glances towards the toilet, and I duck behind the door.

'Don't fucking move,' whispers Milano and we lie still in the shadow. Two of Sampath's gang carry the body of the Fucker, while the Kicker wails and shudders. The Hijacker slams a fist to the side of the Kicker's face and his wail turns to a whimper. They push him down the hall in the direction of the Dispensary and the mob follows. We wait till there is no sound except for the dripping tap and Milano's heart rattling in his rib cage.

I can hear the worms in my stomach talking. These worms talk all the time. I hear them gossiping at night when they think I'm asleep. They are saying they need to find another host, as my body is old and weakening. They must think I cannot hear them. All the prisoners, except for Milano, believe that I am slow or that I am retarded or that I am ill. All I am, is sad. Sad for terrible things that I forgot that I did. That is all. I will speak when there is something worth saying, but I have not found it yet.

Milano listens at the corridor for a long while. Maybe he hears the worms in my tummy. Telling themselves that I'm a waste of time. Sometimes I think that I only exist for the worms in my tummy. Milano strokes my head and smiles. 'Let's go.'

* * *

They call the solitary confinement cell block the Bamuna because of battery acid. It is the cheapest drug available in the prison and, like all the powders and pills circulating in the cells, it is supplied by the guards. The prison administration prefers if a majority of its population is doped, and they don't care if it is pills or powders or battery juice as long as the prisoners stay quiet and refrain from thinking about justice.

Alcohol is considered more dangerous than firearms in these closed quarters and is dealt with severely. The Cook tried to smuggle kasippu through the kitchen supply van. When the guards found out, they cracked his skull on the sink.

The guards controlled the contraband and knew that drunks start fights that spiral into riots that require squads with guns. Neither of us was sorry to see the Kicker and the Fucker tied up and beaten. After the head injury, the Cook started putting roaches into the onion fry and rat meat into the curry. No one complained because it was tastier than the rice water mush, they usually served.

'Outside, dope is an excuse to lock up the poor,' said the Activist whenever he walked past the Garment Factory and smelled the air. 'Inside, it's a tool to neutralize our minds.'

'All very Kafkaesque,' the Prof said to the Cook when I was on Kitchen duty. No one understood him aside from the cockroaches waiting to be deep fried.

Outside the solitary cells is a wall and over the wall is a parked garbage truck. To stop the prisoners in solitary from wailing, the Kicker came up with an idea, inspired by a street drug called Gal Bamuna. If you took a drop of acid from the truck's battery and placed it on a tongue, the prisoner would go silent and immobile for at least ten hours. 'Like a stoned holy man or a gal bamuna, hence the name,' was how Milano explained it to me. Many who received this treatment, reported blinding headaches for months afterwards. But like most of the Kicker's ideas, it yielded results. No one screamed in solitary much after that.

The Bamuna cells were empty in preparation for Kathleen Burnett's Human Rights visit. 'What's the point,' the Nigerian Barber used to complain in guttural Sinhala. 'We have no humans here. Or rights.'

Only one cell had its door open, and this was known as the lair of the Blue Meadow Killer.

'Oi! Malli, where you?' Milano got to the last cell and then the smell hit him. 'Jesus!'

The cell was the size of the cupboard that the Lepers kept their mops in. It was dark and its one window was the size of a bathroom tile. Outside were books, though not like the ones in the Prof's library, these were thick like Father Pieris' holy book and were stacked along the steps. Next to them were three bags tied at the edges and filled with the Blue Meadow Killer's urine and faeces.

In the darkness I smelled smoke, the same smell you got at the Garment Factory when the juveniles were lighting up smack on cigarette paper.

'Jesus Christ malli. Where did you get that?'

At first, all we saw was an orange circle of a beedi in the dark. And a squeaky voice of a man-boy who drowned a beautiful girl in a pool at the Blue Meadow luxury apartments.

'My Ammi's lawyer gave the guard my salary.'

'Your Ammi came?'

'She will only pay my salary if I start my studies again. Bitch.'

The Blue Meadow Killer was to study economics as a part of his appeal case. His mother owned several construction firms and came with a different lawyer each visit. Each time different things were claimed – that the girl was intoxicated and drowned by accident, that the boy was too young to be serving a life sentence, that the President was a distant relative who could be convinced to grant a pardon. After each visit, the boy would bribe the guards for extra smack, and then swim in his own delusions.

'So good no, malli? You can finish your studies.'

'And do what? What can an economist do in hell?' The boy leans forward and the light from the tiny window catches the tattoo on his shoulder.

'You want some. It is top fucking shelf. Not from the guards also.'

'You know about the riot?'

'Heard some buggers shouting. But buggers are always shouting.'

He leans into the light, and I can see that he has smoked more than usual. Only the whites of his eyes are visible as he speaks.

'You told me once that you drove your thatha's Pajero.'

'Have a taste Milano. It's my last bit.'

'Not today thanks. How big was the Pajero?'

'It was a piece of shit. Thathi never gave me the Jaguar to drive.'

'I need someone to drive a truck. Can you do it?'

'What's the point of economics? My Ammi is a fucken idiot. The rich get cars, the poor get cages. Ammi thinks the President will be impressed if I pass an exam. As if he even passed O levels. Why should I get pardoned? Just cos my Ammi's loaded?'

'Malli I agree with you fully. There is no way they will pardon you. Your dead girl's parents are more loaded than your Ammi.'

'So, tell this big escape plan? I dress up in your outfit and drive the kunu truck, and then what?'

'We have two hours before sunset. Before the guards change. No one checks the ID of a kunu kaaraya.'

'If it's two hours, I'll need more smack.'

'No, you don't.'

'And where do I chauffeur you and Poosa? Have you booked a suite at the Cinnamon Grand? Will they valet park your kunu truck!'

The boy laughs without stopping and writhes across the sticky floor like a tapeworm. It is a sound between a cough and a sob, and appears to flit between pain and pleasure. Milano does not even pretend to smile. I listen carefully at the corridor. The Bamuna cell block is never a good place to be caught loitering. Unless you have a mother who owns buildings.

'I'm sure your Ammi can get you on a plane to somewhere.'

The boy finally stops laughing. He places his feet on the wall and his head on the floor. The light catches his scalp as he turns to us and speaks.

'You know humans are the only creatures born helpless without parents. Look at wildebeest calves born in the wild. Those bastards have to run from cheetahs as soon as they are born. I got to watch nature documentaries on the TV in Cell 9.'

The boy's Ammi pulled strings and got him the Hilton. He lasted there a week before he got caught with smuggled vodka.

'If you can't drive, just say so.'

'Most of the losers here never watched TV. Sin also, not their fault. Who gets to choose where they are born?'

'I can't drive, malli. I've told you this.'

'Fine, fine. I'll do this for Poosa, not for you. I'll chauffeur you in two hours. First get me a hit.'

'From where? The place is under siege. The guards are dead.'

'Screw the guards. I got this from the Hilton.'

'Who's in the Hilton?'

'The Very Special Prisoner in Cell 9. Good friend of Ammi's. Take this note to him. He already has the cash.'

'Who is he?'

'Big dude. He owns the bosses. You won't know him.'

'Soodu's gang is raiding the Dispensary and the Sick Room. They won't let me near the Hilton.'

'Who's asking you to go?'

'The riot squad is due any minute. And enough smack for you now. How will you drive?'

Two hands dart from the darkness and grab me by the neck. I feel string tighten on my windpipe and for the first time I see fear in Milano's eyes.

'Poosa can go anywhere in this prison. He can hide in places none of us would think about. He has 9 lives.'

'You. Let. Him. Go. Now.'

'Relax Milla. I know you call me the Blue Meadow Killer. Even though I am not.'

'No one calls you that.'

'Really? Then what's my actual name?'

Milano watches as the Blue Meadow Killer ties the thing around my neck. Without warning, the boy lets out a screech and clutches his stomach. He lets go of me and I leap into Milano's arms and let him loosen my yoke. The boy's cry lasts for much longer than his laugh.

When he sticks his head out of the cell, in between the unread books and the sealed bags of shit, he is gasping for breath and his forehead is beaded in sweat.

'Poosa knows where to go. He has done this before.'

It is true, I have. But never to the Hilton. I didn't look at Milano because I knew what I would see on his face.

'Don't worry Milla,' says the Blue Meadow Killer. 'Poosa can never be caught.

'We have two hours before the guards change.'

'You know why I drowned the girl?'

Milano raises his hand and slaps the wall. It is unclear if he is going to hit the boy with a bag of shit or a textbook or his open palm.

'If you waste my fucking time. I will find your Ammi and feed her these shit bags.'

'I can't remember if I killed her. That's the truth. You know what I'm talking about Milla. Don't you? I don't remember. Maybe I did it, and I can't tell you why. But if I don't get my smack, I might start remembering what happened in that pool at 3 in the morning when I was 16. And then I know one thing for sure. I won't be able to drive even a fucken tricycle for you.'

Milla shakes his head and mutters like he does when he's furious. He grabs me by the shoulder and pushes me into the corridor.

'You better hurry Poosa. If you're not back in an hour I will leave.'

The Hilton is at the other end of the prison, but it isn't far from the Bamuna cells. Not for me anyway. I can make it there and back in 10 minutes if I run, 30 if I stroll. All I have to do is navigates a maze of hells and avoid the monsters that lurk there.

* * *

The worms in my stomach start chattering as soon as I set off. They tell me that I should hide. That it is best to stay where you are. Because there is nothing to escape to. While this may be hell, outside there is only death. But how can the worms in my stomach know so much, when even I can barely remember?

The corridors are empty. I scamper past C block and see prisoners cowering in their cells, though me they do not see. I have a talent for going places without anyone noticing. Which is why they tie things around my neck and send me on errands. Not just the Blue Meadow Killer, I have delivered for the Tamil prisoners and the Foreigners. They pay me with stolen food which I always appreciate. Milano knows nothing about this and would likely curse them and me if he did.

There are yowls and shrieks coming from the Library. I have heard noises like that before. I climb to the window and peep in. The cries come from the Tamil prisoners who are on the floor getting hammered with furniture. Soodu's gang has invaded the Library and outnumbered all the Tamils and their toothbrushes. The Innocent One and the Tall One fight back, while the others lie in balls on the floor while the thugs hit them with chair legs. The Prof, the Activist and Father Pieris are nowhere to be seen.

Usually I would go to the Dispensary and let whoever's there take the money from my neck and replace it with powder wrapped in paper. Scurrying back to cell C with powders around your neck is dangerous work. Every junkie and druggie may try to grab you and snap your windpipe, and it is best not to let them. I always deliver my parcel to the person who sent me. Or my life would be worth less than it is.

I pass cell B and cell A and hear more shouts and blows. I do not go for a closer look. I slink past the Garment Factory where the Lepers and the Dying lie on tables next to sewing machines. This means the Sick Room has been taken over, either by rioters, or by those brought in to stop the rioting. To get to the Hilton without passing the Sick Room would be tricky. For most, but not for me.

As I climb over the roof of the Garment Factory, I spy the Prof and Father Pieris hiding under another table with the Nigerians. Their prison uniforms are black and white and stained in blood. The Activist paces up and down and rants and raves. I see a large gash on his bald head and blood stains on his beard.

If you can jump over roofs, then you are less likely to meet marauding rioters or gun-toting police. As I suspected, the Sick Room was where they are. They sprawl on the beds, drinking cough medicine and murdering songs. These are not members of Soodu's gang, these are occupants of cell A who are now guarding the guards. The tormentors of the general populace lie bound on the floor. The Kicker is shivering, and the Fucker does not move.

From the roof of the Sick Room, I jump to the stairwell that leads to the Hilton. The door is closed, so I walk on the ledge towards the window. The Hilton window overlooks the garbage yard, where the truck is parked. The truck is green and rusted and surrounded by waste from the Kitchen and I can smell it to this rooftop. Beyond that is the sentry post where the guards will change before the sun goes down.

I peer through the window and two hands grab me and pull me into the room. It is the Head Guard who holds a gun and trembles. He lets go of me and smirks as if he has been expecting me. The Head Guard is a much older than the last one. He has only been here a few weeks and has not yet been cruel to anyone. He seems gentler and politer than the last three Head Guards and no one can fathom what he is doing here. The Activist thinks he has been sent to prepare the prison for Kathleen Burnet's visit. Though if Kathleen Burnett visited today, she would most likely be spreadeagled on a Garment Factory table and devoured by the beasts.

The Head Guard barks. 'Poosa! What the fuck are you doing?' He holds me by my wrists and my eyes travel the room. It is the cleanest space I have ever set feet in. It is decorated with posters from a paradise that I have never seen. There is a television, a book rack, a shining desk, a bed full of pillows and a white box on the ceiling which pumps out clean air.

'There's something around his neck,' says a voice from the bed. It is a voice that sounds like a song. Rich and tuneful and sweet. How I imagine the God in Father Pieris' big books would sound like. I escape from the Head Guard's grasp and sit on the floor by the door. He puts down his gun and lunges for me. I let him pull the thing from around my neck before escaping to the corner.

'Sir, it's from that Rich Bitch's son,' says the Head Guard, unravelling the note.

'That didn't take long,' said the voice. 'Give him a bit. Not too much. If he overdoses, that Mother will flatten this place.'

'Might be a good idea sir. Some places deserve to be flattened.'

'Then where would all the crooks go?'

'The usual places I guess.'

I had never heard a guard calling a prisoner sir, as if it were part of their name. I let the Head Guard tie a paper filled with powder around my neck. I look into the shadows that cover the bed and see a small man dressed in a white sarong. I feel I should recognize him, but I do not. He walks over and stokes my head and my back and I do not mind the softness of his touch or the fresh smell of his skin.

'What's happening out there Poosa?'

I look up at him and say nothing.

He looks up the Head Guard. 'What time will the riot squad be here?'

The Head Guard points to the phone which I had not noticed before.

'Shall I call them, Sir Christopher?'

'Don't use my fucking name idiot!'

The Head Guard shrinks.

'Sorry sir. It is only Poosa. Who will he tell?'

He giggles while the Very Special Prisoner stares.

Outside there is the crash of bullets hitting metal. I hear hundreds of boots pounding on concrete.

'That must be them,' says the occupant of the cleanest room I have ever been in. 'You better run Poosa.'

They open the door and let me out and that is exactly what I do.

* * *

I run straight through the corridors like a cheetah, I do not bother with the roof. Behind me I hear boots and bullets. Before me there is silence. The beatings and the screams have stopped and all I hear are my bare feet hitting the sticky floors.

I pass the Kitchen where the knives are, the Dispensary where the dope is, the Garment Factory where the scared are hiding, and the Library where Soodu Sampath's animals crouch in pools of blood. No one sees me or stops me as I pass A cell and B cell and C cell, I do not look at what is in there, for all I can smell is terror and tears.

When I get to the Bamuna cell, the Blue Meadow Killer is shivering. He has stripped down to his underwear and is sweating piss. He grabs at me, but I jump into Milano's lap and let him take the thing from my neck. He hands the paper to the boy who pries it open with trembling fingers and begins sprinkling it onto cigarette foil. He does not pause to say thank you.

Milano changes into his garbage man uniform. He chucks on an orange shirt and throws green shorts to the boy.

'Oi malli! First you put this on.'

But the boy is making a futile effort to get his rusted lighter to work. He flicks it several times and it spits out sparks, and I am afraid that I will be sent to the Kitchen to bring back fire when a flame appears from nowhere and turns the silver paper brown, the powder to smoke and the boy's mouth into a serpent's tongue. He gobbles the smoke like a meal.

'We need to go now!' hisses Milano.

The Blue Meadow Killer laughs as he sprinkles more powder onto the shiny paper. He uses the torn cover of a textbook as a funnel.

'You will never escape your cage. You can run all you like.'

He takes a lungful of yellow fog in through his nose and mouth and his words come out in fumes and splutters.

'The human is the only creature who cages other beings. Even though the whole world is a massive fucken cage, and everything is made of tiny cells.'

He takes more puffs as if he is in a dragon chasing race.

'You'll find nothing out there Milano. It's the same shit like here. Just big bullies and small cages.'

'Poosa got you your stuff! You keep your promise. Or I swear, I will drown your mother in her own fucking pool.'

The boy looks up and grins.

'I'll hold the bitch down for you!'

His laugh begins as a boom, which makes him cough and the cough gets stuck in his throat and his face turns into a balloon and pink snot exits his nostrils and his eyes roll backwards, and his head hits the concrete. His body goes into spasms and stops moving. Milano pulls him up and shakes him and slaps him and wails.

'He's not dead,' says a voice from the corridor. 'But he won't wake for 2 days.'

We turn and see the Innocent Tamil, the Nigerian Barber and the Activist stepping out of the shadow. They all have rips in their clothes, gashes on their bodies, and bruises on their faces.

'That smelt like black tar gold from Ceylon Islands,' says the Activist. 'He is not going to be driving any bloody trucks.'

'What are you doing?' gasps Milano.

'We followed Poosa,' says the Nigerian in Sinhala. 'I will drive your truck.'

'I only made two extra uniforms,' says Milano. 'One for Father Pieris. One for this pile of shit.'

The Nigerian has already begun stripping. He dumps his tattered prison outfit next to the Blue Meadow Killer's heaving stomach and dons the green and orange uniform. The shorts hug his thighs and the shirt barely overs his gut.

'I will drive,' he says as he climbs the mango tree and hoists himself to the roof of the Bamuna cells.

The Activist looks at the Tamil boy and smiles.

'You go ahead putha. I have only few months left of my sentence. I'll meet you outside. You will not survive in here son.'

We hear an explosion and shouting down the corridor. The Activist gives Milano a leg up and he places his foot on the branches of the mango tree. I climb up after him, I do not need leg ups. When we get to the roof, we see the Hijacker and two of Soodu's goons chasing the Tall Tamil boy down the corridor. He runs to the Bamuna cells and shoves the door closed. The Hijacker bangs the door and pounds on it with a pole. And then his face is covered in chocolate slime and yellow acid.

The Innocent Tamil hurls two more bags of shit at the Hijacker and the goons, and each one hits their mark. They are stunned by the slime and immobilized by the stench. They drop their clubs and begin retching. The Activist and the Innocent Tamil pick up the chair legs and bring them down on their soiled spines. Milano pushes me from the edge and towards the parapet.

'Quick, quick Poosa. We have to go!'

Jumping from the roof to the wall wasn't hard, even for Milano. The leap from the wall to the rubbish dump is twice Milano's height though there is a mountain of garbage to cushion the fall. When we get to the truck, the Nigerian is in the driving seat staring at the sentry post.

'You have keys?'

Milano pulls out two toothbrushes, one that's been smoothed into the edge of a screwdriver and the other sharpened into the blade of a knife. He jams the screwbrush into the ignition and pulls out a green wire, a red wire and a white cable. He shaves the ends of the wires with the toothknife and connects the hairs of one to the other.

The engine splutters like the Blue Meadow Killer did an eternity ago, and then clears its throat and lets out a belch. The Nigerian steps on the pedal and gives a grin. First the engine purrs, then the radiator shudders, and then the truck lets out a roar. No one aside from us hears it because there are louder noises muffling the air.

At the far end of the prison, we hear the bullets of the riot squad, though we cannot tell if they are hitting wall or flesh. We hear screams from across the cell blocks as if hell has unleashed all its rabid *parayas* and then we see Soodu's gang on the roof of A cell, dumping piles of books in the centre and setting them alight. They stand around the blaze and sing and hoot and jeer. We hide ourselves in the front cabin of the garbage truck, but they are not looking in our direction. We stare down the setting sun and hold our breath and await the new guards and pray the prison does not break into a ball of fire.

The air crowds with sounds, and it is hard to tell the shouts from the screams, or the bullets from the boots. There is a tap on the driver's window and the Nigerian jumps out of his ill-fitting uniform. It is the Innocent Tamil, his eyes are bloated purple, two black yolks on bloodied eggs. He wears the last garbageman's outfit.

'The guards are changing. Shall we go?'

For the first time since I've known him, Milano looks unsure. He looks to the burning rooftop and the animals chanting and covers his ears with his palms. The bullets make echoes that burst like fireworks and the smoke in the air smells of beedi and blood. The outside wall of the prison stretches the length of the yard and ends at the sentry post. It is caked in dust and grime and has only the one window. The one looking out from Cell 9 of the Hilton.

'Where's the Activist?'

The Innocent Tamil spits. It is unclear if it is betel or blood that exits his lips. It leaves a red stain on the plastic caps on the mountain of rotting rubbish. Then he lets out a sob.

'He's dead. They were after him from the beginning. Maybe they started the riot to get him. So, they could say "Activist killed in prison riot", and no one would ask how. He was out in 3 months. But they got him. This is a filthy fucking world.'

'The new guards are here,' says Milano. 'Let's go.'

Milano hoists himself to the right side of the truck and hangs off the footboard. The Tamil does the same for the left side. It doesn't take acting talent to pretend to be a garbage man. Just a uniform and an averted gaze will usually do. I take my position on the back of the truck before the gaping mouth of this garbage monster. We watch the sentries take their posts and wait for the old guards to depart. Both new guys stand mesmerized by the inferno on the roof and at the prisoners ranting and shaking their fists. They do not notice us until we drive up to the barricade.

Milano shouts out the scripted line over a gate with spikes.

'Officer sir. Please open gate sir. We are getting late.'

He has practiced the banter in front of me many times, He has an answer for every possible interrogation. The young guard opens the gate without even looking at us. This emboldens Milano and I wish for him to shut up, but he doesn't.

'Boss, what's happening in the prison?'

I stick my head out from the back. The street outside is filled with men carrying cameras and well-dressed women speaking into them. The cars have stopped to stare, and the shops are empty of all their keepers. Police in riot gear stand outside the front doors and eavesdrop on the massacre.

I look back to the open window of Cell 9 of the Hilton and see the Head Guard talking to a riot policeman at the doorway. I see them clearly despite the failing light. And even though I am too far away to hear, I can tell that neither are happy. They wave arms and point fingers and bark into the other's face.

The Very Special Prisoner sits on the bed and watches the two-armed men argue. Over what I cannot even guess. After the riot policeman leaves the room, the Head Guard closes the door and places his ear to it. Then he turns around and points his gun at Very Special Prisoner's head. I do not hear a shot, but I see the prisoner fall down.

Whatever noise the bullet makes evaporates into the cacophony and the only one to see or hear it is me. The Head Guard glances at our truck before closing the window, though me he does not see. I turn to look at the sentry guard, who is shouting at Milano.

'Is this a time to be collecting kunu? Get the fuck out of here!'

The other guard opens the gate. 'Get out! Go!'

'Sorry, sir, we will go,' says Milano bowing his head. Then he shouts at the Nigerian driver. 'Drive! Drive! Drive!'

We hold our breath all the way from the suburbs into Colombo's heart. No one says a word until we reach a road called Gregory's. The Nigerian brakes onto the pavement, gets out of the truck and nods at Milano.

'Thank you, my friend. I go now.'

'Where?' says Milano.

'Embassy!' shouts the Nigerian as he sprints to a white castle with a green and white flag at its turret. We look for the Innocent Tamil, but he has escaped without goodbye. Perhaps he dropped off at a traffic light when we were busy holding our breath. Milano swears and curses. He curses the sky and the road and me and the mother he killed and the two boys he orphaned.

Milano gets in the driving seat, and I hop next to him. He shudders and screams and finally puts his foot down. The truck moves slower than I could run, and Milano keeps cursing and swearing and then starts closing his eyes which does not seem like a smart thing to do when driving. I am relieved when we reach a traffic light, and a policeman tells us to stop and asks for Milano's license.

The Police looks at us suspiciously and then grabs me and pulls the thing from around my neck. 'What the hell is this?'

Milano breaks into a sprint but the Police hold on to me and I cannot get away. Milano looks back at me twice though he doesn't stop running. Keep running Milano. Don't come back for me. I don't want you to. You must keep running. You have gold to steal and orphans to feed. You need to run and me you do not need.

* * *

The next day I am photographed by many. They put me in a cell and laugh at me. I am given milk to drink and leftovers to eat. I do not like the attention. I do not like it at all.

They show me a newspaper with a picture of me on the front. I look scrawny and my fur is missing in patches. I look like how I felt when I was pregnant with the litter. The ones I killed, because I knew I could not care for them. My tail looks withered, and my body looks weak. They read the headline for me and chuckle.

'Cat in Remand for Smuggling Heroin out of Prison'

I do not know why it is funny for them. But I get visitors from everywhere, many with cameras, all here to see the Heroin Cat. The worms in my stomach are silent. Maybe they are dead or maybe they escaped aboard the Innocent Tamil.

They release me through the front door, even though I have nowhere to go. Life is tough on the street, and I walk for miles and days, I walk in circles for weeks, looking for garbage dumps next to slimy walls with solitary windows and Very Special Prisoners inside. I cannot remember how long it took me or what I had to do to find my home again. The worst things are always best forgotten.

There is no garbage truck in the yard. Just bags and bags and bags of uncollected crap. I scale the wall and jump to the top of the Bamuna cells and feel a joy that I do not recognize amidst the familiar stenches that welcome me. Each Bamuna cell has an occupant and most I do not recognize. And then I come to the final cell, the one with the open door and I look for the Blue Meadow Killer, but it is not he who is there.

It is Milano. His head is shaven, and he is thinner. He is crouched at the shard of light, reading a book by that Archer fellow. The one with my face on the cover.

'Poosa!' he cries, and I cry too.

I leap into his arms and curl my tail around his body. Because I do not mind living in the dark as long as he is there.

Endthology

THIS IS AN ANTHOLOGY SQUEEZED INTO TWO HUNDRED words. It is told in Lankan onomatopoeia. Words like *jabok!* to denote something huge falling into water. Or *pat-pat!* for things happening quickly. Or *chatas patas!* for stuff exploding. Words that sound like sounds. So, *ting-ting!* Let's begin.

Homegrown terrorists hijack plane with 249 passengers. *Dishum dishum!* Government shoots plane out of sky killing everyone. *Tak-tak!* Government shapes it up with a *human-shields-this-is-war-these-things-happen* argument. People eventually stop *kutu-kutu-ing*.

Story Two. His toenails are filthy so *pat-gaala*. She rejects him so he *gnuru-gnurus* and joins the movement and shoots her uncle who is a *shos-shos* powerful man. So, army brings whole *jing-bang,* and 13 get shot *dading biding*, and down south thousands are burned alive. All because of a dirty toenail. *Hoo.*

Finale. *Thadang!* JVP tell him paste posters or die. *Pataas!* Cops tell him inform on JVP or die. *Zung-gaala!* He hides in the forest and thinks, 'I'm a Sinhala Buddhist, don't you both represent me?' *Hai hooi! Ammo!* He returns to find his wife and children slaughtered. *Chee-chee.* Police say must be JVP, who say must be police. If only this were fiction. *Aiyo.*

Yuri
Nate
Drinkwater
An unpublished interview

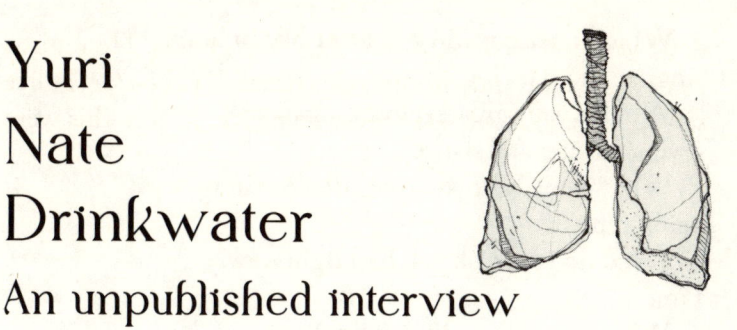

What one word would describe you?
Breathing.
What do you fear the most?
Not breathing.
What do you consider your greatest achievement?
Continuing to breathe.
Which words or phrases do you most overuse?
I mean.
What do you consider the most overrated virtue?
Politeness.
On what occasion do you lie?
When asked strange questions.
Who or what is the greatest love of your life?
Her and her and him and them.
What do you dislike most about your appearance?
My left nostril.
What is your most marked characteristic?
A lack of surprise.
What is your most treasured possession?
My lungs.
Choose a movie title for the story of your life.
I've already given you three.

Which talent would you most like to have?
Singing and dancing.

What is your greatest extravagance?
Trying to sing and dance.

What is the trait you most deplore in yourself?
Being repetitive.

What do you wish you had right now?
Time.

Where would you like to live?
Here.

What is your current state of mind?
Now.

If you could change one thing about yourself, what would it be?
Me.

What is your motto?
Me. Me. Me.

If you were to die and come back as a person or thing, what do you think it would be?
The bass player of U2.

Which historical figure do you admire most?
The writer of the Bible.

What would you be doing in 20 years?
Learning to sing and dance.

What is the first thing you do when you wake up?
Urinate and drink water.

If you had to change your name, what would you change it to?
Yuri Nate Drinkwater.

What was your favourite food as a child?
Pol Roti with lunu miris and dallo curry.

What inspires you?
A solid deadline.

When was the last time you tried something new, and what was it?
Pol Roti with hummus and guacamole.

Who is your favourite hero of fiction?
Inigo Montoya.

What do you most value in your friends?
Breath.

Acknowledgements

Aadhil Aziz
Andrew Fidel Fernando
Ali Shabaz
Alyna Haji Omar
Ameena Hussein
Amish Raj Mulmi
Amy Hempel
Ashok Ferrey
Asvajit Boyle
Avani Wannakuwatte
Avanti Samarasekera
Avtar Singh
Dathika Wickremanayake
Dani Boekel
Deshan Tennekoon
Dilshard Ahamed
Diresh Thevanayagam
Eranga Tennekoon
Glory Salwar
Jehan Mendis
Jhumpa Lahiri
Ken Liu
Lal Medawattegedara
Madina Kalyayeva
Manjula Gunawardena
Marissa Jansz
Mark Ellingham
Michael Meyler
Nandini Nair
Natania Jansz
Neil Gaiman
Poulomi Chatterjee
Prasad Pereira
Roald Dahl
Roger Charles
Romesh Gunasekera
Ravi Eshwar
Ruhanie Perera
Sam Pereira
Sid Dissanayake
Sean Amarasekera
Shanaka Amarasinghe